HOPE UNCHAINED

LIGHT *in the* EMPIRE

HOPE UNCHAINED

CAROL ASHBY

CERRILLO PRESS

Cerrillo Press
Edgewood, NM

LIGHT *in the* EMPIRE

HOPE UNCHAINED

CAROL ASHBY

CERRILLO PRESS

"For I know the plans I have for you," says the LORD.

"They are plans for good and not for disaster,

to give you a future and a hope."

Jeremiah 29:11 (NLT)

And we know that for those who love God

all things work together for good,

for those who are called according to his purpose.

Romans 8:28 (ESV)

May the God of hope fill you with all joy and peace in believing,

so that by the power of the Holy Spirit

you may abound in hope.

Romans 15:13 (ESV)

To my children, Paul and Lydia,
for their love, support, and encouragement.
And especially to my husband, Jim,
who always looks for the good with me.

And most of all, to Jesus.

Soli Deo gloria.

Faith, hope, and love. Three things at the core of a Christian's life.

It is our faith in Jesus as our savior that makes us a Christian. His sacrificial death paid for our sins and set us right with God. That first step of faith is the starting point where our belief in Jesus gives us the right to become children of God.

But it isn't our faith that draws other people to wonder about Jesus. It's how we live out that faith. It's the hope it gives us when our world turns upside down and everything we expected is up in the air or shattered into a thousand pieces. And even more, it's the love we show to people, especially to those who played a role in disrupting our lives.

The life of faith is full of joy, but it isn't free of problems. Jesus himself told us that in this world we would have troubles. But he also said to take heart, for He had overcome the world (John 16:33).

There are times in every Christian's life where it can be hard to face what's happening with hope. Sometimes we get what we feared, not what we hoped for. It can be tempting to focus on the bad, not look for the good that might come from it. But we have God's promise to carry with us through hard times. We have His word that He can work all things together for our good (Romans 8:28).

God is the great healer, but in His own way and His own time. I've lived long enough to have seen how God can bring good things out of what seemed only bad at the time. I've become more patient waiting for that to happen, and I know I won't always see that positive ending while I'm in the midst of the struggle and feeling the pain. Faith and experience both tell me to hope.

Sometimes a difficult time for us opens doors to share with others how the hope God gives us can carry us through. Peter tells us to always be ready to give a reason for the hope we have (1 Peter 3:15). Our hope in a time of trial could be what leads another person to seek God.

Hope Unchained is the story of a woman who has everything taken from her, but she doesn't lose hope that God can bring good out of bad for those who love Him. She shows love to those who had been her enemies, and that turns them into friends and leads them toward faith.

I hope you enjoy this story of God making all things work together for good as much as I've enjoyed guiding Ariana and Donatus toward a future filled with hope and love. May we always face our own difficult times full of the hope that comes from God.

Carol Ashby

Characters

ARIANA'S FAMILY AND FRIENDS

Ariana (16): young Dacian woman taken by Romans as a slave

Diegis (11): Ariana's younger brother, taken by Romans as a slave

Roanna (6): Ariana's younger sister, taken by Romans as a slave

Cotiso: elderly shepherd, member of Didas's house church

Didas: Ariana's father, killed by Roman soldiers

Tamura: Ariana's mother, killed by Roman soldiers

Zapada: Ariana's horse

FULVIUS GRACCHUS FAMILY AND SLAVES

Quintus Fulvius Gracchus (36): tribune of IV Flavia Felix legion

Marcia Philippa (30): Gracchus's wife

Cletus: Gracchus's steward

SERTORIUS DONATUS FAMILY

Gaius Sertorius Donatus (20): ex-legionary, served under Gracchus

OTHER IMPORTANT CHARACTERS

Ursus: gladiator bodyguard borrowed by Gracchus from his general (legate)

Bikili (10): Dacian slave

Cities and Towns

Ad Drinum (13): town near present day Loznica, Serbia

Aquae (14): town near present-day Sarajevo, Bosnia and Herzegovina

Aternum: port town in eastern Italia, present-day Pescara, Italy

Bassiana (9): town near present-day Donji Petrovci, Serbia

Danuvius: Danube River

Delos: island in Aegean that was major slave-trading city for eastern Empire

Dobreta (3): location of major Roman bridge over the Danube

Dyrrhachium (6): major Roman port city on eastern coast of Adriatic Sea, present-day Durrës

Gensis (11): mansio near present-day Lešnica, Serbia

Lederata (2): town with pontoon bridge and naval docks on Danube near Viminacium

Lissus (5): port town just north of Dyrrhachium (6), present-day Lezhë, Albania

Mare Nostrum: "our sea", Roman name for the Mediterranean Sea

Narona (15): port town in present-day Croatia

Sarmizegetusa (Regia) (1): capital city of the kingdom of Dacia, present-day Romania

Singidunum (8): headquarters of Legio IV Flavia Felix, present-day Belgrade

Sirmium (10): capital of Pannonia Inferior, present-day Sremska Mitrovica, Serbia

Thessalonica (15): major port city, capital of Macedonia

Tricornium (7): Military fort on the Danube, present-day Ritopek, Serbia

Viminacium (4): headquarters of Legio VII Claudia, capital of Moesia Superior, present-day Kostolac, Serbia

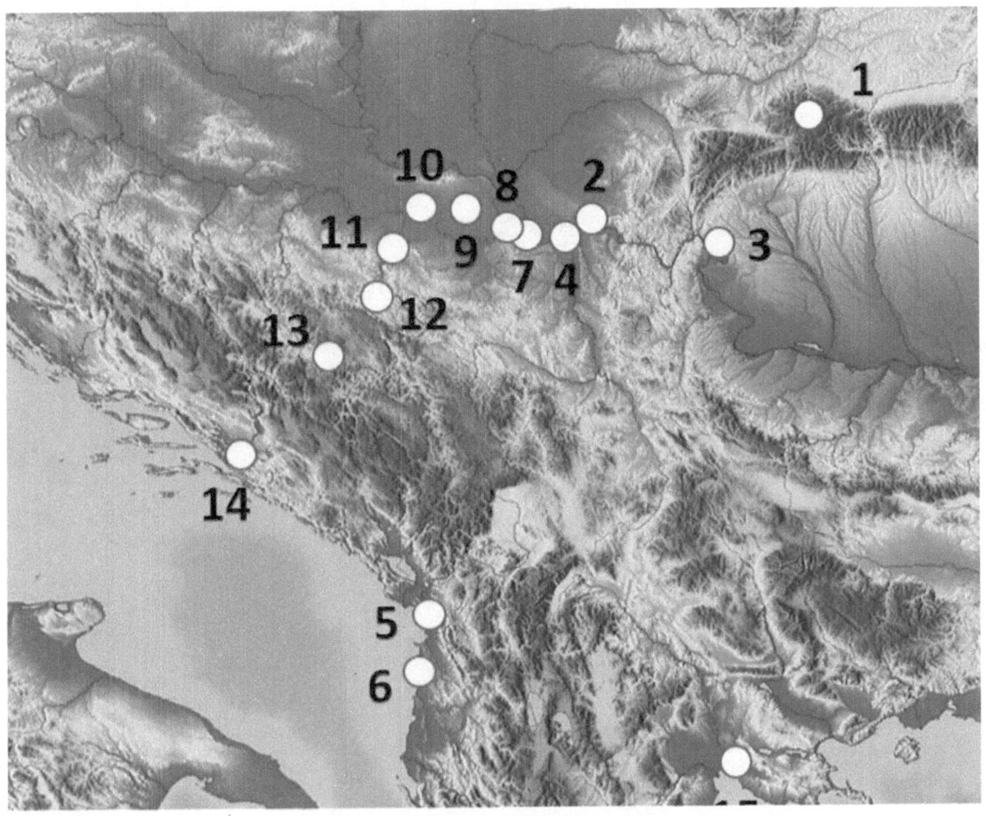

Chapter 1

Giving Her Word

Sarmizegetusa, Dacia, AD 106

Hand resting on his sword, the tribune rode slowly along the cages. When he reached the one where Ariana stood among the young women aged twelve to twenty, he reined in. His ice-cold eyes scanned the group, and a shiver ran up her spine.

The girl beside her shoved Ariana forward and slipped behind another taller girl. A futile move. There was no escape from what lay ahead. Front of the cage or rear, they were all slaves of the conquering army of Rome.

Ariana swallowed the lump that kept rising in her throat. The same fate awaited them all—the auction tomorrow, a long walk to the coast to board the slave ships, and a voyage to a life of bondage.

A flick of the tribune's fingers summoned the Greek in charge of their cage. The Roman spoke quiet Latin, and it drew an oily smile from the Greek.

"All who speak Greek, come forward." The trader's command was in Greek. Should she reveal she understood and join the dozen girls who worked their way forward to stand closer to the bars?

She'd prayed a thousand prayers for deliverance. Was this an answer, or just one more time her cries brought no response?

One deep breath and she stepped out with the others.

The tribune's gaze, which had swept past her before, locked on each girl in turn. One of the youngest stood next to Ariana, and her rapid breathing pulled Ariana's attention from the tribune's frown. She took a half step sideways and clasped the terrified girl's hand. Then she moved it behind her back so the Greek wouldn't see. When she interlaced their fingers and gave a gentle squeeze, the girl's breathing slowed.

The Greek moved back by the officer, and again Latin words were spoken between them. The Greek's smile turned wooden before he shrugged.

The stallion fidgeted, and the Roman leaned forward to pat its neck. He nudged the horse closer to the cage.

"Any Christian, step forward." The Roman's Greek was edged with anger as he scowled.

Ariana closed her eyes and fought to slow her own breathing. There would be no auction for her, no sea voyage.

Jesus, whatever comes, give me strength to show how one of Your own lives...and dies.

She took two steps forward. With shoulders squared, she raised her chin and looked straight into the tribune's eyes.

"I follow Jesus as my Lord."

The scowl relaxed into a frown. He pointed at her, then turned emotionless eyes back on the Greek. She didn't need to know Latin to understand what he said. The Greek unlocked the door and motioned for her to come out.

She stepped past him as he relocked the door. With a short strip of leather, he bound her wrists. The tribune tossed him one end of a rope, and he tied that to her wrists as well.

The officer nudged his horse into a walk, and the rope jerked her forward. She stumbled but caught herself before she fell. Like a sheep being led to slaughter, she followed him away from the cages.

For sixteen years, she'd known the love of her family and her God. Rome had taken her loved ones, but no one could take her from Jesus. Perhaps it was a mercy to die for her Lord rather than live as a Roman slave. But fear still flickered through her, and her chin quivered. Then she clenched her teeth and drew a deep breath. For whatever lay ahead, God would give her strength.

The pace of the tribune's horse was only a walk, but Ariana still found herself almost jogging to keep up. She'd walked perhaps a quarter hour when the legion field camp loomed before her.

An earthen wall more than a quarter mile long rose at least ten feet above the wide trench dug in front of it. A row of pointed stakes rose above the wall, and Roman sentries walked slowly behind them, flashes of sunlight reflecting off their armor. She scanned left and right, looking for the tall poles of the execution field and the crossbars holding the bodies of dead and dying men. She saw none, but maybe it was on the other side of the camp.

Or maybe that wasn't where the tribune was taking her. Her breath came faster, and her heart raced as dreaded possibilities danced in her mind.

Then he turned down a road that led up a hill to an area of large houses once occupied by the wealthy who chose to live a few miles outside the capital city. Homes of the people who used to buy Father's horses...before the Roman soldiers killed him and took them all.

The Greek-style house to her left, where she'd led a mare while Father led two more, stood vacant with its gate torn from its hinges. With each house she passed, the blood pounding in her ears drowned out the silence.

She heard distant voices speaking Greek, not Dacian. The man who rode through the gate fifty feet ahead had the dark, short-cropped hair of a Roman, not the full red mane of a Dacian.

Her lips tightened. The conquerors had occupied the homes of the conquered, and nothing would ever be the same. She swallowed hard and forced back the tears. Father and Mother dead, her younger brother dragged from her side and her little sister torn from her arms as the Romans sorted their newest slaves by age and gender...nothing would ever be the same. Everything had changed—except her God.

She turned her eyes skyward. *Please, God. Diegis and Roanna... protect them.* She closed her eyelids...and walked into the rear of the tribune's gray stallion.

Her eyes popped open as the horse shied away from her. The tribune reined in and jerked on the rope to draw her close. She bowed her head, as expected of a slave. But he pressed his foot against her throat and lifted her chin until her eyes looked into his.

"Listen carefully, Christian, and speak only truth if you want to live." His words were quiet with a hard edge. "I have heard that your kind make the best slaves, that you can be trusted to work when no one watches and that you never try to kill your masters. Is that true?"

His dark brown eyes bored into her as his foot dropped back to his horse's side.

Ariana swallowed. She knew the commands of Paul to serve as if serving the Lord, and a follower of Jesus would never murder. But what did the tribune want her to say?

"If we obey God's commands, it's true."

His brow furrowed. "Is it true of you?"

"I try to obey my Lord Jesus."

His horse shifted sideways, and he pulled on the rope to draw her close again.

"The garrison that will remain at your capital when the rest of the legion leaves is under my command. My wife came from Moesia to join me." His mouth curved into something that was part smile, part frown, but his eyes stayed unreadable.

"A *cisium* accident right after she arrived…" His jaw clenched. "The legion's chief physician says she'll never walk again. I must be with my troops every day and some nights, and that leaves her alone with a steward I've only owned a year and a household of slaves I don't fully trust. She needs someone who will watch over her like I would.

"I took you from the cage because you admitted you're a Christian, and I expect you to do exactly what a Christian slave is supposed to do."

The tribune's eyebrows dipped, and his mouth shifted into full frown. "But you are not to tell my wife anything about your god. I do not want her deluded by stories about a man who came back to life after being crucified." A snort accompanied his sneer. "I want no stories of how your dead teacher healed people when he was alive. None of that really happened, and I do not want my wife's hopes raised and then crushed when she isn't healed."

His eyes chilled. "I'll have you nailed to a cross like your teacher if you fail to obey me in this."

An ironic laugh rumbled in the tribune's throat. "They say Christians always keep their word, so give me yours."

Ariana stared at his horse's feet as her heart raced. Never speak of her Lord?

The tribune leaned over and seized her chin. He tipped it up to put her face close to his. "Swear to me, Christian."

His face was hard, but deep within those warrior eyes, worry about the woman he loved revealed a heart capable of more than cruelty.

"I will do my best to serve her as you wish."

His eyes narrowed as he stared into her own. Finally, his curt nod confirmed his acceptance of her promise.

"You will tell no one I chose to bring a Christian into my household. As far as anyone else is concerned, I brought you because I want to give my wife a slave to stay with her at all times and help her while I'm away, and I thought a young one would cheer her up when she was sad."

His eyes clouded. "She has begun saying she should just die so I could remarry. I know she's thinking about suicide. You are to prevent that at all costs. If you fail, crucifixion will take you to join her in the underworld."

Sadness lingered in his eyes, but his lips curved into a weary smile. "Your word again, Christian."

"I will do my best to protect her, even from herself."

He released her chin and sat upright in his saddle. "You'd better hope your best is good enough." He glared down at her. "That god of yours may command forgiveness, but he is not my god. I am not a forgiving man." His finger stabbed the air and stopped on her forehead. "Do not forget that."

He nudged his horse to resume their climb.

With every step, relief and anxiety warred within her. Was this tribune saving her from the terrible fate she'd thought certain or leading her to one far worse than she feared?

Chapter 2

ALL HE WANTS

Ariana's climb ended far up the slope where a fine house over-looked the gardens of the houses below it. When the tribune guided the stallion through the gate, a boy of about eleven scurried over to take his horse.

She scanned the stableyard, and her throat tightened. Not far past this house, a cart track turned off the road. A few miles down that shortcut through the woods and she'd reach her family's horse farm. A few miles but it might as well be a thousand.

Two years ago, she'd stood under that beech tree. For his son's sixteenth birthday, the nobleman who owned this house bought a young gray stallion. Was it the one the tribune rode now? Were father and son both dead, like her mother and father? Were the family's younger children in the cages with Diegis and Roanna?

God, please help me stop thinking about what's gone forever.

A man near her father's age strode toward them. His curly hair was nearly black, and he wore a tunic, not trousers. "Welcome home, master." His words were Greek, but not like Dacians spoke it. His bearing was too proud to be anything but steward.

The tribune tossed him the end of the rope. "Get this one cleaned up. She's my wife's new handmaid."

The steward scanned her head to foot and back. He opened his mouth as if to speak, then said nothing.

"Say what you were thinking, Cletus." The tribune swung his leg over the horse's neck and slid off.

The steward blew out a breath. "Red hair, gray eyes, that shirt and long skirt...this one is Dacian. Of course, you know best, master, but one of the Syrian girls might be...safer for Mistress Marcia."

Ariana startled when the tribune's fingertips lifted her chin to force her to look into his eyes. Without a word, they repeated his threat. "This one will serve well. She knows what will happen if she doesn't."

A quick dip of the steward's head was followed by a practiced smile. "What do you want to call her?"

"Your name?" The tribune released her chin.

"Ariana."

Cletus cleared his throat. "A name change makes new slaves more obedient."

The frown returned as the tribune's eyes locked on hers again. Then one corner of his mouth lifted.

"She'll do exactly what she should once she's been told what that is. I'm going to speak with my wife before I return to my troops. Have Ariana ready for me to present to Marcia before I leave."

As the tribune walked toward the house, Cletus used his dagger to cut first the rope and then the leather thong. "Do you understand Latin?"

Ariana shook her head. She knew some words, but not enough she'd call it understanding.

"Greek?"

She nodded as she rubbed where her wrists had been bound.

The steward sheathed his dagger. "You are now the property of Quintus Fulvius Gracchus, Tribune of Rome. You will be serving his wife, Marcia Philippa. You will address them as master and mistress and me as steward. I expect immediate obedience at all times, or you will be punished. Understood?"

"Yes, steward."

One sniff and his nose wrinkled. He pointed toward a cistern. "Wash that stench off." His hand swung toward a rope where clean tunics hung drying. "Then put on one of those, and be quick about it. Tribune Gracchus is not a patient man, and he said to be ready when he returns."

"Yes, steward." A quick bow and she headed toward the cistern.

God, let the tribune taking me from the cage be Your will, not his own idea. Please give me courage and strength to serve as if I'm serving You.

Gracchus strode through the enclosed courtyard of his Greek-style house. The bedrooms and women's room lined the U-shaped balcony. Windows made them cheery while providing delightful views of the nearby mountains, but they were unused since the accident.

The Dacian king had taken enough Roman money in the twenty years since his treaty with Domitian. Decebalus and his nobles should have used some to build Roman-style houses with peristyle gardens and everything on the ground floor. But a search for a proper home for his injured wife turned up nothing.

Gracchus had ordered a corner of the stone courtyard to be covered with a canopy so a couch and large pots of flowers could be Marcia's garden oasis during the day. His office on the ground floor had been converted into a bedroom with bright fabric draperies and a view of the activity in the courtyard.

He hadn't been home since yesterday morning, and her new garden was a welcome sight. When he entered the bedroom, Marcia lay with her back turned on life, her eyes fixed on the small window at ceiling level that let in light but kept out thieves. At the click of his hobnailed shoes on the mosaic flooring, she looked back over her shoulder. She dredged up a smile, but her eyes remained sad.

He took a chair from the wall and sat to get down to her level. "How are you feeling?"

"The bruises don't hurt anymore."

"Good. The courtyard garden is ready. Have you tried it?"

"No. It's too hard to get there."

"Cletus will have someone carry you out."

"I haven't felt like it." Her brow furrowed. "You're usually with your troops midday. Is something wrong?"

"No." He took her hand and caressed the back with his thumb. "I have a present for you, and I wanted to bring it to you right away. It isn't something my men need to see with me."

"Is it a dagger?" Her eyes brightened as she asked the question. "I might need one...to protect myself."

Gracchus fought a frown. There was only one thing she would do with a dagger.

"No. You don't need a dagger, but I did get something even better for your protection. A special gift that will keep me from worrying about you during the day when I can't be here."

She turned her hand in his and entwined their fingers. "I don't need special protection. The gods have already turned against me. If I should die soon, they'd only be answering my prayers. You deserve a wife who can give you sons. A young healthy woman, not a worthless cripple like me."

"Stop saying that. You're the only woman I want. It was your intelligence and fire that attracted me when your brother introduced us, not your pretty face and figure."

Her eyebrows rose.

"Not that you weren't pretty, because you were. You still are, but you're much more. That hasn't changed."

Her lips twitched, and a wry smile crept out. "You were the first man who wasn't afraid of me after hearing my ex-father-in-law's lies. You likened me to the Sarmatian cavalry women who cut down their enemies as easily as any man and would never let a husband beat them."

He touched her cheek. "Your warrior spirit...that's what caught my eye and then my heart."

Her face brightened. Then her gaze shifted to her legs, and sadness quenched the glow. "But this is something I can't conquer. Even the greatest warriors get defeated. Then it's time to die."

"No." His jaw clenched. "No Roman soldier stops fighting until his commander orders it. You'd still want me if I came home wounded beyond healing. Don't ask me to do less. Do you hear me?"

Tears filled her eyes as her mouth quivered. Then she drew a deep breath and nodded.

But did that nod mean she'd continue to fight, or only that she'd heard?

He slipped the strap holding his *gladius* over his head and hung it on the chair. He set his dagger on the seat. After releasing the clasps on the side of his body armor, he removed the cuirass and set it on the floor.

Then he scooped Marcia into his arms. She buried her face in his shoulder and wept silent tears. He lowered himself onto her couch, setting her in his lap so he could wrap her in both arms.

When her shuddering sigh signaled her tears were over, he kissed her temple.

"Caring for you is my privilege."

"This gift for my protection." Her smile was sad. "What is it?"

"I got a new slave to be with you at all times when I can't be here. She understands Greek well and will have no other duties than serving you."

"Is she young and pretty?"

He shrugged before resting his palm on her cheek. "Typical young Dacian. It doesn't matter what she looks like. I got her for you, not me. I have the only woman I want."

"Dacian?" Her lips curved into a wry smile. "A strange choice if you want to keep me safe."

"Never doubt that." His lips brushed her forehead. "This one is unusual. She knows what I expect, and she'll do it."

He stood and placed her on the couch, adjusting the pillows for her to sit up and covering her legs. "I'll get her, and then I must return to camp."

As he walked past the chair, he picked up his dagger and gladius and dropped the strap over his head. Sharp edges might prove too tempting.

Gracchus paused at the door to offer an encouraging smile and received a shaky one in return. When he stepped out of Marcia's view, his smile flipped into a frown. The Christian knew what he expected, and she'd do it...or she'd be on a cross.

Chapter 3

The Special Gift

Ariana stood in the stableyard and shivered. The slave tunic only covered her upper arms and barely reached her knees. Her own shirt sleeves had brushed her wrists, and her skirt reached her ankles. Her finger traced the garland of flowers Mother had embroidered around the neck before rolling the shirt and skirt into a bundle to wash later.

As the steward walked toward her, his gaze settled on the clothes. She held the bundle closer.

Cletus looked at her front and back. "Master Gracchus should think you're clean enough to show the mistress, but one of the housemaids will show you later how they bathe to suit Roman masters."

He snatched the bundle from her, and when she reached to get it back, he slapped her.

"You are the slave of Tribune Gracchus, and a slave owns nothing.

You only need what he provides." He tossed her shirt with Mother's beautiful garland to the stable slave. "Burn this."

Ariana blinked hard to stop the tears. She knew Jesus's words. Don't cling to treasures that thieves can steal. Lay up treasures in heaven. But that shirt wasn't a treasure because it was worth money. Mother's love was sewn in every leaf and flower of the garland. A Roman soldier had killed her mother. Now a soldier's slave would burn Mother's gift of love.

Gracchus emerged from the house without his body armor. The white tunic with two narrow purple stripes made him appear less frightening, even though he still wore a sword and dagger and skirt of leather strips.

Then she looked at his face. Tightened mouth and stormy eyes chilled her like an early spring rain. With a curl of his fingers, he summoned her, then stood with legs spread and arms crossed.

She walked over to stand in front of him, eyes downcast.

"Look at me, Ariana."

She obeyed, and up close, what had looked like anger was clearly worry.

"After I give you to Marcia, you are to stay with her all the time." He spoke softly, as if he didn't want others to hear. "Watch her closely, but don't let it seem like you are. You will report what you see when I return home."

His gaze settled on the brass dagger at his hip. "She just told me she wants to die." His eyes shifted to lock on hers. "If you want to live, make sure she stays alive."

"I'll do all I can to keep her safe."

His mouth twisted. "Keep her safe, master. I'm master; she's mistress. Don't forget to say it each time you speak to us. Obey her quickly in everything except when her safety is at risk. I want her to feel in control again. She has a warrior's heart, but this accident has defeated her."

"I'll try, master."

Master Gracchus spun on his heel and led her into the house.

Ariana followed him through a courtyard bright with flowers into a dim room. She hung back, but he snapped his fingers and pointed at the spot beside him. She moved closer, and he gripped her upper arm.

"This is Ariana." His eyes locked on hers. "You are to help your mistress with whatever she wants. Serving her well is your only duty for now."

Ariana raised her eyes to the mistress's face. A beautiful woman, probably in her early thirties. Dark brown eyes swept her from head to foot, then returned to her husband.

"I'd rather have a dagger."

The tribune bent over to kiss her forehead. "A warrior fights until the commander says stop. I'll ask what you had her do when I return."

He lifted the sword strap over his head and hung it on a chair. Then he dropped the cuirass onto his shoulders and latched the clasps along his ribs before draping the strap across his chest. After he placed the red-plumed brass helmet on his head, he lifted Mistress Marcia's hand and kissed her palm.

"I expect to be home for dinner."

As he strode past Ariana, his eyes once more gave the command she didn't need to hear. He'd promised death on a cross if she failed, but even without that threat, she would try to obey Apostle Paul and serve as if serving Jesus, her Lord.

◆

Marcia watched her husband leave, then closed her eyes. He deserved so much more than she could give him now.

Quintus had transformed her life since he'd first come to her father's house in Viminacium. Trajan had withdrawn his legions to winter camps south of the Danube during the First Dacian War, and Quintus had come to see how her brother was recovering from his injuries.

That was five years ago, but she could still hear her brother's drunken banter as they reclined at dinner. "Tribune Quintus Gracchus, a man afraid of nothing, on or off the field of battle. It's been a decade since death ended both your marriages. I'd wager you two would be ideal for each other."

Quintus had turned his eyes on her, eyes that watched and read everyone while revealing none of his own thoughts. "My wife died bearing our only daughter. It's a sad thing when husband and wife are parted so soon after marriage."

She'd laughed at him. "That depends on the marriage. The early end of some is a sure sign of Fortuna's favor. The only good that comes from some unions is children. Having a child is worth any pain. But my dead husband's father took mine as soon as he was born and banned me from ever seeing him. My restored freedom came at too high a cost."

His face didn't change, but deep in his eyes she saw the question. He was new in town. He hadn't heard the vile lies spread abroad that she'd poisoned her first husband. His interest in her would die as soon as he did.

The steward had heard her yell that she'd kill the brute she'd married if he ever tried to beat her again. She'd hit him with a lampstand, stunning him before fleeing to her father's house. He'd died alone in the night, choking on his own drunken vomit. Then his father brought charges of murder. Only revealing all the hidden bruises had convinced the judge to say it wasn't proven that she poisoned him, but even if she did, he deserved it.

Their son was born seven months later. At least his grandfather chose to let him live instead of abandoning him to die. But maybe if, as *paterfamilias*, he had refused to raise her son, she could have had her maid secretly follow and bring her baby home after they left him for the dogs.

For ten years, her father-in-law had insisted she was a poisoner, and no Roman was willing to risk the old man's wrath by marrying her.

No Roman until Quintus. The next time he came, he said he'd heard the rumors. Had she killed her husband? Then, with arms crossed, he waited. She'd told him what really happened. Those eyes that missed nothing bored into her; then his lips curved into a smile. "I admire the warrior women of the Britons and Sarmatians. They'd never take a beating without fighting back. Why should a Roman?"

Within a month, they'd married. She'd dreamed of giving him many sons, but now...She looked at her useless legs, and the tears she struggled to hide when he was with her broke free.

Chapter 4

WHAT STILL REMAINS

The new slave went to the dressing table. She opened the drawer and withdrew a handkerchief. Without a word, she handed it to Marcia and stepped back.

Marcia buried her face in the linen square until the torrent of tears turned into a trickle. When she finally lowered the wet cloth, the girl was standing silently by her couch, arms hanging, hands clasped.

Marcia's brow furrowed as she looked at the face of the Dacian girl who'd been torn from all she'd known and made a slave. She expected to see hatred burning in those eyes. Long-time slaves learned to mask hostility, but a new young one...her true feelings would show through any mask.

But the gray eyes of Quintus's "special gift" were strangely peaceful. If that was a mask and any emotion was peeking through, it was sympathy.

"He told you to watch me, didn't he." It was a statement, not a question. She should never have asked for the dagger and revealed her desire to die.

"Yes, mistress."

"That should bore you beyond endurance. All I can do is lie here and wait to die."

"Perhaps not, mistress. One of my neighbors is...was an old woman. It was hard for her to stand and harder still to walk, but she wove baskets to sell and sewed clothes for her grandchildren." The Dacian's gaze dropped to the floor before rising to Marcia again. "When you lose something, no matter how precious, you can decide to go on with what still remains."

Marcia released a delicate snort. "A Roman matron runs her husband's house, bears his children, and visits with other women who do the same." Her mouth turned down. "All that requires a good pair of legs."

A trace of a smile warmed the girl's eyes. "But you still have good hands. Is there nothing a Roman matron does with those?"

Marcia's eyebrows shot up. A slave questioning her like an equal? She couldn't allow it, even if the question was valid.

"My husband said your name was...?"

"Ariana."

"Ariana, mistress. Do not forget to address us properly as master and mistress, and do not presume to tell me what to do."

Ariana dropped her gaze to the floor. "Yes, mistress."

"That's better. Now leave me. Go to Steward Cletus, and he'll tell you what to do."

"I can't do that."

Marcia frowned. Such impertinence. "Your master told you to help me however I want. I want to be alone."

The girl's eyes widened. "But the tribune told me I was to stay with you at all times. I can't do both." A pause, then the girl's breath caught. "Mistress. I can't do both, mistress, and I have to obey the master."

"He gave you to me. You'll obey me first."

Panic filled Ariana's eyes before she closed them. Two fast, deep breaths, then her breathing slowed. When her eyes reopened, the panic was gone.

"I'll stand over there by the door. I'll be so quiet it will seem like I left. Please let me obey you both that way, mistress."

Marcia closed her eyes and rubbed her forehead. If Quintus discovered the girl had left the post he'd assigned her, he'd be furious. A tribune of Rome expected to be obeyed instantly by all who reported to him, and failure guaranteed punishment. Except with her, he was not a patient man.

"Go stand by the door. I'll call you if I want you."

"Thank you, mistress." Ariana's quick smile almost drew one of her own.

As her guardian walked away, Marcia sighed. Quintus's gift would keep him chained to a woman who could no longer give him what he deserved.

A slave should never have presumed to question her, but the girl's question played at the back of her mind. What could a Roman matron still do with two good hands?

Gracchus trotted into his stableyard and slid off the stallion before the stable slave reached him. He dropped the reins and strode into his house.

Marcia asking for a dagger...his lips tightened. He'd barely brought the Christian in time to protect his beloved from herself, and maybe the report the girl would give him tonight would help him discover what would make Marcia want to live again.

When he stepped into her room, Marcia was asleep on the couch, facing away from the door. His head snapped sideways at the soft sound by the wall. Ariana stood holding a finger to her lips as she tipped her head toward the door. He stepped back into the courtyard, and his new slave followed him.

He crossed his arms. "Report."

Ariana focused on his feet as she bit her lip. After a deep breath, she raised her eyes to his. "Right after you left, she cried."

He rubbed his forehead. Not what he wanted to hear.

"But it wasn't anything you did, master. It was over what she thinks she's lost. She doesn't yet see what she still has."

He removed his helmet and tucked it under his arm. "What she lost?"

"Yes, master. Without her legs, she thinks she can't run your house or raise children. But that's not true." She opened her mouth, then closed it and looked down again.

"Look at me." Her eyes focused on his again. "When I say report, I want all you've seen and what you think about it, not just what you think I want to hear."

She nodded. "Someone tried to make it nice, but that room feels like a prison. If she could get out of it and go wherever she wanted, she could run the house. Maybe a chair on a low platform with wheels that I could push or pull...or something like that."

He tipped his head. An obvious solution once he thought about it. "I'll tell Cletus to get something made immediately. What else?"

"Nothing yet. She didn't want to talk to me much. I mostly stood by the door while she slept."

He tipped his head toward Marcia's door. "Resume your post while I clean up. Then I'll take over. When I'm gone at night, you'll sleep in her room. Cletus will get something set up for that. He'll also tell you where you'll sleep when I'm here."

"Yes, master." A quick dip of her head, and she slipped back to her place on the wall.

As he went upstairs to deposit his armor in the bedchamber he'd made into his office, hope that had nearly died started to grow. After only half a day, his new slave was already proving his wisdom in finding a Christian to watch over his greatest treasure.

Chapter 5

WHERE SHE'D RATHER BE

Day 2

The pinkish gray of dawn greeted Ariana when she opened her eyes. She and two house slaves shared the tiny room next to the kitchen. The girl who helped the cook made no effort to be quiet as she rose and even stepped on Ariana as she left for the kitchen.

But it was a big improvement on the filthy slave cages.

Thank you, Lord, for bring the tribune to claim me. Please protect Diegis and Roanna and bring someone kind for them as well.

Well, the tribune wasn't exactly kind. He wouldn't hesitate to kill her if she failed to protect the mistress. But for a Roman, at least he didn't seem too cruel.

When she closed her eyes, the mistress's desolate face drifted into view. *Show me what to do to help the mistress.*

She rose and readied herself for another day of service to a woman who didn't want her there. As she approached the mistress's room, the master's voice reached her.

"Stop saying that. You are not a burden. You never will be. I won't divorce you to take another wife, and you will not shame me by trying to divorce me."

He sounded angry, but worry and frustration often sounded like anger.

Ariana pressed her back against the wall outside the mistress's room and froze. A husband and wife needed privacy, especially when they argued. But the tribune had ordered her to watch the mistress whenever he wasn't there. She couldn't go beyond earshot to give privacy, or the mistress would be unwatched when he left her room.

But it might be dangerous for him to see her there. Frustrated men who don't follow the Lord often strike out. The tribune would never hit his wife, but he might hit her.

"Please, Quintus. This can't be what you want. Let me go." The mistress's voice broke.

"I've never lied to you." The tribune's voice had softened. "Believe me when I say you are still all I want."

Silence fell and lasted much too long, so Ariana peeked into the room. The tribune sat on the couch, Mistress Marcia in his lap, his arms around her. His eyes were closed as his cheek rested on her hair.

Ariana slipped away from the door. She'd given the tribune her word that she would protect his wife because she feared him. She had no doubt he'd kill her if she failed. But fear of losing his beloved had spawned that threat, not the cruelty of an officer of Rome.

God, give me wisdom to find the way to help them both.

As Ariana adjusted the mistress's pillows so she could sit straighter, she smiled. Mistress Marcia had gone from wanting her to stand at the wall like a statue yesterday to asking for a fresh drink and some dried dates this morning. And it wasn't only to get her out of the room so the mistress could try to kill herself.

Ariana had put all the jewelry and sashes that might be long enough to strangle someone in the dressing-table drawers or the heavy carved chest. They were too far for the mistress to drag herself to them before Ariana could pass the message to the cook to get the food delivered and then return.

But asking for some food was a far cry from wanting to live. This bedchamber was gloomy enough to depress even a cheery person. It was time to get Mistress Marcia out of the dark and into the sunshine again.

"Mistress, as I was coming back from the kitchen, I saw the prettiest yellow flowers in the courtyard. There's a couch out there under a canopy. The tribune ordered it put there for you."

The mistress shrugged. "It's not worth the effort to get there."

"But won't he be disappointed when he learns you haven't used it?" Ariana swept the room with her hand. "I know they tried to make this room nice for you with the bright draperies, but it feels more like a cage than a room fit for a mistress. It would be a nice surprise for the tribune to find you waiting for him among the flowers when he returns home."

"It makes no difference where I am." A downturned mouth accompanied the shake of Mistress Marcia's head. "A soldier's wife spends too much time waiting for him to return. When his legion shifted from battle to occupation, I couldn't wait to see Quintus, so I decided to surprise him here. We had less than a week together before the accident crippled me." Pain filled the mistress's eyes, but she raised her chin. "And now I can't wait to die. My husband needs a different wife. Divorce is out of the question, but my death will set him free."

Ariana's hand flew to her chest. "I don't think the tribune wants to be free. Any man who wanted to be rid of you would never have come himself to the slave pens to pick out your new maid."

The mistress's brow furrowed. "Why did he pick you over the rest?" She scanned Ariana head to toe. "You're not big enough to carry me, and you're not pretty enough to tempt most men. Some special skill?"

Ariana dropped her gaze to the floor. Telling Mistress Marcia the real reason might put her on a cross. "You'll have to ask the tribune why."

"Hmph." The mistress fingered the elegant fabric that covered her legs. "He never lies to me, but he doesn't tell me everything. Did he tell you?"

"I won't lie to you either, mistress." She fixed her eyes on the mistress's face. "I'm sure the tribune had his reasons. He must have thought it best."

Mistress Marcia's lips tightened. "Best for me. Certainly not best for him, even if he won't admit it. But I'll convince him. Most men don't know what's best for them. Even when they think they want something, you shouldn't give it to them when it's bad for them. You should make the people you care about do what's best for them, not you."

Ariana tipped her head and donned a smile. "So, if I think it's best for you to get out of this dark room and give the tribune pleasure when he comes home, I should make you go into the courtyard?"

"Don't talk nonsense. I'm your mistress, and no slave should try to make me do anything."

"I know I shouldn't, mistress." Ariana closed her eyes and bowed her head. *God, help me convince her she wants to live so I won't have to die.*

When she lifted it a few moments later, she stared into Mistress Marcia's eyes. "But how do I explain to the tribune why you're not in the courtyard with the flowers when he told me he wanted you there? You are mistress, but he's master. If you don't care where you are and he does, please let me do what he ordered."

"Was your father a politician? If so, he trained you well for convincing negotiation." A wry smile lifted one corner of the mistress's mouth.

"No, mistress. Father raised beautiful horses. I loved helping him." It took all her will to shove back the image of him dying as the Romans led their horses away.

A deep breath was followed by the mistress's deeper sigh. "If Quintus bought you to cheer me up, he wasted his money, even though you're trying. But I can wait to die under the canopy as well as in here. Tell Cletus to send someone to carry me."

When Gracchus entered his courtyard that evening, he glanced toward the canopy and froze. Marcia was lying on the couch with Ariana standing behind her. As he redirected his steps toward her, Marcia smiled. Not quite a happy smile, but not as sad as the ones he'd been seeing.

Before he reached her, she held out her hand. "The flowers are lovely, and you were right that I'd find it pleasanter out here."

A quick kiss of Marcia's hand, then he summoned Ariana with a curl of his fingers. She walked around the flower pots to reach him, then looked directly into his eyes as she stood before him. Not the right attitude for a slave. He'd warn her later.

He put his helmet on the girl's head and hung his scabbard strap around her neck. Then he loosened the clasps on his brass cuirass and took it off. When he held it out to Ariana, she wrapped both arms around it.

Her eyes widened. "It's so heavy."

"Protection has its price." The corner of his mouth turned up. "And its reward. Put those in my office."

A quick dip of her head, and his Christian headed for the stairs. His smile broadened as he turned back to Marcia. The girl had forgotten to say 'master,' but he'd remind her later. He wanted nothing more at that moment than to enjoy the rekindling light in his beloved's eyes.

Chapter 6

PROTECTING THE MISTRESS

Day 3

Ariana picked up the tray holding the remains of Mistress Marcia's lunch of grapes, bread, and cheese. Before the next meal, she would speak with the cook. Someone had put a knife on the tray instead of slicing the cheese before serving.

She'd cut the cheese herself and slipped the knife in the back of her belt before placing the tray on the small table where the mistress could reach it.

Maybe the kitchen slaves didn't know the mistress wanted to kill herself, or maybe they just didn't care. Her lips tightened. Maybe they knew and hoped she'd do it. Whatever was true, she'd make sure it didn't happen again.

The mistress was relaxing on the courtyard couch, her arm draped across her forehead, when the squeak of a poorly greased axle made Ariana turn.

A man Ariana had never seen stood before her. Behind him, a wicker chair cushioned with fat pillows sat on a wooden platform. Four solid wooden wheels that were half the size of those on a farm wagon turned on two axles that supported the platform. Behind the chair, a crossbar would let someone push. At the front, a rope was looped and tied to make a harness that slipped over the man's shoulders.

The corner of Ariana's mouth turned up. When the tribune said he'd get something made right away to help the mistress move around, he knew how to deliver.

"Look, mistress. The tribune gave you something that will let you get out of the house."

Mistress Marcia raised herself on an elbow for a better view. "I've never seen anything like that before."

"Let's try it out. In the stableyard, there's so much for you to see: trees and a vegetable garden and the people working for you. Just outside the gate is a view of the mountains."

Ariana stepped aside and waved toward the mistress. "Please put Mistress Marcia in the chair."

The man who made the delivery dipped his head before scooping the mistress into his arms and depositing her in the chair. Then he stepped back, awaiting instructions.

Ariana adjusted the pillows beside and behind her. "Comfortable?"

Mistress Marcia rubbed her lip. "It's no worse than the couch."

"Then let's go see the mountains."

The man slipped into the harness and pulled the mistress out of the courtyard, through the stableyard, and out the gate.

Before them stretched the mountains that Ariana had loved since she was a little girl. She drew a deep breath and closed her eyes. For a moment, she felt almost free.

"Anything else?" The man's voice drew her back to reality. She opened her eyes and was once more the slave of the tribune and his wife.

"No. Thank you."

He stared at her and held out his hand, as if expecting some money. She had nothing to give him. Neither did the mistress.

"Go ask for the steward if you're supposed to be paid now, but if the tribune already paid for this..." She sucked air between her teeth. "He's not a man I'd want to get angry by cheating him."

With a frown, he turned and stomped back down the hill.

Mistress Marcia's mouth curved into a wry smile. "I see your father taught you more than how to raise a good horse, and you're right that Quintus won't tolerate dishonesty."

"Every good man values the truth."

The mistress's smile turned cynical. "You're too young to know what makes a good man."

"It isn't only age that gives us wisdom, mistress."

Mistress Marcia's mouth opened, then closed without her speaking. Her gaze locked on something in the distance, or maybe on something only in her mind. Then her shoulders drooped.

The mistress was a Roman noblewoman, the wife of the man who commanded the soldiers who'd taken everything from her. But the despair in the mistress's eyes still broke Ariana's heart. *Lord, he'll kill me if I tell her You are the truth and the source of any wisdom worth having. But she needs to know. Please reach her with something other than my words.*

After letting her gaze rest for a few moments on each peak on the skyline, Ariana turned her eyes onto the large houses now occupied by Romans on the hill below them. A group of six men in Dacian clothing entered the stableyard of one a quarter mile away. A man with straight

Roman hair and dressed in a tunic walked over to them. When they grabbed the man's arms and yanked them behind, her breath froze. When a Dacian slashed his throat, she gasped. The dead man crumpled, and the Dacians entered the house.

"What's wrong?" The mistress's voice sounded too calm for her to have seen.

Ariana slipped into the rope harness and pulled the chair back through the gate. A two-wheeled farm cart half full of straw stood near the stalls. Two mules watched her straining in the harness.

"What are you doing?" Alarm raised the pitch of the mistress's voice as Ariana stopped beside the cart.

"They're killing Romans down the hill. I'm getting you out of here before they come."

A strange spark lit Mistress Marcia's eyes. "Just give me a dagger and let them come."

Ariana shook her head. "The tribune told me you have a warrior heart, but now is not the time or place for you to do battle. I won't leave you here to die."

"I order you to let them kill me."

"But the tribune ordered me to protect you. I can't do both, so I'm going to obey him."

One of the house slaves was taking down the dry laundry. Ariana ran to her. She snatched a slave tunic from the basket and pressed it into the woman's hand.

"Put this on the mistress to hide her fine tunic. Take all the ornaments out of her hair and let it down. Then part it in the middle, tuck it behind her ears, and tie it at the back of her neck, like mine."

The woman's eyes widened. "Why?"

"Someone's going to kill the mistress if I don't get her out of here right now, and she must not look Roman."

A gasp, and the woman hurried to the mistress to help.

The stable boy stood with his mouth open as Ariana hurried over. "You harness one mule; I'll do the other. Then we'll yoke them to the cart."

By the time the mules were harnessed and yoked, the mistress was ready to load. Ariana climbed into the cart while the stable boy and laundry woman took her from the chair and handed her to Ariana.

"Stop trying to save me. I don't want to be saved." The mistress twisted as far as she could. "Where's Cletus?"

"I won't stop, no matter what he says." Ariana jumped down from the cart. "We'll need some food. I'll be right back."

The day's bread had just been pulled from the oven by the kitchen door. Ariana scooped up three loaves and tossed them in a basket. She scurried through the kitchen into the storeroom between it and the dining room. There she grabbed a wheel of cheese and several handfuls of dried dates and a bag of raisins.

On her way back through the kitchen, she paused by the cook. "There are men down the hill killing Romans. Find Steward Cletus and warn him."

She ran out the door and past the clothes lines, snatching a sheet as she passed. She set the basket in the cart by the mistress and covered her legs.

Ariana had barely climbed into the cart when Cletus ran out of the house and seized the halter of the right-hand mule.

"What do you think you're doing? Get out of this cart."

"They were killing Romans down the hill, and they could be here any moment. Tell the tribune I'm taking the mistress to my home to protect her, and we'll be back as soon as I think it's safe."

Two slaps with the reins and the mules broke into a trot, leaving Cletus staring at her, open-mouthed.

She turned the cart up the hill, heading for the shortcut through the woods that lead home.

"Take me back this instant." Anger simmered behind every one of the mistress's words.

"I can't do that. Not until I think it's safe. If we meet someone who isn't in a Roman uniform, don't say anything. Your words will betray you as Roman."

"I don't care. I'm ready to die so Quintus can be free to remarry. I have nothing worth living for."

"But we'd both be killed, and I don't want to die yet. I've only seen sixteen years. And there is always something worth living for. I don't want to die just because you can't see the reasons why you should want to live."

The hill grew steeper, and Ariana slapped the reins to keep up their pace.

"What does a slave like you have to look forward to? Being so young only means that many more years to suffer." Mistress tugged at Ariana's arm. "You're not very pretty, but men don't usually care. My husband says I'm all he wants, but how long can that last?" Her sigh was slow and deep. "You should hope he'll keep you when I'm gone. He's always gentle with me. He won't enjoy causing you pain, like some men would. That's the best you can hope for."

"While you are still alive, there is always hope for a better future."

The mistress ended the conversation with a delicate snort.

Ariana kept the mules at fast trot until the trail to her home appeared ahead. She slowed the mules to a walk to make the sharp turn off the main road. Fifty feet down the trail, she reined in.

"Why are you stopping? Are we going back?"

"No, mistress. I'm going to brush away our tracks coming off the road. In case they saw us leave and plan to follow, I don't want them to know where we turned off."

With a fallen branch, she swept away the wheel tracks. Then she climbed back in and urged the mules to a trot once more.

They'd gone about two miles when the group of four men sprang from the trees and blocked the path. Ariana's gasp turned into urgent prayer. The tribune would never know. "God, protect and deliver us. We are in Your hands."

The mistress grabbed the back of Ariana's tunic. "Wh—"

Ariana reached back to touch the mistress's shoulder as she whispered, "Don't speak, mistress. They're Dacian."

She reined in, and the leader stepped forward to take the halter of the left-hand mule.

"A fine Roman cart pulled by even finer Roman mules." His leering eyes scanned her as a sneer twisted his lips. "And a pair of fine Roman women for our pleasure."

Ariana met his gaze and straightened her spine. "I'm Dacian, not Roman. I was trapped in the Roman slave pens, but I'm free again." She shifted her gaze from his eyes to the mules. "But it is true they are fine mules. They're the only thing my mother and I have after I escaped the house of a Roman tribune who threatened to kill me."

He looked in the cart and saw the mistress. "Your mother?" His eyes narrowed.

It would be hard to find a woman who looked more Roman than

Mistress Marcia. *Please, God! Cover her with Your protection. Don't let him see what's so plainly before his eyes.*

"She has suffered so much since the Romans came. She used to walk and talk and be a happy woman, but now..." Ariana squeezed her eyes shut, as if she was trying not to let a tear escape. "Please. I'm only trying to take her home. Father was killed by the Romans, my little sister and brother taken to be Roman slaves. It's all been too much for her. If I can only get her home...maybe..."

As she thought of Roanna, alone and frightened somewhere with a slave trader doing who knew what, genuine tears filled the wells of her eyes.

The first tear trickled down. "Maybe I won't have to watch her die, too. Please..." She stared at him, pleading in silence while praying fervently, and the teardrops began forming tracks in the dust on her cheeks.

Next to the leader stood a man the same age as Father. He placed his hand on the leader's shoulder. "She could be my own daughter. We're better men than the Roman dogs. Let her keep the mules and go."

The leader's mouth twitched. A curt nod followed. He released the halter and stepped back. "The path behind us was clear of Romans, but hurry anyway. When you get home, hide your animals if you can."

"Thank you so much! I don't know how we'd make it without them."

"Go, and Zalmoxis protect you from Roman dogs."

She slapped the reins, and the mules moved forward. "I will never forget your kindness."

When the men were out of earshot, the mistress tugged on her tunic sleeve. "What did you tell them? Did I hear you call me your mother? We look nothing alike. Were they blind or fools?"

"I didn't say it, but I let them think you were. God protected us and made them see only what He wanted them to see. But even if you were my mother, I could do no more than I'm doing. Perhaps they saw that and thought of their own families. Mercy is thought a virtue among some men. Not all men are cruel."

The mistress's laugh was hollow. "Not like Roman men, you mean. If my husband were merciful, he would have let me die in the wreckage instead of making me live as a cripple. I'm only half a woman, and who wants that?"

"Your husband loves you. He's happy to have what you call half a woman if that woman is you."

"What do you know of what makes my husband happy?" She swept her hand over her legs. "No man could want this."

"I know he told me I was to make sure no one hurt you, not even yourself. If I fail, he promised me a cross to die on."

The mistress jerked on Ariana's arm to make her look back. "He said what?"

"I'll die on a cross if I let you kill yourself. He knows you want to, and he's afraid you'll try."

A leafy branch brushed Ariana's shoulder. A quick lift of her arm kept it from hitting the mistress's face.

"Why does he think a slave like you can keep me from doing it?"

"He doesn't know whether I can, but he's willing to hope. He thought the threat would make me afraid not to stop you."

"Are you still afraid? He can't touch you now. It's just the two of us here. You could toss me to the side of the road, and he would never know. No one would know."

"I would know, mistress. I gave him my word that I would do all I could to protect you. I keep my word."

The mistress said nothing, so Ariana turned back to face the mules.

"You're a strange one." The mistress's voice was low. "You could leave me and be free. It makes no sense for you to stay."

"No sense to you, mistress, but I have a reason to stay that he forbade me to tell you."

"And if I order you to tell me?"

"I can't tell you. I gave him my word on that as well."

Chapter 7

Where is Home?

Many years with the legion had hardened Gracchus against the sight and smell of death, but his first view of the corpse of his neighbor's steward in a stableyard not a quarter mile from his own ripped into him as if he'd never seen one before.

When a bleeding slave brought word of the Dacian attacks in the elite neighborhood to the legion camp, Gracchus had joined the cavalry troop as it rode out to kill whoever was responsible. They found no trace of the murderers, only the bodies of two Roman families and a handful of slaves who hadn't run away.

Gracchus swung his stallion toward the gate and signaled four of the troop to follow him. At a gallop, he led them up the road toward his greatest fear. His crippled beloved could never have run from the danger. She would have been like a lamb chained for slaughter by a pack of wild dogs.

He entered his stableyard with sword drawn. Silence greeted him.

He slipped from his horse and ran into the house's courtyard. A quick glance showed no Marcia under the canopy, and he trotted to the door of her room.

No Marcia. Even as relief over not finding her body raced through him, panic over what might be happening now snapped at its heels.

"Cletus!" His bellow should awaken even the dead.

He spun, sword ready, when he heard the steward's office door scrape the cobblestones behind him. Cletus's head peeked out, then the whole man followed.

"Master." Cletus drew a deep breath and blew it out as he walked toward Gracchus. "You came in time. I had everyone grab what they could of value and barricaded us in. The Dacians beat on the door, but it held. I was afraid they'd gone to get something to burn it down."

Gracchus walked to his steward and slapped his shoulder. "You did well." Then he stepped past and entered the room. He wanted nothing more than to hold Marcia close and tell her she was safe. He would place guards on the house to keep her that way.

He scanned the room. No Marcia. Most of his slaves were there, but not the Christian.

Three strides and he towered over his steward. "Where is my wife?"

"Her maid took Mistress Marcia to hide at the girl's house after she saw men killing Romans below us. She took the mistress and some food in the mule cart."

"Where is her house?"

The blood drained from Cletus's face. "The way she said it, I was certain you knew. She said to tell the tribune she was taking the mistress to her home and would return when it was safe. Then she drove the mules at a fast trot up the hill. There were already men coming up the road, so I herded everyone into my office as soon as they left."

Gracchus backhanded Cletus with all his strength, and the steward staggered backward. "Why didn't you ask exactly where she was going? Why didn't you send someone with them?" His hand shook with fury. He forced himself to take several deep breaths as Cletus cowered before him.

"Ask all the others if she told any of them where she came from."

Cletus dropped his head. "Yes, master." He sidled toward the office, holding his cheek after he turned his face away.

Gracchus paced, then dropped onto the couch under the canopy. He buried his face in his hands. Marcia kidnapped by her own slave, the very one he bought to keep her safe from herself. He raised his head and stared through the courtyard door into the stableyard.

Well, maybe not kidnapped. The girl had sworn to protect Marcia. If she hadn't taken her, he might have come home to her ravaged corpse. But could he trust the word of a Christian when she was no longer where he could deliver on his threat to kill her if she failed to protect his wife?

He strode into the stableyard and mounted. With a flick of his hand, he signaled his men to follow. Then he cantered out the gate and up the road. Trotting mules were no match for his stallion. He should catch up quickly if they stayed on the road.

But if they didn't... He sucked air between clenched teeth.

He urged his horse to a gallop. If he didn't find them on the road, they shouldn't be gone more than a day...if the Christian was keeping her word. If Marcia wasn't back by tomorrow, he'd start the hunt.

He clenched his jaw until it hurt. If Ariana let anything happen to Marcia, he would drive the nails into the girl's wrists himself.

A path trod mostly by horses can be rough going in a two-wheeled cart, but it was no worse than Ariana expected. She'd jiggled and bounced and jostled into her brother and sister more times than she could count as they rode in the back of their cart to Sarmizegetusa. The ride seemed smoother on the driver's seat, but she'd give anything to be jouncing in the back again while her father drove.

She closed her eyes. Well-trained mules didn't need guiding when the bushes brushed the side of the cart and there was nowhere to go but forward.

God, what am I going to find when I get home? It's been more than a week.

She squeezed her eyes tighter to stop the tears. The Romans had stabbed Father when they came to take the horses and slit Mother's throat when she ran to him. The last thing she saw as the soldiers bound her wrists and led her away was Father sliding his hand across the bloodied dirt to touch Mother's fingertips.

Father and Mother were with Jesus, but would she have to bury what was left of their bodies when she reached what once had been home?

One wheel rolled over a fallen branch, and the jolt when it hit the ground again drew a pained grunt from Mistress Marcia.

"I'm sorry, mistress. I wish we'd had time to put a mattress in the cart to soften the ride."

"How much longer before we get to wherever you're taking me?" Weariness, not anger, colored the mistress's voice.

Ariana pointed ahead. "See where the bushes pull back? It's just beyond there."

But what lay just beyond? A place of refuge for a day or two or a nightmare to be endured before evening fell?

The mules pulled the cart into the clearing. It took every bit of courage Ariana had to turn her eyes toward the spot where her parents died.

Her whole body relaxed as she released the breath she'd held too long. Mother and Father were gone. She scanned the farmyard. In a shaft of sunlight past the empty corrals, an upended rock stood by a long mound of bare dirt. Two curved lines, touching at one end and crossing at the other to make a tail, had been scratched onto it.

Thank You, God, for this mercy.

Only someone from their house church would have placed the fish there. But who had survived and was still free?

She looped the reins around a stick by the seat and climbed down.

Mistress Marcia reached to grab Ariana's arm and missed. "Where are you going?"

"To make sure it's safe to go inside." She took the mistress's outstretched hand and squeezed. "I'll be right back."

As she walked toward the house that was no longer home, a small patch of red caught her eye. Once more, tears stung her eyes. Roanna's favorite doll, dressed in the colorful scraps left over when Mother made Father's new shirt, lay at the base of the dog rose Mother had planted by the house.

She scooped it up and tucked it into her tunic. Would she be allowed to keep it if she took it back to the tribune's house? Or would it join Mother's beautiful embroidery in the fire? A slave owned nothing. That's what Cletus had said.

With her hand on the tunic she wore but didn't own, she held Roanna's treasured toy close. Maybe it was better to leave it behind. Maybe someday another family would move into their house, and another little girl would love the doll as Roanna had.

Lay up no treasures on earth. Jesus had warned that nothing on earth lasted.

Lord, help me let go of what I must. Keep my eyes on the treasures in heaven with Mother and Father and You.

◆

Marcia surveyed the rough-hewn house that was to be her residence until Ariana deemed it safe to go home. A rock foundation half as tall as a man had steps leading down to the door of a half-buried basement. The foundation supported a rectangular house made of boards. Each wall had one or two small windows. Stone stairs led up to a porch. The thatched roof over the porch was supported by five wooden poles and wooden crossbeams. A railing of close-fitting wooden slats enclosed the front and sides of the gated porch.

Ariana climbed the stairs to the porch, then entered the door. It was only a moment before she came back out. Then she went down the steps and through the door that opened into the basement.

As she returned to the cart, the girl kept her sad eyes from meeting Marcia's own.

"No one has been staying here." A long blink, and Ariana looked once more at Marcia's face and offered a weak smile. "It should be safe for us to stay here overnight. It might be safe for me to take you home tomorrow or the next day at the latest. By then, the soldiers should have come and chased away the ones who were attacking the houses the Romans had taken."

"Our house was already empty when Quintus moved in. The others probably were as well."

"Yes, mistress." Ariana tipped her head down, but not before Marcia saw the pain in her eyes. Her house was empty, too. Not because it had been taken, but because everyone had been taken from it.

Marcia shook her head to toss those thoughts aside. In war, there were those who won and those who lost. The Dacian king had asked for this war by sending his men across the Danube too many times to plunder Roman Moesia. Roman citizens had died in those raids. Now he'd lost, and his people would pay the price. Ariana was lucky Quintus claimed her before she was sold to who knew what kind of man.

But whether the house was empty or not wasn't the main obstacle to staying. She eyed the steps up into the house and down into the basement.

"I see a problem. How will you get me up or down those steps? You're even smaller than I am."

Ariana's head swung, and she looked at the house before turning her eyes back on Marcia. "I'll find a way. Somehow my God will provide."

Marcia's hand swept that thought away. "Gods don't provide. They don't care what happens to us."

The words were scarcely out of Marcia mouth when—

"Ariana!"

The deep male voice made her jump. She and Ariana both turned toward the sound.

"Cotiso!" Ariana ran to a man dressed in tight woolen pants, a linen shirt hanging halfway to his knees, a studded leather belt, and a long sheepskin coat. His gray hair brushed his shoulders, and his trimmed beard framed a huge smile. She wrapped her arms around his chest. "I'm so glad they didn't kill you, too."

Marcia's mouth turned down. Surely her friend's appearance was only a happy coincidence. But might it be something more?

◆

As her friend's arms tightened around her, Ariana fought tears.

But for the first time since the Romans came, they were happy tears, not sad.

Cotiso rested his hand on the back of her head. "I was grazing the flock in the high meadows. When I saw the smoke from the fires in the capital, I came down."

She looked past him at the four sheep just inside the forest edge.

"What happened to the flock?"

"I left them with the dogs and Rigozus on the mountain. A man by himself could draw a Roman sword. An old man with four aging ewes..." He shrugged. "I look harmless and too old and poor to bother with."

Her gaze followed his to the fresh grave.

"I buried all those from the fellowship that I found." He moved her away enough to look at her face. "I'm glad Diegis and Roanna weren't among them."

Ariana swept some tears from her cheek. "They were taken to the slave pens with me. I don't know where they are now." Her lip quivered.

Cotiso pulled her back into his arms and rested his cheek on her hair. "Wherever they are, God is with them. Although we can't see it now, God can make everything work for good in the end."

"I know, and He'll give me strength to bear the bad while I wait for the good."

When he released her, he tipped his head toward Marcia. "Who is this?"

"My new mistress, Marcia Philippa. A tribune took me from the slave pens to serve his wife. She was crippled after she came here to join him. Some men were killing the Roman families down the hill from us, so I brought her here." She lowered her voice, but Mistress

Marcia was so close, she'd probably hear anyway. "In a day or two, I have to take her back."

"Oh, Ariana." Cotiso's voice turned quiet. "And be a slave again?"

Ariana's nod was slow. "I gave the tribune my word I'd protect her."

Cotiso closed his eyes and shook his head. A deep sigh, and then he reopened them. "I'll help you while you're here."

Chapter 8

WHY SUCH MERCY?

Marcia had spent her whole life in elite Roman circles, and she had mastered the art of letting no one see her thoughts. But she was hard-pressed to keep the amazement these two triggered off her face.

She was at the mercy of two Dacians. How could they be showing her so much kindness? Ariana could have been free, but she was determined to keep her word to Quintus. That would keep her a slave. Cotiso had just buried many of his friends, people killed by the men Quintus now commanded, yet he was treating the enemy's wife like a neighbor needing help.

Mercy was not considered a virtue by Romans. From all she'd heard, Dacian warriors were no different. What was wrong with these two? Maybe not wrong, but why were they so different from anyone she'd known before?

Cotiso rested his hand on Ariana's shoulder. "What can I do?"

"I'd like to get Mistress Marcia out of the wagon. I think the porch bench would be a good place for a while." She climbed up to the cart seat, then stepped over the wall into the back. "I can get her to the edge for you to pick her up."

Marcia tightened her lips. "I'm not a sack of grain. I have arms that still work."

Ariana's quick smile met her words. "I'll move your legs; you move the rest of you."

When Marcia reached the back end of the cart, the shepherd scooped her up and carried her toward the stairs. Ariana scurried ahead into the house and came back out with two cushions. Then she pulled the bench away from the wall and angled it into the corner. "One to sit on, one for your back, and it should be quite comfortable."

Cotiso lowered her into the corner and stepped back.

It wasn't quite comfortable, but Marcia gave them a nod and a smile. Ariana was doing the best she could with what was there.

"Will that do for a while?" Cotiso's smile seemed genuine. "I need to tend to the sheep."

"It will. Thank you."

He squeezed Ariana's shoulder before going down the stairs and walking into the trees.

"Mistress."

Marcia raised her eyebrows to invite her maid to speak.

"I need to put the mules in the corral and give them water and something to eat. Call me if you need something."

Marcia's nod of dismissal sent the girl down the stairs as well.

The mules Ariana was caring for—they should have been stolen by the band in the woods. The leader should have seen her as the rich Roman matron she was. Ariana claimed her god had protected them.

But if Ariana's god had the power to protect them from robbers, why hadn't he protected her and her family from Roman troops? Maybe the gods of Rome were more powerful, but Marcia had never seen them help her. Except for Quintus wanting her, Fortuna had frowned on Marcia all her life. They'd barely married when he left for war, and just when she'd expected to reunite and enjoy life together, the accident had destroyed all hope for that.

Zalmoxis, god of the Dacians, hadn't protected his worshippers from Rome crushing them, so how could Cotiso say his god would make everything work for good in the end? Gods didn't care about those who worshiped them. All her life, she'd performed the rituals exactly when and how she should to please the gods. None had shown her favor. The gods or fate had taken her legs and left her a life not worth living.

Her gaze settled on Ariana, and Marcia rubbed her lip. It felt like she'd lost everything, but Ariana saw things differently. Marcia saw crippled legs. Her maid saw working hands. Marcia saw a woman who'd become a burden to her husband. Ariana saw a woman so beloved that her husband would do anything to keep her safe.

When you lose something, no matter how precious, you can decide to go on with what still remains. That's what Ariana had said. Maybe she was right.

The bleating of sheep drew Marcia's gaze. Staff in hand, Cotiso called to them, and they ambled over. Quick words too quiet for her to hear were exchanged between the shepherd and Ariana before Cotiso opened the gate of an empty corral. While he forked hay into a manger from a pile behind the corral, Ariana carried buckets of water to fill the trough. When he called the sheep again, the flock headed through the gate. Once they were in, Ariana closed it.

Then, with his hand on her shoulder and her smiling up at him, the pair walked toward the house.

A slave who'd just lost her freedom and family and a man who'd buried too many friends. How could they seem so at peace?

Marcia lay on the bed in the corner as the sounds of night settled around her. After their meal of bread and cheese, Cotiso had gone to sleep in the stable, and Ariana had climbed into the loft that reached halfway across the small main room.

Ariana had wished her a good night's sleep, ending with a subtle reminder that Quintus would crucify her if anything happened to Marcia. Those pleading eyes— it was impossible not to promise she wouldn't try to kill herself before they returned home.

It had been an exhausting day, but sleep eluded her. Quintus must be worried to the point of distraction about where she was.

Then the silence of the house was broken. Quiet sobbing, like she'd done so many times in Quintus's arms, came from the loft. Whispered words that she couldn't understand followed the tears. Ariana must be praying to the Dacian god.

Words in the darkness offered to deaf ears. That's all a plea to the gods was.

Then the names began: Diegis, Roanna, Cotiso...and Marcia.

Her brow furrowed. Ariana had included her with the names of those she loved.

And for some reason she couldn't explain, that warmed her heart.

Chapter 9

A Different Kind of God

Day 4

Ariana awoke to the gray of early dawn and rapid thuds on wooden planks. A muffled voice calling her name was followed by more pounding. She scampered down the ladder and opened the door.

Cotiso stepped inside and wrapped her in his arms. "Praise God you're safe."

"What's wrong?" Fear colored the mistress's voice behind her.

He released her. "The mules. Someone just stole them. I heard the sheep bleating. When I went out to check, I saw a man riding one mule and leading the other toward town. I gave chase, but he got away." His lips tightened. "I should have slept outside."

Ariana touched his hand. "But then he might have killed you before he took the mules. We probably don't need them."

"But how will we get home?" For the mistress, fear had shifted to worry.

Ariana walked to her bedside. "If we don't get back today, the tribune will send out searchers tomorrow. It might take a few days, but they'll find us here. It's only a few miles back to the road." She offered the mistress a shaky smile. "Nothing will stop him from finding you, but he might not be pleased with how I've protected you."

One corner of Mistress Marcia's mouth turned up. "He will when I tell him he should be. Except for him needing a different wife, we mostly agree." Her brow furrowed. "But if it takes them several days, what will we eat? You only brought a little, and there's nowhere to get more."

"That won't be a problem." She walked into the storeroom and returned with a quiver of iron-tipped arrows and a bow.

Ariana stepped between the bow and its loose bowstring to rest one curved tip of the bow on the outside of her right foot and the central grip against the back of her left thigh. With a slight forward bend, she pulled the second bow tip forward as she slid the bowstring into its groove.

She barely suppressed a chuckle at the look of amazement on the mistress's face as she stepped free of the strung bow. "Mother was a Sarmatian horse-warrior before marrying Father. She taught Diegis and me how to shoot from a running horse. On foot, I can hit anything. Even if a rabbit's running or a big enough bird flies slow, it will soon be in the stewpot."

She fingered the string, and her smiled faded. "She often said Father showed her how much better it was to kill rabbits than men."

Ariana's gaze shifted to the mistress. It should be Mother on that bed, not the wife of the Roman whose men had killed her. *God, give me strength to love even the wife of my enemy, and help me serve her as if serving You.*

"There's dried vegetables stored under the house and both barley and wheat. I'll make a stew for tonight."

"I'll stay with Marcia while you hunt." Cotiso opened the door.

Ariana paused in the doorway. "I'll be back as soon as I can."

◆

As soon as Ariana's footsteps faded, Marcia turned toward Cotiso. "Will she come back?"

"She said so, and she will. She'll never break her word."

"That's what she said when she refused to leave me yesterday. She'd given her word to my husband that she'd protect me."

With a silent smile, the shepherd sat at the table. He clasped his hands and rested his forehead against them. The silence that fell between them grew uncomfortable.

"Cotiso?"

"Yes?" His hands dropped to the table.

"Ariana's parents...did you know them well? How did a Dacian horse breeder marry a Sarmatian warrior?"

Cotiso leaned back in the chair and rested his hands on his stomach. "Didas grew up in this house. His father led our fellowship then, and Didas led after his father's death. Tamura, I knew her since she married him.

"They met in the capital when he was selling horses. Tamura and many from her clan were cavalry for Decebalus. Didas was telling some people about Jesus. She came over to look at his horses and started listening. Then a man showed up carrying his son. The boy was near death, burning up with fever. As Didas prayed for him, the fever left, and the boy walked home like he'd never been sick."

Marcia's brow furrowed. Telling people about Jesus? So Ariana was a Christian. No wonder Quintus had said she was unusual.

"Right away? Like he'd never been sick?" Her frown deepened. "Does any god have that kind of power?"

Cotiso's crooked smile lit his eyes. "God can heal anyone from anything when it fulfills His purpose. Sometimes fast, sometimes slow. Jesus raised people from the dead. So did Apostle Paul by God's Spirit working through him." He leaned forward to rest his arms on the table. "Like you, Tamura wanted to know what god had that kind of power, so she asked Didas to tell her about Him."

Marcia fingered her lip. Quintus had always teased her about how much she thought like the warrior women.

"He'd barely started when her captain signaled their troop was leaving. She asked if he'd come the next day and tell her more. He did, and after several more times, she wanted his God to be her God, too. When she told her father she no longer believed in the Sarmatian gods, he was angry. When she declared she followed the one true God, her clan banished her."

"Don't the Sarmatians have many gods? Couldn't she have just added one more?"

He tried to keep his lips straight, but his eyes laughed at her question. What was so funny?

"Not as many as you Romans. Only seven...a god of war like your Mars, fire, water, some others." His eyes turned serious. "But God tells us He's the only true God of all people everywhere. He created the heavens and earth, everything and everyone on it, and He commands us to worship only Him. He calls us all to follow Him: Dacian or Roman, man or woman, slave or free."

Marcia rubbed her lip again. Only one god for all people everywhere? Worship—she knew what that meant. She'd been doing that all her life with the gods of Rome. She still did, even though Quintus said they weren't real. But what did it mean *to follow*? Did Cotiso's god move from place to place?

"Where would I find this god so I could follow him where he was going next?"

His eyes were laughing again, but this time a warm smile accompanied them.

"We don't find Him like that. He's not in a town or a temple that we have to go to. He meets us where we are. He's here right now. He wants us to know Him and love Him like He knows and loves us. But from the beginning, people have made choices based on pride and selfishness that build a barrier between us and Him. A barrier we can't tear down by ourselves."

"Not even if we want to? Isn't there some ritual we can perform that will gain us access through the barrier?"

That was supposed to work with the gods of Rome, as long as the ritual was performed exactly right.

With tightened lips, Cotiso shook his head. "No. God is holy and perfect, and we're broken by the selfish, prideful choices we've made. Our choices and the things we do because of them are called sins. They keep us separated from God. And nothing we can do, no ritual, no animal sacrifice, can change that."

"Couldn't he just pretend the barrier wasn't there?"

"Truth doesn't go away just because we pretend it isn't true. We can't cross the barrier our sins have built, but He did something that could." Cotiso's mouth curved into a smile as his eyes focused on something past her.

"What did he do?"

His gaze settled back on her. "So we could be with Him, He came as a man, Jesus of Nazareth, to die as payment for the sins that keep us from Him, and now all who believe in Jesus as the One Who saved them will live with Him forever."

Coming as a man to die for people? Believe that man saved them and then someone could live forever with that god? This was nothing like what she knew of the Roman gods who took human form only for their own pleasure and cared nothing for a person like her.

"Tell me more."

"Jesus tells us we must love God with all our hearts and minds and other people like we love ourselves. Loving others, including our enemies, that's hard for anyone. We need God's Spirit to help us do it. But for some, like Tamura, making that choice carries a higher cost."

He sucked air between his teeth. "All Sarmatians train to be warriors. A young woman has to kill an enemy before she can marry. When Tamura decided to follow Jesus, she refused to kill anymore, so they cast her out. Her father sent her away with only a horse and her bow. When Didas heard, he found her and brought her to join our fellowship. He married her to give her a home, and their love grew strong and deep after they wed. Ariana was their first child. Then Diegis and Roanna." His hand swept the room. "This was a house filled with joy."

A sigh escaped him. "The love they shared...it blessed all of us who knew them." His eyes saddened when they turned toward the open door and the grave that could be seen beyond it. "He was holding her hand when I found them." His jaw clenched, then he turned his gaze back on Marcia and forced a smile. "I know they're together forever with Jesus, but I'll miss them until I join them."

With her hand over her mouth, she stared at him. The god Ariana said had protected them from the robbers. The god who'd led a war-rior woman to abandon everything with no regrets. The god Cotiso believed would bring good from bad, even when it was impossible to see how that could be. He sounded so different from the gods of Rome.

Chapter 10

REAL POWER

"Last night..." Marcia rubbed her mouth. How best to ask him? "Ariana was talking in the dark. I don't understand much Dacian, but I'm sure she was talking about her brother and sister and you. And then she named me."

Cotiso's smile warmed. "She was asking God to protect us."

"She did that when the robbers wanted the mules. 'Protect and deliver us' is what she said. 'We are in your hands.' And after they let us go, she said your god made them."

"He probably did."

"When we first got here and I asked how she would get me into this house, she said your god would provide. Then you walked out of the woods."

"So God did provide, as she said."

"But those could be coincidences. Healing the boy with the fever, that took real power. Her father prayed, and the boy was healed." Her sigh was deep and slow. "If the soldiers hadn't killed him, he could have prayed and maybe my legs could have been healed."

Cotiso leaned forward and rested his arms on the table. "Didas didn't have special power to heal. He asked the Holy Spirit to heal the boy. Every follower of Jesus has the Holy Spirit living in them. The Spirit gives us special gifts, and one is healing. Any Christian can pray for healing."

"Are you saying you have the power to heal someone?"

He raised his hands, palms toward her, as he leaned back in the chair. "No man has that power. It's God's power. I can only ask God to heal, and sometimes He does."

Marcia's pulse quickened. "Will you ask your god to heal me? If he does, I'll make him the chief of all the gods I worship."

Cotiso's headshake was emphatic. "God can't be bribed or bargained with. He doesn't want to be one of many you worship. He's told His people we must worship only Him. The rest aren't really gods, anyway. Only God is real. Only He has the power to give us eternal life, saving us from the penalty for our sins."

His eyes turned serious. "If I ask God to heal you, do you believe He can?"

"If he really is the one true god, then yes. I believe he can, but I don't know why he would want to. I'm not one of his worshipers."

"None of us deserve anything God gives us, but He gives it anyway. Do you truly want me to pray for your healing? Nothing may be the same afterward."

Nothing the same? Marcia drew a deep breath and blew it out. Her life since the accident was in shambles. Quintus was the only good thing left, and he deserved so much more than she could give him now.

"Yes. What do we need for the ritual?"

Cotiso's eyes lit as if he thought that funny. "No ritual. I just talk with God."

"That's all? Just talk? No offering of money or an animal?"

The Roman gods required payment before their priest recited the ritual prayers, although Quintus always said that money made its way into the priest's own purse, not the treasure chests of the gods.

His silent laughter expanded from his eyes to his lips as a smile grew. "He made the heavens and the earth and every living creature on it. Why would He need your money? It's only our hearts He wants, hearts that love and obey Him."

"But I don't know your god. How can I love him? I don't know what his commands are. How can I obey them?"

"Right now, you don't, but you could, if you want to."

Marcia fingered her lip. The boy with the fever hadn't known or obeyed their god either, but Didas's prayers still brought healing.

If their god healed her, how could she not want to love and obey him? Only a fool would turn away from a god with real power, and she was no fool.

Marcia took three deep breaths, blowing each out slowly. "I'm ready for you to pray."

He walked to her bedside and placed his hand on her forehead. She closed her eyes.

"Dear God, Father of my Lord Jesus, send Your Holy Spirit on Marcia to heal her legs. Open her mind and heart toward You, and when she's ready, claim her as one of Your own."

Heat coursed through her body, and peace flooded her mind. It only lasted a few moments, but when she opened her eyes, Cotiso stood beside her, hands raised, head tipped back, eyes closed.

"Cotiso?"

He lowered his arms and turned his warm gaze on her.

Her heart beat faster. "I think your god did something."

"I know. I felt the heat. Now wiggle your toes."

She looked down at her feet and sent the command. Tears sprang to her eyes even as her grin grew. The twitching of her toes declared the power of the One True God. The power of Ariana's God, of Cotiso's God, of the God she wanted to know and love as He loved her.

She willed her right knee to bend, then her left. Slowly at first, then faster until she was shuffling her feet back and forth under the sheets.

Laughter bubbled up from her inmost being and overflowed into the room. It swept over Cotiso and caught him up in the joy of it all as he laughed with her.

She swung her legs off the bed, and the small woolen rug by the bedside tickled the soles of her feet.

Arms held out for balance, she stood. She wobbled a little, but nothing was going to stop her now. She shuffled one foot forward, paused to regain her balance, then slid the other forward to join it.

Her laughter burst forth again and echoed around the room. "Thank you, God!"

Her eyes swam in joyful tears, and Cotiso took the hand she held out to him. "God has healed your body. Are you ready to hear what Jesus did for you? If you decide to believe in Him, your life will never be the same. It's not a safe choice, but He'll also heal your mind and soul."

Not a safe choice? She'd always been one to choose what was right, not what was safe.

"Tell me everything."

Chapter 11

LOVED AND WHOLE

Ariana entered the farmyard, rabbit in hand. At the foot of the stairs, she laid the rabbit down and ran her hand along her mother's bow. It was a thing of beauty, with its sleek, curved wood combined with horn and sinew to give it a springy strength that wood alone couldn't achieve. It felt good to shoot it one last time, just as Mother had taught her. She would leave it beneath her bed with Roanna's doll.

As she lifted her foot to climb the stairs, the mistress's laughter drifted out the door. Then Cotiso's deep chuckle joined it.

Ariana bounded up the stairs and into the room. Mistress Marcia sat at the table, leaning on her elbow, while Cotiso leaned back in his chair, arms crossed and a big grin on his face.

The mistress turned at her footsteps. "Ariana. That didn't take long. But now you're back, we have a surprise for you."

Ariana raised her eyebrows and waited.

When Mistress Marcia rose to her feet and took two steps toward her, Ariana's mouth dropped open, then curved into a grin as big as the one the mistress wore.

The mistress laughed. "You should see your face. Your God healed me. Cotiso has been telling me about what Jesus did when He died on the cross, and I've confessed my sins and accepted Him as my Savior, just like the two of you."

She closed her eyes and raised her arms before dropping them and hugging herself. "I feel wonderful...like a new person, loved and whole."

With her arms spread, she turned full circle. Still a little shaky, but almost a twirl. "Cotiso told me that you and your brother Diegis memorized the gospels written by Luke and Apostle John and many of the letters from Apostles Paul and Peter. He said you'll be able to answer any questions I still have after we go home to Quintus. I can hardly wait to hear everything you're going to tell me, and I can get papyrus to write it down as well."

The tribune's name sent a shiver up Ariana's spine. As soon as he learned of the mistress's new faith, he might crucify her for his wife becoming a Christian, even though she wasn't the one who told her about Jesus. But the delight on Mistress Marcia's face still brought Ariana joy. Healed in both body and spirit, she would always know the joy of being a child of God.

"Ariana."

Ariana shook her head to stop the dread images of the future.

Mistress Marcia's brow furrowed. "Why didn't you tell me it was possible to be healed?"

Ariana dropped her gaze to the floor. What could she say? She'd promise the tribune she wouldn't tell the mistress anything about Jesus or his miracles of healing.

Silence curled around them like a snake before the mistress inhale sharply. "Quintus ordered you not to, didn't he? That's the second promise you made him that you refused to break."

Ariana's shrug answered without words.

The mistress rested her hand on Ariana's shoulder. "You don't have to be afraid. I can convince Quintus to do almost anything as long as it doesn't violate his sense of honor. I can make him see that the only honorable thing to do for the woman who kept his wife alive and helped her become happy and whole again is to spare her. He should be willing to free you and let you continue to stay with me as my companion."

She sat at the table again. "As soon as his men find us and we get some more mules, we can go home. I can't wait to surprise Quintus."

"But we don't have to wait, mistress. As soon as you feel ready, we can walk back."

"How far is it?"

Cotiso leaned forward to place forearms on the table. "Not as far as you think. It's half as far as you drove if we cut through the woods. I can escort you back before I return to my flock."

Ariana's gaze dropped to the mistress's feet. Her shoes were white felt embroidered with threads of gold and colored silk. "In the loft, I have some shoes that will cover all your foot and stay on with straps that wrap up your leg." The sandals Cletus had given her weren't fit for forest travel either, but she would wear her mother's spare pair.

"Quintus gave me these right after the accident." Mistress Marcia sat and pulled one off. She traced the gold needlework. "He tried to convince me I'd need them when I walked again." She slipped off the other. "And I will, but not on a forest trail."

"If the tribune's men find us today, you won't have to walk."

"And in case they don't, I'll walk some today to get used to it again. Then we'll have a delicious stew tonight and walk home tomorrow if they aren't here by lunchtime." She set the felt shoes on the table. "You should pack anything special you'd like to keep from here and bring it home."

Ariana's eyebrows rose. "Do you think the tribune would let me keep Mother's bow and arrows?"

Mistress Marcia's laughter echoed in the small room. "He's always said I remind him of the warrior women of the Britons and Sarmatians that he admires so much. How could he possibly object to having the bow of a Sarmatian warrior in our house? Maybe you can teach me to shoot to justify his admiration." Her smile broadened. "But not from a running horse."

Ariana's own smile grew. She'd also take Roanna's doll, a shirt her mother had embroidered, Father's knife in the wooden sheath he'd decorated with a carved fish, and the small vellum codex that Diegis had made with some of his favorite parts of the gospel of John. Not treasures to anyone else, but precious reminders of the ones she loved most and would join someday in heaven for a blessed reunion in the presence of their Lord.

"I'll get the shoes, and we can take your first short walk." With a heart lighter than it had been since the Romans took everything, Ariana climbed into the loft.

Life would never be like it had been before Mother and Father were killed and the rest of her family made slaves. But God could bring good out of bad. The tribune had been His instrument for saving her from a life of slavery and Mistress Marcia from a future life in hell. He could bring good to Roanna and Diegis as well, even if she never knew how. And that would be her prayer until they met again, on earth or in heaven.

When she came back down, she knelt to wrap and tie the laces around Mistress Marcia's calves.

When she finished the first, the mistress lifted her foot and admired the shoe. "I can hardly wait to see Quintus's face when I walk into the house in these. He's so funny the way he goes from smiles to frowns and back again. He can be quite intimidating at times, but underneath he has a loving heart."

Ariana kept her head down to hide her face. A loving heart for his wife. For others, he had a warrior heart, and he expected to be obeyed. She had obeyed him, but would he think so when his wife came home a follower of Jesus and she was the only one there for him to blame?

Day 5

The next day, no soldiers had come by lunchtime. Marcia watched Ariana wrap a few things in a cloth and place them, along with her shoes, in the basket. The remaining food went into a sack for Cotiso to take back to the high meadows.

Then Ariana hung the quiver on her shoulder, picked up the bow and basket, and headed down the stairs. Cotiso also went down ahead of Marcia and offered his hand to steady her as she carefully descended, one step at a time.

"Which way?" There wasn't any path that was obvious to Marcia.

Cotiso tipped his head toward the trees past where the track entered the farmyard. "We just work our way through the woods for a while, and then we'll reach a footpath."

He called to the sheep, and they followed him into the trees. Marcia took her first step toward home, and Ariana fell in beside her.

They started out moving slowly enough that the sheep had time to graze, so it wasn't a tiring pace. But when they reached the footpath, Cotiso began walking faster.

"Are we going too fast?" Concern tinged Ariana's voice.

"Not for my legs, but…" As they moved closer to home, she'd started to think more about Quintus's likely reaction to the revelation of her faith. He'd be thrilled to see her walking, but coming back a Christian…that was going to be a problem for him.

She sucked a breath between her teeth, then sighed. "Quintus is very loyal to Rome. He doesn't believe in the Roman gods himself, but he isn't going to be happy that I've embraced a faith whose followers won't take part in the state cult. I know I can't offer incense to the genius of the emperor and the gods of Rome ever again." She plucked a leaf and tore it in half. "I want him to experience all the joy and peace from God like I have, but at first, I'm sure he won't want to listen to my reasons for making that decision."

Ariana's mouth pulled sideways into a wry smile. "That's been a problem for so many that Apostle Peter already told us what to do in one of his letters. When a husband doesn't want to believe and follow God's word, his wife can win him over."

Marcia's eyebrows rose. "Even a man so sure of himself as Quintus? How?"

A shrub covered with buds stood by the path, and Ariana plucked one that had started to open. "By pure and respectful conduct, treating him as having the authority God has given him as husband. The more he sees of the presence of God in the way you live, the harder it becomes for him to deny God is real." Slowly, she peeled the bud open to reveal the petals inside. "First he'll wonder, then he'll ask, and then he'll yield."

She tossed the flower aside and fingered her bow. "It works the same way for a woman who doesn't believe when a man who cares for her does, like when Mother turned from the Sarmatian gods to Jesus. She wondered about Father's God when she saw His power to heal. She came back to ask about Him, and soon she saw He really was God. Then she wanted to follow Him."

Marcia nodded as her smile grew. That was exactly what would work with her husband who questioned until he was sure of the truth and then acted on it.

Almost too soon they reached the hilltop overlooking Marcia's house. "That's where we live."

"Then this is where I leave you." Cotiso opened his arms, and Ariana threw herself into them. "May God bless and protect you until we meet again."

Ariana wiped the corner of her eye. "Until we meet again, in this world or the next."

When she stepped back, he took Marcia's hand. "I'll be praying for you to grow in your knowledge and love of our God."

Marcia's smile wavered, and she blinked back tears. How could she say goodbye forever to the man who'd led her to Jesus?

"When you bring the flocks down in the fall, you must come see us. I may have many questions for you."

"Ariana can answer them all as well as I can, but I will come see how you are doing and report how Ariana's part of my flock is faring." He squeezed her hand before letting go. "Now you go down there and make your husband happy again. Then lead him to Jesus to make him joyful as well."

He called to his sheep and headed back the way they'd come.

Marcia flicked away the single tear that had escaped and squared her shoulders. "Let's go surprise Quintus."

Chapter 12

Destined to Fail

Quintus's horse was lathered when he galloped into his stable-yard and reined in. Stone-faced, he had received the report at camp from his men who had searched for Marcia. He'd mounted his horse and ridden out immediately.

But he wasn't made of stone, and he didn't want to expose the ragged, raw wound in his heart to the watchful eyes of fellow soldiers who didn't need to see their leader's weakness when they needed him strong.

He swung his leg over the stallion's neck and slid off. Three steps toward the courtyard entrance and he froze. Nothing awaited him there. It never would now Marcia was gone.

He closed his eyes and fought the urge to drop to his knees and pound the ground. A tribune of Rome knew how to face death. He'd stared it down for years...but never over someone he loved.

And he didn't even have her body for proper funeral rites. He'd sent out his best trackers. They'd found the path through the woods that was barely wide enough for his cart to pass. They'd followed the wheel tracks to a house and found the cart there. The mules had been unhitched and put in a corral with hay and water.

Fresh but cold coals in a firepit revealed where something had been cooked the night before. Tracks from a small flock of sheep or goats came from the woods and entered a second corral. Fresh hay and water for an overnight stay, then the flock headed back into the woods on the other side of the clearing.

But no one was there. The mules had gone back up the path with hoofprints spaced like one was ridden and the other led. And behind the corral...a grave, fresh but at least several days old.

Christian slaves were supposed to work when you didn't watch them and never kill their masters. But the one he chose had kidnapped and killed his beloved, hidden her body somewhere, and stolen the mules to get away. By now she could be anywhere. He'd never catch her to make her suffer before he took her life, as she'd taken Marcia's.

He strode into the courtyard and under the canopy. In the midst of the flowers that were meant to cheer her, he dropped onto Marcia's couch. He removed his helmet and set it beside him. Elbows on his knees, he buried his face in his hands.

"Quintus."

It was Marcia's voice. His mind was playing cruel tricks on him.

"Quintus." The voice seemed closer.

He raised his head and opened his eyes. Marcia and her slave were walking toward him.

He shot to his feet. Marcia was walking! Six steps and he had her in his arms. He crushed her to his chest and rested his cheek on her hair.

"Too tight, dearest. I can't breathe."

He relaxed his hold and stepped back, leaving his hands on her arms lest she somehow vanish if he didn't hold her.

"What happened to you? Where have you been?"

"Oh, you mean this?" She stepped free of his grip, held out her arms and slowly twirled.

He rolled his eyes. "Of course I mean that. You're walking again. How is that possible?"

"Ariana took me to her house when the men were attacking the houses below us, and her God healed me there."

◆

The smile on Quintus's face froze. When it flipped into a frown, Marcia's breath caught.

Fury darkened his eyes. They locked onto Ariana as frown turned into scowl. In all their years together, she'd never seen him so angry.

Ariana was too close, and he seized her arms. She cried out as his grip tightened. "You did exactly what I forbade. You broke your word to me, but I won't break mine to you."

Marcia grabbed Quintus's arm and jerked one hand off her. With the other hand still gripping Ariana, he turned to face Marcia.

"Don't hurt her. Ariana kept her word to you completely, both in protecting me from harm and in not telling me about Jesus. I ordered her to let them murder me. She refused. I told her to dump me beside the road and leave. She refused, even after I told her no one would know. She said she'd given you her word to protect me, and she never broke her word. When I demanded to know why she wouldn't leave me and be free, she wouldn't tell me because she'd given you her word. She never even spoke the name of Jesus until I already believed in Him. You can't punish her for what she never did."

"Well, if she didn't tell you about him, then who did?"

She rested her hand on his cheek and stroked it with her thumb. "I'm never going to tell you. Then you won't have to do anything about it, no matter what official policy might be."

A huge sigh drained his lungs. His whole body relaxed as he released Ariana's other arm. "There's been nothing but the truth between us, so I'll spare her...this time." His brow furrowed as his mouth turned grim. "But you've made a dangerous choice. You must not let anyone know you've turned from the Roman gods. There's no way to know when a provincial governor or emperor might decide to kill Christians." He drew her into his arms and whispered into her hair. "I couldn't bear to lose you."

She snuggled in. "I feel exactly the same." Then she pushed back a little. "Now about Ariana."

His smile flipped into a frown.

Marcia pushed the corners of his mouth up with her fingertips. "You look quite frightening when you do that," Her hand dropped to his chest. "But I know what a generous heart lives in here. I want her freed to live with us like my daughter."

"That's not necessary."

"But—"

He placed his fingers on her lips. "I took her from the slave pens before she was sold the first time. No official records show she was ever a slave. The number of slaves delivered to the ships will equal the tally when they left here. If anyone notices they're one short of the original count, they'll assume she died before they left. You can keep her with you as long as the two of you only talk about your god with each other. No one must learn either of you are Christians."

His fingers traced her jawline. "I'm glad your legs have healed, but that only means the legion physician was wrong about the injury being permanent. It was only a matter of waiting long enough for the healing to occur in the natural way of things."

"That's not true. It was a miracle from Jesus. I felt the Spirit of God moving and—"

Again, he placed his fingertips on her lips. "I don't want to hear that again. No god is real. The stories about Jesus of Nazareth healing people and raising them from the dead are just that—stories. Any man executed on a Roman cross is most certainly dead, and dead men don't come back to life and heal someone seventy years later."

He kissed her forehead. "But you can believe what you like as long as you don't let anyone but Ariana know what you believe."

His smile was too indulgent, but a quiet voice inside Marcia's head told her to let it pass...for now. "If that's what you want."

"It is." After pushing back some strands of her hair, Quintus fingered her ear. "I'd rather spend the whole evening with you, but the legate planned a dinner for all his officers. I need to return to camp now, or I'll be late."

Marcia wrapped the man who loved her more than she ever deserved in her arms and stood on tiptoes to kiss him. "Wake me when you get home."

With a grin that promised more than words could express, he stepped back. "Nothing could keep me from doing that."

As Quintus walked past Ariana, he paused. He started to frown; then his mouth relaxed. "Take care of Marcia until I return, but I'll need no report from you tonight."

His gaze lingered on Marcia until her cheeks warmed. "I'll get one myself."

When her beloved placed his helmet on his head and strode into the stableyard, Marcia knew exactly what she would do. Apostle Peter had explained how to live when married to an unbeliever, and she would win Quintus over, no matter what it took.

She was now a child of God. With both Ariana and her praying for Quintus to understand what Jesus had done and turn to Him in faith, his plan to ignore the Son of God was destined to fail.

Chapter 13

A Fitting Reward

Day 6

When Ariana came to help her dress, Marcia had already pulled the sheets from the couch she'd slept on since the accident.

"Quintus won't be coming home until very late tonight. I want to surprise him by moving our room back upstairs. The master bedchamber has such a lovely view of the mountains at sunrise. This was his old office."

She picked up one of the history scrolls he'd brought to entertain her when she couldn't walk. "I could have his things moved back in here, but maybe he likes the view from the second floor better. He's placed his desk so he can look up from whatever he's working on and see the mountains."

She picked up two more scrolls and cradled the stack like a baby. "You're going to be living here with us permanently. Anyplace else would be too dangerous for you. You should go this morning to your old house and bring back everything you want to keep before someone else takes it."

"I would like to have the things in my mother's trunk." Ariana's smile was sad. "What she wore before she met Father, the embroidered tunic she wore at their wedding, her knives and Father's woodworking tools that I could someday give to my son. I can take the other two mules and bring back the cart."

"That's a fine idea, but you're not going alone. Cletus will send one of our men with you, armed to discourage any trouble. Caprius should do."

Ariana's smile drifted toward a grin. "He needs to be able to ride well if he wants to keep up with me. I prefer a horse, but riding a mule fast is almost as fun." The smile faded. "We had such beautiful horses. The gray the master rides...if he took it from this house, it was one of ours."

Ariana's eyes glistened too much, and Marcia drew her into her arms. "He had that horse in Viminacium." She blinked to halt the tears burning in her own eyes. "I'm so sorry. I wish I could undo what happened to your family."

She moved Ariana to arm's length. "But like you and Cotiso told me, God can bring good out of bad for those who love Him. I'm praying for that." She squared her shoulders. "Let's go find Cletus."

It was almost lunchtime when Ariana drove the cart into the courtyard, and Marcia strolled over to see what she'd decided to keep. Her eyebrows lifted at the pile that almost overflowed the cart Ariana had used to save her.

A small trunk was buried under three saddles, some fleece pads, several woven saddle coverings, and a collection of bridles.

Ariana met her raised eyebrows with a grin. "Scythian saddles are more comfortable than Roman ones."

Caprius climbed down and took a few stiff steps. "Where do you want everything, mistress?"

"Upstairs in Ariana's room, one door down from the master's chamber, but get two of the others to carry her trunk up. Find another trunk to store all these horse things." She gauged the stack again. "Maybe two trunks."

"Yes, mistress." His steps were slow and deliberate as he walked away.

Ariana snapped the reins and drove the cart to where it was usually parked. Then she began to unhitch the mules.

"It took a long time to go five miles and return." Marcia stroked one mule's nose.

"I took pity on Caprius and let the mules walk all the way. He was bouncing too much at the trot and looked scared half to death at the canter. I think he'll still be sore tomorrow." A wry smile accompanied her shrug.

One of the men came to finish unhitching, and Marcia stepped back. "I've had some changes made to the women's room while you were gone. Come and see."

She led Ariana up the stairs into a brightly lit room directly across the courtyard from their bedchambers.

"A Roman matron usually spends her time overseeing the household, visiting, shopping, and weaving. But Cletus has been running the household well without my help, I don't know anyone I want to visit, and what had been the market area of the capital has mostly been destroyed. That leaves weaving, but there doesn't seem to be much need here."

"We could weave for some who are unable to weave for themselves. Winter is coming, and so many lost everything in the fires in the city."

"I'll get some looms of different sizes set up." Marcia paused. Her next words might hit too close to Ariana's wounded heart. "Most of the healthy people were taken as slaves. But there must be some, maybe the old and injured, who were left behind, and maybe some orphan children too small for the slavers to want. We can start weaving and figure out who needs what we make later. Quintus might know how to find those most needing help."

Ariana walked to the window and leaned against the frame. She pointed toward the east. "From here, I can almost see home."

Marcia joined her, and the silence stretched out too long.

"I wonder where Cotiso is. How am I going to introduce him to Quintus when he comes to visit after he brings the sheep down for winter? I don't want Quintus suspecting he told me about Jesus and prayed with me. But maybe by then Quintus will be open to hearing about God, and it won't be dangerous."

She rubbed the back of her neck. "Or maybe we should meet Cotiso at your house."

"Do you really think just visiting would be that dangerous?"

"Oh, yes. Quintus told you he'd crucify you for telling me about Jesus, and he would have. I want him to share this joy, but he's not a man who will change his mind quickly without logic and evidence. If I try to move him too fast, he'll dig in and never yield."

The corner of Ariana's mouth lifted. "You make him sound like an old mule we had. Smart and a hard worker when he wanted to be. But if he got something into his head, nothing would turn him."

"Exactly, but don't ever tell him I said so. I'm glad he was too stubborn to give up on me or let me give up." She pushed back a strand of Ariana's hair. "God brought him to the cages to get you at the perfect time for me."

"God can bring good from bad. It can be hard to remember that sometimes. Master claiming me was a gift from God for us both."

Marcia began stringing a loom, humming as Ariana worked at the loom beside hers. Quintus had called Ariana a special gift, and he couldn't have spoken more truly. Ariana was the most precious gift he'd ever given her. But what gift could she find to bless her new sister and friend?

Day 8

Two days later, Ariana helped Marcia dress, then accompanied her to the triclinium. The tribune had already eaten most of his breakfast, but when they entered, he shifted on his couch so Marcia could recline next to him. Ariana resumed her place by the wall, ready to serve.

"Come join us." Marcia pointed at the couch next to theirs.

Ariana glanced at the tribune in time to see his mouth twitch. He wasn't ready to see his former slave act like his wife's equal, so she sat on the edge of the couch instead of reclining. She'd never reclined while eating, so sitting was better anyway.

"You're no longer my slave, Ariana. You'll be Marcia's companion, and anything she wants you to do is fine with me. Your quick action saved her from certain death. That has earned my deepest gratitude as well as your freedom."

Marcia shifted on the couch to look at his face. "Gratitude isn't a strong enough word for what I feel. I'm deeply in debt to her for...

everything. She deserves a special reward." Her eyes turned on Ariana. "Is there anything you want?"

Ariana's back straightened. Anything? Only to have her family alive and happy together again. She opened her mouth, then paused. That must wait until their reunion in heaven, but maybe part was possible.

"I'd like to find Diegis and Roanna and set them free, too."

Quintus rose from his couch. "A reasonable request. Find Cletus and bring him to my office. I'll send him with you to the pens this morning. He'll buy them. Then bring them here. It's safer if you all stay in my house while Dacians are still being collected to sell."

He bent and kissed Marcia.

Ariana darted from the room ahead of him. Her heart leaped as her feet flew. Diegis and Roanna, lost to her forever, had just been restored. Cletus should be moments away in the courtyard or his office. But the sooner the tribune gave the order, the sooner her brother and sister would be by her side again.

Chapter 14

Maybe Not Too Late

To Ariana, the walk down the hill to the road that led to the castrum seemed to take forever. Cletus strolled when he should have been striding. Diegis and Roanna were waiting for her, and she and Cletus would be running if she had her choice.

As they turned onto the road leading from the legion camp to the slave cages, a cavalry troop rode toward them. A mesh of small metal rings covered their torsos while pants came halfway down their legs. Many were blond with well-trimmed beards framed by the cheek guards of their helmets. With large oval shields and swords half again as long as the one the tribune wore, they approached at a trot, and Ariana's shoulders tensed.

Blue shields, not red. Chain mail, not bands of metal, but these were still soldiers of Rome, like those who murdered her parents.

Cletus stepped off the road to let them pass, and Ariana fidgeted as he simply stood there.

The troop slowed to a walk. As they neared, one turned to the rider next to him. "Looks like they left one."

Cletus stepped in front of her and frowned at the cavalryman as he rode by.

When the last pair of horses passed, Cletus stepped back onto the road, and they resumed their trek that would bring freedom to those she loved.

When she saw the tops of the cages above the row of tall shrubs, she sprinted across the field toward them, leaving Cletus behind to walk the longer distance on the road. She pushed through the bushes as their branches tugged at her tunic.

And when she stepped into the clearing beyond, she dropped to her knees as the wail escaped her lips. A torrent of tears swept down her cheeks, and sobs shook her whole body.

Everyone was gone.

"Ariana." She startled when Cletus's hand gripped her shoulder. "That's enough. Get up."

Her gasping sobs turned into silent teardrops. With a shuddering sigh, she swept the tears from her cheeks before she stood.

Cletus crossed his arms. "There's nothing to be done here. It's time to go home."

Home? She swallowed a sob still trying to escape. Home was a silent cottage at the edge of the woods where two fresh graves lay past empty corrals.

He turned and started walking. Her feet stayed fixed in place, her gaze sweeping the empty cages.

"Ariana. Come."

She glanced at him over her shoulder and fixed her eyes on the bars once more.

"Come now." A hint of irritation colored his voice. "They're gone, and they won't be coming back."

As though in a dream, she turned and followed. A nightmare, not a dream. One from which she'd never awaken.

Her whole body drooped as she trudged past the castrum for the second time that day. A week ago, she'd followed the tribune to his house, uncertain of what lay ahead for her, afraid of what waited for those she loved. Today, she walked the same road to a place that wasn't home, but in time, with Marcia there, it might feel like it.

But Roanna and Diegis were walking a road to a life of slavery, and she'd never see them again.

God, why didn't You let me rescue them? Why did You let me hope?

When she knew she could do nothing, she'd accepted what had to be. Life without hope was impossible, but hope first raised and then crushed hurt more than she knew how to bear.

When they entered the courtyard, Marcia was waiting for her. One look at Ariana, and she opened her arms wide. Ariana stepped into them, and Marcia held her close.

The sobs Ariana thought she'd conquered wracked her body once more as she clung to Marcia. Marcia's arms tightened around her...but they weren't Mother's arms. Marcia was her sister in Christ, and she was becoming a friend. But her hugs could never fill the aching emptiness in Ariana's heart. Only God and time could do that.

When the sobs finally faded away and she stepped back, Marcia pushed a strand of hair behind her ear. "What happened?"

"They're gone." Ariana's voice quavered as she swept a fresh tear away. "Everyone is gone."

"But that doesn't mean you can't find them. They'll be walking to the coast for shipping to Rome and other places. They can't have left more than a week ago. We can catch up with the slave caravan and buy them. The moment Quintus gets home, we'll plan what to do."

"We can?" The heavy darkness that had wrapped around Ariana brightened.

"Of course we can. We'll catch up and buy them and bring them home with us."

Ariana managed a trembling smile, and Marcia pulled her into her arms again. Ariana rested her head on Marcia's shoulder and closed her eyes.

Hope was a precious gift from God, and Marcia's words filled Ariana's empty cup again. Surely a tribune of Rome would know how to get two Roman captives freed.

Quintus walked into the courtyard to find Marcia and Ariana sitting among the flowers. Marcia rose the moment she saw him.

"I'm so glad you're home. Ariana went to buy Roanna and Diegis, and they'd already left. I intend to go after them, but I'll need a raeda for that.

"You're not going after them. It's too dangerous."

She squared her shoulders. "I don't care about the danger. I want to rescue them."

"I won't have you putting yourself in danger. Even if you tried, you'd never catch up with them. If they left right after I got Ariana, they have a week's head start on you, and they don't travel much slower than a carriage. It's only three weeks to the ports from which they ship the slaves. You'd have to follow them all the way to the coast. By the time you get there, they'll already have been sold and shipped out."

"But we have to do something." Fists on her hips, a determined set to her jaw—Marcia was ready for a fight.

"I can catch them on horseback. I can go by myself and get them." Hope colored Ariana's voice.

Marcia slipped her arm around Ariana's shoulders. "That's an excellent idea."

Ariana's eyes brightened. "Riding that distance is nothing. I can catch them before they reach the sea."

He released his helmet strap and placed the helmet on the couch. "It's a terrible idea. It wouldn't be safe for you to go alone. Some are still collecting Dacians to sell. You could end up a slave again."

"I'm willing to risk it to free them."

"You might be, but I'm not." He glanced at Marcia. "I'm not going to risk Marcia losing you."

"Please, Quintus. There must be some way." Marcia drew Ariana closer as both sets of eyes brimmed with tears.

Marcia never used tears as a weapon to get her own way, and it took a lot to make her cry. If it meant that much to her...

As he rubbed his jaw, a slow smile formed. "Perhaps there is. I know the right man to keep her safe and make certain the search is successful. Donatus served as my orderly for almost four months. I'll speak with him as soon as possible tomorrow. If he can go with her, they might be able to start the journey the day after that."

Marcia wrapped her arms around his chest and squeezed the breath out of him. "I told Ariana you'd know what to do." She stood on tiptoes to kiss his cheek. "You always do."

"Not always, but I do this time."

He scooped up his helmet. As soon as he put his armor in his office upstairs, he'd return to enjoy the company of the woman who made even a bad day end well.

Day 9

When Gracchus rode into his stableyard that evening, Marcia and Ariana sat in chairs under the portico. He wasn't even off his horse before Marcia was beside him.

She craned her neck to look past him and out the gate. "I thought he'd be with you. Is he coming later?"

"I told my new orderly to find Donatus. At the end of the day, he reported that he searched all over the camp and hadn't found him. Even a donkey would know better than to look for a discharged legionary inside the camp itself."

He rolled his eyes. "I only chose the man because Flaccus said he'd used him as an orderly and his work was extraordinary. It is—extraordinarily bad. I should have been suspicious when I heard laughter after I left Flaccus's office."

He lifted his helmet off and handed it to the waiting slave. "I've given him a list of places to look tomorrow. Donatus should be at one of them."

"But what if he doesn't find him? Can someone else go with her? We can't wait too long."

"No. This trip needs a man who can assess any situation and change plans at a moment's notice if needed. I could name others who could do that, but I also want a man I trust completely. That's a list of one." He kissed her temple. "I know how important this is to you. It will be worth the extra day to have Donatus as her escort."

"Well, if you're sure..." She wrapped her arm around his and led him toward the house. "I want nothing to happen to Ariana, and that requires the best."

Ariana stood under the portico, biting her lip.

Gracchus paused beside her. "You don't need to worry. You'll be traveling twice as fast as the slave caravan. There's plenty of time to catch up with them."

A quick exchange of glances with Marcia, and the Christian nodded.

The corner of his mouth turned up. "I know you two will be praying I find the right escort, even if I tell you not to. But you can stop. I already have without any help from your god."

Chapter 15

DONATUS

A taberna near Sarmizegetusa, Day 10

Gaius Sertonius Donatus sat in the back of the taberna, tracing the rim of his cup of cheap wine with the middle finger of his left hand. He took a small sip, then returned the cup to the table. His finger resumed its tireless circling.

He wanted to drink himself into oblivion. But that would take more than one cup of wine, and he restricted himself to one cup a day. That was all he had money for, and if he didn't find work soon, he wouldn't have enough for even one.

His right forearm rested on the table, palm up. He placed his left hand on the scar near the elbow and pressed hard. Sometimes that helped the pain, but not today. From the elbow to just above his wrist, the ache that was his constant companion made him want to pound his fist on the table.

But it would have to be his left fist. The knife that had pierced his leather armguard hadn't gone in deep, but it was deep enough to damage the nerves that let him control his right hand.

That had been almost four months ago. He'd killed the Dacian who crippled him with a left-handed thrust with his dagger. The man had sneered and spat in his face before the life drained from his eyes, but who had really lost that fight?

He took another sip. The wine was half gone.

He'd planned on twenty years in the legion and a pension at discharge that would let him get a farm and start over. At thirty-eight, he'd still be young enough to start a family and build a new life.

But two years was all he served. That Dacian hadn't taken his life, but he might as well have.

Tribune Gracchus had served with Donatus's centurion uncle when the tribune was no older than Donatus. Out of regard for his uncle, the tribune made Donatus his orderly while the physician waited to see if the damage would heal.

But a week ago, the physician pronounced it permanent, and he'd been given an honorable discharge for medical reasons. He'd received his last pay and a few words of gratitude for his service to Rome. There would be no pension, no farm, no family...no life as he'd imagined it.

For the last six days, he'd been looking for work, but no one wanted to hire an ex-legionary with one good hand.

Another small sip, and he traced the rim again. His uncle had taken land in Germania as his pension... a two-month walk and half an empire away. His father had died in Rome, and there was no home left to take in the cripple he'd become.

As he lifted the cup for a final sip, the soldier who'd replaced him as Gracchus's orderly entered the taberna and scanned the room. His gaze locked onto Donatus, and he strode to the table.

"Gaius Sertorius Donatus?" He spoke it as a question, even though Donatus had spent several hours explaining the tribune's responsibilities and how he expected his orderly to help.

"Yes." His cup paused in midair.

"Tribune Fulvius Gracchus wants to speak to you immediately."

"About what?"

The orderly raised his chin to look down his nose. "I don't question my tribune's commands...and neither should you."

"He's not my tribune anymore." He brought the cup to his lips and drained the final drops. "But he is a man who deserves respect whether he has authority over me or not." He rose. "I'll speak with him now."

The orderly spun and marched toward the door, and Donatus followed. Gracchus was a man who deserved utmost respect. But what could the commander of the occupation garrison want with a castoff like him?

The legionary camp

As Donatus walked past the legionaries manning the *castrum*'s gates, it felt like he was coming home. The orderly led him to the office he knew better than his escort did and knocked.

"Enter." The familiar tenor of Gracchus's voice made it feel like he still belonged there.

The orderly pushed opened the door, and Donatus walked in.

"Leave us." The orderly's mouth turned down, but he left, closing the door behind him.

Gracchus pointed at a chair by his desk. "Sit."

It creaked as Donatus lowered himself onto the seat he'd wiped clean so many times.

His former commander leaned back in his chair. "It's good to see you again, Donatus. How is civilian life treating you?"

"As I expected."

The tribune's lips tightened as he nodded.

A plate of rolls, cheese, and fruit sat beside the wax tablets the tribune had been reading. He pushed it toward Donatus.

"Eat the rest of this while I attend to something before we talk." He rose. "I'll be back shortly."

When the door closed behind him, Donatus popped the first grape into his mouth. The sweet juice shot across his tongue, and he reached for another. A cluster of grapes, many slices of cheese, and two rolls later, the empty stomach he'd started to consider normal was contentedly full. This was one day he wouldn't need to spend some of his rapidly shrinking supply of money on food.

He heard Gracchus telling the orderly to take some wax tablets to the legate before he reentered the room. The tribune's chair squeaked as he lowered himself into it and leaned back with arms crossed.

"You're probably wondering why I sent for you. I need a man I can trust to help my wife's friend solve a problem. Two denarii a day and expenses paid. Are you available for two weeks at least and maybe as long as five? You might have to travel as far as the *Mare Nostrum* and back."

One month's pay for two week's work? "Yes, but I don't have a horse."

"Not a problem. I'll provide horses for the party."

"Then I'm available."

"Good. Where are you staying?"

The only place he could afford was a room shared with five other men. Every night brought at least one change of roommate. He slept there, but he tried to be last asleep and first awake. Drop his guard at the wrong time, and he might not awaken at all.

Before he could frame an answer, Gracchus leaned his arms on the desk. "It doesn't matter. You'll need to leave promptly tomorrow, so tonight you'll sleep at my house. Let your landlord know you're moving out, and bring everything you want to keep back here. You'll accompany me when I go home."

Gracchus rose, and Donatus stood as well. "I'll explain your assignment fully when we get there and you meet Marcia's friend. My wife will want to make sure you're both well fed and rested before you leave. I hope the trip will be short, but you might be riding fast and far."

"Whatever you need, tribune, I'm glad to do it."

"Gracchus, not tribune. You don't report to me now." A slap on Donatus's left arm was accompanied by a warmer smile than he'd ever seen on his commander's face. Gracchus took a step toward the door, then glanced back. "Get your things and wait here in my office. My thanks for your willingness to still serve."

As he watched the tribune stride away, Donatus's whole body relaxed. A good meal, a safe bed, and enough money to carrying him for two months or more if he was careful after he returned.

He'd cursed his fate and would have sworn the gods, if they were real, had all turned against him. The future was still bleak, but at least for the next two weeks, he didn't have to worry about what the next day held.

It took less than an hour for Donatus to prepare for the trip. Everything he owned was wrapped in his red military cloak with a rope looped around it and knotted to form a strap for slinging across his chest. It lay on the floor by the row of chairs while Donatus paced, his bad arm cradled by the good one. He'd tried to use his right hand more than normal as he made the knots, and he was paying for that now.

A legionary could march all day in full armor with all his equipment and still dig the defensive trenches around the camp they built for a single night. He was still fit for the marching, but he forced himself to sit. He stretched out his legs, crossed his arms, and dropped his chin.

One of his roommates last night came in drunk with a swollen lip, a black eye, and a shirt much better than the one he'd left in. Donatus had stood his share of guard duty. Going to sleep was cause for execution. He'd stood guard last night so the drunken brawler wouldn't kill him for his cloak and almost-new military sandals.

He woke with a start to find Gracchus standing before him, eyes laughing. "You can sleep tonight. Let's go."

Gracchus scooped up the cloak and handed it to him. He followed the tribune into the stableyard to find three mares and the tribune's stallion saddled and waiting. Gracchus's hand swept toward them. "Pick the one you want for the trip."

Donatus knew how to ride, but he was no horseman. They looked equally good to him, so he took the closest one.

The stable hand clipped lead ropes to the halters of the other two.

Gracchus's gaze settled on Donatus's right hand. Then he signaled the stable hand. "Tie one to the other one's saddle, and give me the lead."

Donatus glanced at his fingers that couldn't even grip a rope and fought the sigh. His one good hand was needed for controlling his own horse, not helping the tribune with the others.

Gracchus mounted and started at a walk. Donatus nudged his horse to come alongside his new employer.

"Do you have much experience riding?" Gracchus sat his horse like it was part of him.

"Enough." But that had been with two good hands. Saddling the beast was going to be a problem. Was Gracchus second-guessing his decision to hire him?

One corner of Gracchus's mouth curved. "My wife's friend has more than most and will probably want to care for the horses. You won't need to do more than ride."

The tribune nudged his horse into a trot, and Donatus stayed at his side. A kick took the stallion to a canter, and Donatus kept pace. He caught the sideways glance of his commander and the nod that accompanied a twitch of his mouth that was almost a smile.

Donatus relaxed in the saddle. He'd passed Gracchus's test. He might need help getting a horse ready to ride, but he would make certain this expedition was a success, no matter what it took.

Chapter 16

The Assignment

The Gracchus house, Evening of Day 10

Donatus and Gracchus rode uphill past the houses of the Dacian elite, now mostly empty. At the top of the hill, Gracchus turned through an arched gateway into a stableyard. The stable man stood talking with a woman grinding grain, but he stopped mid-sentence to approach the riders.

"Welcome home, master." He gripped the stallion's halter as Gracchus swung his leg over the horse's neck and slid off. Then he took the lead rope from his master.

"The three mares should be saddled and ready in the morning when my stallion is."

"Yes, master."

As the slave led the three horses away, Donatus dismounted and led his mare to an empty stall.

"Leave it. Stabularius will take care of them all. Come meet my wife and her friend."

A pair of carved doors stood open, and Donatus followed the tribune through them. In one corner of the inner courtyard, pots of flowers surrounded a couch and two chairs. Reclining on the couch was a pretty Roman woman. Beside her stood a red-haired slave in a long tunic.

A smile lit the Roman's face, and she rose to meet them. "Welcome home, dear. I see you've brought the solution to our problem."

"I have. Gaius Sertorius Donatus, my wife, Marcia Philippa." The tribune's gaze shifted to the red-haired woman. "And her friend, Ariana, whose problem you'll be solving."

Donatus froze his face, but was he quick enough to conceal his shock? On the last day he served the tribune, Gracchus's wife couldn't walk, and that was supposed to be permanent.

Yet she stood before him, arm around the waist of a young woman with red hair and gray eyes. The friend of the commander's wife was a Dacian. Trapped in this house, how had she even met one, let alone have one become so good a friend the commander would hire him to help her?

Both women were smiling at him, and he returned a smile as he tipped his head to acknowledge the introduction. But was that Dacian's smile as fake as his own, hiding some sinister motive that was dangerous for the commander?

Gracchus's mouth curved into a contented smile when his wife stepped forward and took his hand.

"Dinner is ready." Her eyes turned from her husband to Donatus. "I hope you're hungry. I asked the cook to prepare enough for five."

His smile turned genuine. He hadn't been on limited rations long enough for it to show, but this wife of a military man understood.

"Thank you."

Gracchus waved his hand toward the triclinium. "Let's eat. I'll explain your assignment in detail after we dine, but I won't keep you in suspense that long. You'll be escorting Ariana to find and free her brother and sister before they get taken somewhere on the slave ships."

Donatus's nod acknowledged the task ahead, but it wasn't what he would have chosen. Every time he reached to do something with his right hand, only to find it impossible, his hatred for Dacians flared. As conquered people, it was only right that they be sold as slaves to pay for what the war had cost Rome…and him. To spend two, maybe five weeks helping one Dacian free two more? His jaw clenched.

But if it was important to the best commander he'd ever served, he would do it. And a man in his position couldn't turn down any honest job if he wanted to keep eating.

When they entered the triclinium, Gracchus walked to the central couch of the three arranged around a low table. He sat and swung his legs up to recline for dinner.

Donatus drew a deep breath. He hadn't grown up reclining when he ate, and now that his right hand was useless, reclining on his left side made eating impossible.

He felt Marcia Philippa's gaze upon him. Then she turned to the girl carrying platters from the kitchen.

"We're going to sit at the table tonight."

"Yes, mistress." She set the plate she carried on the table with six chairs around it and moved what was already by the couches to the table.

Palm up, Marcia Philippa swept her hand toward the table. "Please sit, Donatus."

He took a chair on the long side of the table, and Gracchus settled into the chair on his left at the head. Marcia Philippa sat beside her husband and directly across from him, and the Dacian took the chair beside him.

The slave filled Gracchus's goblet with watered wine and waited.

He took a sip and nodded. "You can go. I'll call if I need you before the next course."

She set the pitcher on the table. A quick bow, and the girl left the room.

Donatus reached for the pitcher, but before he touched it, a small hand came from his right and grasped the handle. The Dacian stood, then picked up his goblet and filled it. She placed it close to his left hand before filling first Marcia Philippa's and then her own.

Gracchus picked up the two forks that lay atop the salad and served himself. His wife did the same.

But before Donatus could grip one fork and balance his serving on it, the Dacian took both and placed an ample serving on his plate.

"Would you like more, Donatus?"

"No. That's enough."

He managed to stop the frown, but he couldn't control his eyes. It was more than enough because it wasn't her place to be deciding what and how much he would eat. He wasn't a small child who needed his mother to serve his portion and cut up his food.

But when the second course was served, she did it again. The third course was pastries that could be picked up with a left hand as easily as with a right, and she left him alone.

It was bad enough the Dacian insisted on helping without being asked. Each time he raised his eyes to the tribune's wife, she was watching him as well. Did she also see him as someone who needed help with the simplest things, not as a man who could take care of himself and her friend?

When the pastry course was finished, Gracchus rose. "Come to my office, and I'll explain the details of your assignment."

Donatus followed the commander up the stairs and into an office with a view of the mountains through an east-facing window. Gracchus's hand swept toward the chair in front of the desk as he settled into his own.

"Ariana's brother and sister were among those taken in the last shipment of slaves. They left for the coast seven days ago. Marcia wants to buy and free them, but that means a hard ride to catch up and make the purchase before they board one of the slave ships."

"Which port?"

"That's something you'll have to find out in Viminacium." He reached into a drawer and took out a leather purse. The jingle when he bounced it in his hand proclaimed the large sum inside.

"This should be enough to buy at least three adult slaves. Her brother and sister are eleven and six, so they should cost much less, but I don't want to risk you having too little to make the purchase when you find them."

From the same drawer, Gracchus withdrew a papyrus sheet. "This instructs garrison commanders and local officials to give you whatever assistance you need."

Donatus took the document and scanned it. The wax seal bearing the imprint of Gracchus's signet ring certified its author and his authority to command their help.

"You'll be in charge." Gracchus leaned back in his chair and crossed his arms. "But you should listen to Ariana when she offers advice. She's unlike any young woman you've met. She's very important to Marcia, and that makes her important to me. I want her well protected and brought home safely whether you find her brother and sister or not."

"I'll do everything in my power to make that happen. Is she likely to run away?"

"She's not a slave now, but she wouldn't run even if she was. She's already proven that."

Gracchus stood. "Your room is past my own and two doors down. I'll take you now."

They walked down the balcony together. When they reached the door to the master bedchamber, Gracchus gripped the door handle and paused.

"You'll be leaving early. You have a hard ride ahead of you tomorrow, so you should get the rest of the sleep I interrupted in my office."

"That was only because I stood guard to stay alive last night."

A grin punctuated the laughter in Gracchus's eyes. "That won't be a problem here. Sleep well."

He opened the door, and as he stepped into the room, Marcia Philippa's welcoming voice reached Donatus before her husband closed it.

Donatus entered his own room and sat on the bed. He loosened the laces and slipped off each caliga. The click of hobnails hitting the floor was muffled by the bedside rug. Then he stretched out and placed his good hand behind his head.

A pillow-soft bed with no drunken guffaws or angry voices signaling the start of a fight. No creaking floorboards as someone crept toward you while you tried to decide if it was an attack or just a roommate trying to reach his own bed without waking anyone. What man wouldn't get a good night's sleep in the tribune's house?

Half an hour later, he knew the answer. His arm ached abominably, and the long nap he took in Gracchus's office had taken the edge off his fatigue.

Still, it was the best night he'd had in a very long time. He welcomed the chance to earn some money, but even more he looked forward to doing something to help the man he respected more than any other. A man who deserved gratitude for postponing his discharge as long possible. A man he would do his best to serve well, even as a one-handed man.

Chapter 17

The Medicine He Needs

The Gracchus house, Day 11

Donatus hadn't had such a hearty breakfast since his last morning at the castrum. After a night of undisturbed sleep, it felt good to have a full stomach again. Gracchus had shaken the bowl of hard-boiled eggs a little as he held it out, an obvious command to eat another one or two or even three. Before taking a bite, he dipped one into the sauce Marcia Philippa had insisted he taste.

"You can see why that's Quintus's favorite." His hostess's smile broadened when he dipped it again as he nodded.

The steward entered and cleared his throat.

"Speak, Cletus." Gracchus swirled his goblet and took a sip.

"The bodyguard from the legate has arrived, master."

The tribune wiped his mouth and folded the napkin before placing it by his plate. "Take him to the kitchen and feed him if he hasn't already eaten. I told the cook to have some food packed for the journey. When he's through eating, he can get that tied to one of the saddles."

Donatus's gaze followed Cletus until he left the triclinium, then it shifted to Gracchus. His commander had hired him to help the Dacian. That would include protecting her...or so he'd thought. He'd practiced long and hard to gain enough skill with a sword using his left hand. He could hold his own against an ordinary swordsman now.

But Gracchus obviously didn't think he had what was needed.

Donatus picked up the last grape. Once firm and juicy, it might have made good wine. No more, but it also wasn't a raisin that could keep for many months and still satisfy a man's hunger. It was only a wrinkled grape. Too much like his life.

Gracchus's wife touched her husband's hand. "Thank you for arranging that, dear. I know you said it wasn't necessary, but I feel much better with two men going with Ariana. I don't want her left unprotected if Donatus must go where she can't stay beside him."

Donatus looked away to hide the start of a smile. At least two people still saw him as a capable man.

"I'm not the warrior my mother was, but I'm not entirely helpless. I expect an uneventful journey and success in getting Diegis and Roanna freed." The Dacian's voice was melodic, but Greek words with a Dacian accent would never sound as good to Donatus as Latin.

Gracchus's wife took the Dacian's hand and squeezed. "That will be my prayer until I see you safely back here."

Donatus watched the two of them over the rim of his goblet. How had a Dacian slave become like a younger sister to his commander's wife?

And how could Gracchus trust one of the enemy like this?

His eyebrows had lowered, and he was frowning at the Dacian. A mistake in the presence of her friends. He forced his face to relax.

But not before Marcia Philippa caught him watching, and her smile dimmed.

Two weeks of double normal pay while doing something for the tribune who'd helped him stay in the legion as long as he could—he could put up with the Dacian for that.

"It's time to go if you want to travel a good distance today." Gracchus rose. "We'll leave you women to your tearful farewells, but don't take too long."

Marcia Philippa slapped his arm. "We'll share more than tears, but you two need to leave if you want us to hurry. I want to pray for safe travel and a speedy return."

Gracchus's 'hmph' was not the response Donatus expected. "Do what you feel you must, then come to the stableyard. I need to leave, and so do they."

With a flick of his fingers, he commanded Donatus to follow him from the room.

Donatus glanced back at the women as he stepped through the doorway. Heads bowed, they were holding hands while their lips moved silently. A strange leave-taking, but who was he to say how to talk to a god? He never did it himself. They probably didn't even exist. And if they did, they certainly didn't care about him.

When Donatus and Gracchus entered the stableyard. Ursus, the legate's gladiator bodyguard, was waiting.

"Donatus is in charge of this expedition, and you are to help him in whatever way needed." The tribune's commanding voice invited no questions.

"Yes, tribune." The gladiator looked straight into Donatus's eyes as he spoke. Then his gaze settled on Donatus's right hand. The flare of his nostrils that followed was subtle, but it conveyed more than any words a slave would dare speak.

They stood waiting for several minutes with Gracchus's frown growing deeper. "It's taking the women a long time."

As he spoke, Marcia Philippa and her friend came through the courtyard gate.

Donatus's jaw started to drop, but he stopped it. Ariana was dressed as a Sarmatian warrior. She had rust-colored trousers tucked into leather boots and a blue long-sleeved tunic. From chest straps and a belt hung a dagger, a short, curved sword, and a bow in a scabbard with a quiver of arrows. She carried a fleece pad, Scythian saddle, and padded saddle blanket.

His eyes narrowed. The Sarmatian cavalry fought for Decebalus. Had the tribune hired him to help an enemy?

But a quick glance at Gracchus revealed he was almost as surprised.

Marcia Philippa laughed. "You should see your faces. She's not what you're thinking. Ariana's mother served the Dacian king before she married, but Ariana's only the daughter of a retired warrior and a horse breeder. I thought it best for her to dress for riding."

Gracchus's chuckle drew Donatus's eyes. "With her armed like that, a man would have to be a fool to make her angry. Simply looking at the three of you should frighten away any would-be robbers."

The Dacian looked down at her dagger and sword, then raised her eyes to Gracchus. "I'm no warrior."

"You don't have to be. Battles can be won before the first sword thrust by looking stronger than your enemy."

Donatus crossed his arms. "You look ready to ride. It's time to head out."

"I won't be more than a moment." She walked to the white mare, the smallest of the lot, and set her burden of fleece, blanket, and saddle down. It nuzzled her, and eyes closed, she rested her forehead against its cheek. When she looked at Gracchus, her eyes glistened. "I raised Zapada from a foal. Thank you for bringing her back to me."

The corner of Gracchus's mouth rose. "I didn't know. I only asked for three good horses."

"You got me one of the best."

She loosened the girth of the four-horned Roman cavalry saddle and lifted it to the ground. After placing the fleece wool-down on the horse, she tossed the Scythian saddle frame on its back and guided the breast band over its head. She tightened the cinch and secured the leather strap running across the rump under the tail. She finished by placing the padded blanket over the frame and tying the rolled blanket and her personal bundle at the rear of the saddle.

Offering a smile first to Gracchus and then to Donatus, she took the reins. "I'm ready."

A hand on his shoulder pulled Donatus's gaze from the Dacian to Gracchus. "I told you she was unlike any other woman you've met."

"And you were right." Donatus's mouth wanted to turn down, but he forced it into a subdued smile since that was obviously what Gracchus wanted. "But it's time for us to leave."

Before he could mount, the girl was seated astride the mare, looking as if she was born there.

"I'll return with her and her family as soon as I can."

Gracchus rested his hand on the mare's neck. "I expect you will."

He stepped back, and Donatus kicked his horse into a trot. The hoofbeats of two horses sounded behind him, and he headed out the gate.

The morning sun warmed his face, and a gentle breeze ruffled his hair. It felt good to be a man with a purpose again, even it was only to help a Dacian find her brother and sister to set them free.

◆

The trio rode through the gate and headed south. With a sigh, Marcia rested her hand on Quintus's crossed arms.

"Is Ariana is going to be safe with Donatus?" She bit her lip. "The way he looks at her…like she's the enemy."

He freed one arm and patted her hand. "I couldn't have chosen a finer young man to send with her. If he hadn't been crippled, he would soon have become a centurion, like his uncle. He gave me his word that he'll take care of her. He would die protecting her if that's what it takes to fulfill his promise. He's learned to use a sword left-handed. He'd still be lethal in a fight."

"Let's hope it doesn't come to that. I'm sure you know best, but he's so angry and bitter."

Quintus drew a finger along her jaw. "Then Ariana will be good for him. He's not that different from you when I brought her here."

"I'll be praying that you're right."

"You do that." His lips brushed her temple. "Just don't tell anyone which god you're praying to."

Marcia wrapped her arm around Quintus and led him to the outer gate. As she watched Ariana and her two escorts start down the hill, she began her prayers for the success of their quest, safety for all of them, and special protection for Ariana. Her gaze fixed on Donatus. She would offer special prayers for him to escape the despair she knew too well. Quintus might be right. Time with Ariana might be exactly the medicine he needed.

Chapter 18

Donatus turned his horse south and settled into a fast trot. They hadn't gone even a quarter mile when her voice reached his ears.

"Stop."

His mouth curved down. They'd only just started. What could possibly be her problem? Whatever it was, it could wait. He nudged his horse into a canter.

"Donatus." Her voice carried greater urgency. "Stop!"

Before he could rein back to a trot, she was there beside him, moving in rhythm with the mare as if she were a centaur instead of a horse and rider.

"Ursus can't do this."

He slowed to a walk, with her matching his pace perfectly.

"Do what?"

It was bad enough Marcia Philippa had decided he needed help.

But if he was stuck with the bodyguard, the man should at least be able to do what was needed.

"He can't ride at the trot and canter. He bounces too much when we're trotting. And when we're cantering..." She lowered her voice to scarcely above a whisper. "He looks scared half to death."

"There's nothing I can do about that."

"But there's something I can do. Let me lead while I teach him how to keep from bouncing and show him a couple of tricks to stay firmly seated when we ride fast."

His lips tightened. Her request was not unreasonable. It was hard on both horse and man if Ursus didn't know how to ride anything but a walk.

He took a deep breath and blew it out with a huff. "Do it."

She wheeled her horse and rode back to Ursus. When the two caught up with him, he waved for them to go past.

Her voice was quiet enough that he couldn't catch the words. Ursus's face turned toward her, and his eyebrows dipped to turn his customary frown into a scowl. But as she kept speaking, his shoulders drooped, his back sagged, and his legs dangled as he leaned back. She nudged her horse into a slow trot, and his followed.

As she sped up, he started to bounce, and she slowed the pace to a walk. He relaxed again, and she took him back to a trot. He went longer without bouncing. At the first bounce, she slowed and got him relaxed again. The time between each start and stop lengthened until the bouncing disappeared.

The pair reined in and waited for him.

"We can go as fast as you want now." The smile she gave her student was returned as a cocky grin.

Without a word, Donatus kicked his horse and trotted past them. She moved up beside him, and Ursus moved to her other side.

A horse could go a long distance at a trot without tiring. Farther than a man could stand to ride one. Farther, at least, than he could ride one. But maybe not farther than the centaur-woman riding too close for him to forget she was there.

They'd been riding for half a day when Donatus raised his hand to call a halt by a clear stream. It was time to eat a light lunch while they watered and rested the horses. But he decided to stop for one more reason. From elbow to wrist, his arm had gone past ache to agony.

He slipped from his horse and handed the reins to Ursus, receiving the usual veiled distain in response. The bodyguard's arrogance rankled, but Ursus and the Dacian would be his companions for two to five weeks, and it wasn't worth starting a fight he couldn't win.

A short stroll up the stream brought him to a towering beech. He leaned against the trunk and tipped his head back. With his eyes closed, he cradled the arm tightly against his chest.

"Donatus." The tone of her voice was soft and rather pretty, but its Dacian accent still aggravated a sore spot deep inside him.

He opened his eyes. "What?" He didn't care what the answer was.

"I think I can make it hurt less. Let me help you."

He ground his teeth to hold back the curses he wanted to speak to this Dacian. But she was the friend of his commander's wife, and that required showing her respect he didn't feel.

"Nothing can help this. You think you know more than a legion physician?"

"Not about many things but about this...maybe."

"What makes you think that? What do you know about battle and blood and getting men healed so they can fight again?"

Her jaw clamped, a mirror image of what his must have looked like. "I watched Roman soldiers stab my father so they could steal our horses and slit my mother's throat because she ran to him." Her chin quivered, but the tears pooling in her eyes didn't escape.

He froze, his gaze locked on her face as she fought emotions he'd felt himself.

Then her face relaxed. "Mother was Sarmatian. She was a warrior before she married Father, and she cared for battle wounds. She taught me something that might help you."

His eyes narrowed. "What?"

"Our neighbor broke her arm, and for a while her fingers stopped working, like yours. Her arm was hurting all the time, but Mother knew how to massage it. It helped, and she taught me how to do it."

Before he could reply, the pain surged, quenching the angry words bubbling up within him.

"If it was your horse hurting, you wouldn't refuse to let me help her. Why won't you let me help you?"

As much as he wanted to, he couldn't argue against her logic. "What would you do?"

She stepped closer and held out her hand. "Rest it here."

With his palm up, he offered his forearm, and she placed her hand underneath his elbow. When the fingertips of her other hand first touched his skin, he flinched.

"I'm sorry. I have to apply pressure, so it might hurt more at first." As her fingertips probed around the scar, he held his breath. "But soon it will feel better. Breathe, and let your arm relax. My arm will support it."

She began making small circles as her fingertips pressed into his muscles. As she pressed harder, the flames of pain flared, then started shrinking.

Her free hand wrapped around his arm, placing her thumb on the scar. With pressure that started light and deepened, she kept making circles, and with each one, the pain faded a little.

He lifted his gaze from her fingers to her face. Her eyes were closed, and the hint of a smile played at the corners of her mouth.

She stopped too soon. What had been almost unbearable pain had calmed to mild discomfort.

Her eyes opened. "Better?"

"Some."

"The pain might come back, but we'll do this every time we stop and just before you sleep. Before we finish our trip, I'll teach you how to do it yourself."

One quick nod with no words was his answer. He wanted to learn how to stop the pain himself, but there was something about the way she touched him. It was more than the pressure of fingertips that soothed his sore muscles. And as she released his arm and stepped back, there was something about her peaceful gray eyes that soothed the sore spot deep inside.

Many hours in the saddle found Donatus and his party in broken woods. He'd planned to camp until they crossed into Moesia. Most of the villages along the road had been abandoned as the Roman army advanced, and few people had returned. Many who did were now in the slave caravan with the Dacian's family.

She had been riding beside him as they passed through the first abandoned village. When he glanced at her, her jaw was clenched.

When she realized he was watching her, she turned her face away. After the second village, she dropped back to ride beside Ursus.

Why that bothered him...he couldn't explain. He shouldn't care what she thought.

They topped a low hill to find the road crossed a rock-bottomed stream below them. At the water's edge, he dismounted. Crystal-clear water gurgled across yellow and orange and brown pebbles. With his cupped left hand, he scooped up a drink. Cold and fresh on his tongue, he savored it before swallowing. Two more handfuls, then he slipped his aching arm into the cooling flow.

Hoping it would quench the pain, he closed his eyes. It helped a little, but the only thing he'd found that helped a lot was the massage at lunch.

Ursus and the girl caught up and joined him at the water's edge.

Donatus stood and gripped his forearm, placing his thumb on the scar. Like she had, he pressed while making circles, but the ache remained.

"Would you like me to do that?"

The soft voice just behind him made him jump.

He looked at her over his shoulder. "Yes."

Her left hand on his elbow, his arm resting on hers, her right thumb making circles that worked even though his didn't—it was what he needed, even if she was Dacian.

He watched her thumb. It seemed to be doing exactly what his had, but her circles did something his did not. His gaze lingered on her closed eyes and slight smile. For some reason that eluded him, that smile distracted him from his problems like her fingers calmed his pain.

The pain was mostly gone when she stopped.

"Better?"

"Yes." His single word broadened her smile. He tipped his head toward the stream. "We'll camp upstream out of sight of the road. That should be safe enough. Ursus will take first watch. I'll take second."

"I can stand watch, too."

One corner of his mouth lifted. "I'm your bodyguard. So is Ursus. It's not your place to stand guard against attack. You said yourself you're no warrior."

She opened her mouth, but no words came out. Then her eyes narrowed as her focus moved from his eyes to something past him. A slow turn, then she strolled to her horse. She pulled the bow from the scabbard that she'd hung from her saddle and an arrow from the attached quiver.

An icy calm stole the warmth from her smile. The speed with which she nocked the arrow and drew the bow bounced his head back. Only in battle had he seen that. The whoosh of the arrow as it passed too close to his ear made him flinch and brought his hand to his gladius. Had she tried to shoot him or deliberately missed him?

She slipped the bow back in the scabbard and mounted. A kick to the ribs, and her mare trotted to the edge of the trees. She alighted and pulled the arrow from a rabbit, wiping it clean on the fur before returning it to the quiver. She gripped the rabbit's hind legs and held it high.

When she rode back to him, she handed Ursus the rabbit as she passed.

A smile lit her gray eyes when she reached him. "I'll cook rabbit on a spit for dinner. Then I'll take whichever watch you give me."

He stared at her.

"Please let me help. I'll wake you at the slightest sign of trouble."

"Third watch for you."

The smile she gave him triggered one of his own...until he quenched it.

◆

Ariana had unsaddled and hobbled her own horse, as had Ursus. She watched Donatus as he tried to use his bad hand to uncinch his saddle. She took a step toward him, ready to help.

His eyes lifted to meet hers, and his eyebrows plunged. His scowl stopped her midstep. She drew back, and his gaze returned to the cinch.

His eyebrows dipped repeatedly as his left fingers worked to loosen the straps. They finally released the cinch, and it hung loose under the mare's belly. He lifted the saddle enough to slip his right arm under it and dragged it off the mare's back.

As he walked away, the aura of confidence that surrounded the tribune wrapped around him, too, as if he could do anything asked of him. Maybe that aura was something all Roman soldiers had, something that remained even when it was no longer true.

He dumped the saddle where they'd be spreading their blankets and took the hobbles from the bag tied to it. When he returned to the mare, he crouched beside her. He placed his limp fingers on the back of her foreleg. As he positioned the hobble, she moved forward. Still crouched, he moved with her. Once more, he rested his useless hand on her leg. She took three steps forward, and his jaw clenched as he stood to follow her.

Ariana's eyes followed the pair. She could offer to hobble the horse, but the scowl over her single step prevented that.

Ursus moved to Donatus's side. "Tribune Gracchus said to do whatever you needed." His sinewy hand wrapped around the hobbles. "You need me to do this."

Donatus's jaw muscle twitched, but he let Ursus take the hobbles. "Do it."

He turned and walked away without looking at her. But the aura had dimmed, and his shoulders weren't quite as square, his chin not quite as high.

And she was sorry.

Chapter 19

CROSSING THE BORDER

Just north of the Danube, Day 14

Three days of travel had brought Ariana and her companions near the southern border of Dacia. Three days of devastated villages and missing people. Three days of riding next to a Roman soldier who seemed oblivious to the suffering his army had brought on innocent people whose only crime had been having a king who challenged the might of Rome and lost.

Yet she couldn't keep herself from wanting to help him each time he tried to do something made impossible by his crippled hand. The way his jaw clamped when the pain in his forearm flared toward unbearable made her long to see him free of such suffering. Although he didn't speak it, his gratitude each time she massaged his arm and prayed for his pain to subside showed in his eyes.

Jesus had said to love her enemy, and He didn't say she could pick and choose which enemies to love with undeserved kindness. She didn't deserve the love of Jesus that had saved her. Love freely given was both His gift and His command.

She glanced at Donatus as he rode beside her. He held his right arm tight against his chest, another sure sign it was time for a massage.

"Donatus."

The eyes he turned on her had changed over the last three days from hostile to almost friendly. "What?"

"The grass is good here, and there's a stream ahead. I think it's time to rest the horses for a while. Time for me to treat your arm, too."

A smile, quickly quenched, warmed his eyes even after it vanished. "They can rest while we eat as well."

Ariana led the way to a fallen tree at the edge of the lush meadow. She alighted, and waited for Donatus to dismount. "Arm first, then lunch."

She held out her hand, and he offered his arm. As her thumb began the circles, her heart began the prayers for his healing.

It could be another week before they caught up and rescued Diegis and Roanna and another two weeks before they returned to Marcia.

She glanced at his face and found his eyes focused on her moving thumb, the trace of a frown on his lips. The frown relaxed into an almost-smile as the pain faded away.

Loving her enemy got a little easier each time she did it, and only God knew what that love might do to the heart of a warrior before they completed their journey and said goodbye.

Lederata, Moesia Superior

As they topped a hill, a river wider than any she'd even imagined stretched out before Ariana. Her hand flew to her mouth. How were they ever to cross?

Donatus's mouth curved into a bigger smile than she'd seen before. "The Danuvius, northern border of the Roman Empire. At least it used to be. The northern boundary of Dacia is our new border."

He reached across her horse's neck to point. "We'll cross it there, then head west about ten miles to Viminacium."

A string of boats, connected to each other with heavy wood beams and planking, were tied to brick towers in the middle of the river. Donatus kicked his horse and trotted ahead.

Her jaw clenched. Dacia was part of his empire now, but at what cost? Ariana nudged her mare, and Ursus followed.

Donatus slowed to a walk when he reached the bridge. At least twenty men in battle armor stood by the brick arch that was four times a man's height and at least as wide. On each side were large cross-bow-like weapons. Two soldiers stood beside each with giant arrows already loaded.

Donatus leaned toward her. "*Ballistae.* You're good with a bow, but those can shoot an iron bolt through a wooden door at three hundred feet."

Ariana bit her lip and looked away. She closed her eyes, only to have visions of her father lying at the feet of a man in that same armor with a bloody sword in his hand and her mother falling away from the metal-clad soldier who'd just killed her.

She fought the tears, but one escaped. To keep Donatus from seeing, she'd turned her face toward Ursus. With a man on each side of her, she couldn't hide from both.

The gladiator's face was impassive, but a flicker of sympathy lit his eyes.

As they drew closer, one soldier holding a long stick with a brass knob stepped forward. His gaze raked their trio, and when it settled on Ariana, his hand dropped to his sword as his mouth curved into a frown. Two men behind him drew their swords.

She swallowed hard. Marcia had thought it wise to wear her mother's clothes for the long ride, but that made her look like Sarmatian cavalry. Some of them had fought the Romans for Decebalus.

Donatus slipped from his horse and took a rolled sheet from the case tied at the back of his saddle. With the scroll in his left hand, he spread his arms in a peaceful gesture.

"I'm on special assignment for Tribune Gracchus of the IV Flavia Felix. We wish to cross here."

With his teeth, he pulled the end of the bow, releasing the string that kept the sheet rolled.

The soldier read the papyrus as Donatus held it. Then his eyes returned to Ariana.

The soldier's Latin was spoken too quickly for her to catch all he said, but Sarmatian and enemy were all Ariana needed to understand.

Two more men unsheathed their swords.

She started to chew her lip but stopped before the soldier with the staff saw her.

Donatus smiled as he shook his head. She caught some words about her belonging to Gracchus and the legate of the IV owning Ursus.

The soldier scanned the sheet once more, then nodded. Swords returned to scabbards, and Donatus handed her the string and sheet. While he mounted, she rolled it tight and retied the string so he could use his teeth to untie it. Then she slipped it back into the case he'd taken it from.

He tipped his head to the soldiers as they rode by. Under the arch and onto the boat-mounted bridge, they rode three abreast.

The rushing water slipped past the boats and under their feet, its murmurs echoing in the scaffolding, making background music to the rhythmic thuds of their horses' hooves.

When they reached the halfway point, she touched Donatus's shoulder. The river's song would conceal her words from any but her companions.

His face turned toward her. "What?"

"Did I hear you tell them Gracchus owns me? He doesn't, you know."

"He partly does, and that keeps you safer. You belonging to Gracchus and Ursus belonging to a legion commander is why you're still armed."

His thumb massaged the scar. "Any Roman sees an enemy when he looks at you. A Dacian who doesn't belong to an important man would not be welcome in Moesia right now. Even if you aren't Tribune Gracchus's slave now, you were, and a freed slave still has obligations to her former master."

"I didn't know that. I was a slave in his house less than a week."

His eyebrows rose. "Less than a week and the tribune's wife was so determined to help you? Are you a sorceress or something else who cast a spell on her?"

"No. I only cared for her as I should." She stifled a chuckle at his 'or something else.' That described her perfectly, but Gracchus hadn't told her she was allowed to tell Donatus what she really was.

◆

Donatus's thumb rested on his scar and made several circles. For three days he'd been trying to figure out what Ariana did that worked so well. He was no closer to the answer than he'd been the first day.

He glanced at her, riding in silence beside him. There was something different about her, and it wasn't just her being Dacian.

Was it something she'd done while caring for Marcia Philippa that helped the tribune's wife walk again? He didn't believe in the gods. He didn't believe in the sorcerers who claimed to wield their power. The way she almost laughed at the suggestion, it was clear she didn't either.

So why that strange smile and the closed eyes every time her thumb did what worked?

His mouth twitched. He was finding her on his mind more than he wanted. Time for a distraction.

"Ursus."

The gladiator moved up, trapping the Dacian between them.

"Is this the bridge where you crossed into Dacia?" Donatus made the question friendly. As a one-handed man, he'd never gain the gladiator's full respect, but some men would serve those they liked more loyally than those they respected. It was a long way to the coast, and if danger struck, he needed someone covering his back.

"No. I was already bodyguard to your legate, and we crossed at the Dobreta bridge." A plank creaked under the weight of big man plus biggest horse. He tensed. "I like something solid, not this. I can't swim." He eyed the swirling water to both left and right. A quickly suppressed shudder, and his usual impassive demeanor returned.

Dacius checked his own chuckle. He tried not to laugh at what a man couldn't do, especially since...

"I served a year on this stretch of the Danuvius before the invasion, so I helped build that bridge. Two of the twenty pilings and the wooden arches. If you look over the edge at the twelfth piling, you'll find the bricks marked with IV Flavia Felix that my century laid. Best bridge on the river, but it was better we cross here."

"Why?"

Ariana's quiet word drew his gaze. "The road passes through a legionary camp on both sides of the Dobreta bridge." His mouth twisted into a wry smile. "Getting a Sarmatian cavalry woman and a gladiator armed to fight through two camps without a problem…" He sucked air between his teeth. "Perhaps the tribune's letter wouldn't have been enough."

"You could have done it, but I'm glad we crossed the boat bridge. I've never seen anything like it."

"There's another between here and Dobreta. It's only ten miles to Viminacium now. We'll reach it right after lunch." He kicked his mare to a trot, and they headed west on the Via Militaris.

But her words played at the back of his mind and brought a slight smile to his lips. Maybe there were three people who thought of him as a capable man.

Chapter 20

A Difficult Choice

Viminacium, capital of Moesia Superior, Day 14

As Ariana and the men rode along the river plain, they passed orchards, fields, and vineyards worked by men in tunics. The workers had a mix of blond and red and dark hair, but always a dark-haired man with darker skin like her Roman escort oversaw the work. Most had a coiled whip hanging from their belt, and some were armed. A few workers were close enough to see their eyes, and the despair behind them tore at her heart.

Thank You, God, that Diegis and Roanna will never have to be like these. Thank You for bringing me to Marcia and for the tribune loving her enough to set us all free.

Set back from the road were houses larger than her king's palace. They made the tribune's house look like a cottage. At every stream, a stone bridge arched over the flowing water. Like the army that built it, the Via Militaris let nothing stand in its way. For their horses' comfort, she had them ride on the softer dirt beside the stone-paved road.

Finally, gray walls rose in the distance, walls a of city that dwarfed the Dacian capital she'd visited many times selling horses with Father. Walls that Roanna and Diegis had seen in despair when they had no hope for freedom. But next time they saw those walls would be different. They'd be free, reunited as a family, and heading home.

Donatus glanced at her and caught her smiling. "Your first time in a Roman city?"

"Yes."

His usually straight lips curved into a smile. "This is the provincial capital, so a man can get or do almost anything here. Stay close, and you'll be safe with us."

Safe with them? His words triggered unease. Dressed as she was, how dangerous was this Roman stronghold that was headquarters of one of the legions that had destroyed her peaceful world?

Dread had engulfed her on her first approach to the legion camp in Sarmizegetusa, but its dirt embankment with the deep ditch in front and the wall of stakes on top seemed almost inviting compared to the stone fortress that rose ahead of them. Glints of sunlight flashed off the armor of the soldiers patrolling the stone wall. A wide paved road ran between the fortress wall and an equally imposing wall that circled the city.

Donatus sat straighter, his chin raised as Roman pride lit his eyes and triggered another smile. "Viminacium. Emperor Trajan headquartered here before we crossed into Dacia." He pointed at the fortress. "Headquarters of the VII Claudia, but my century of the IV Flavia Felix was also stationed here before the final campaign. We'll be passing by the IV's headquarters in a few days."

Dressed as a Sarmatian warrior, her thick braid of Dacian red hair declared to all she didn't belong in a Roman fortress town. She felt the eyes, some curious, some hostile, that were directed toward her by the dark-haired men they passed. She nudged her horse to move closer to Donatus. Ursus moved up to put his horse between her and those who didn't like her being there. The tribune had been wise to forbid her going alone to recover Roanna and Diegis. Marcia had been wise in asking him to give her two escorts.

The first gate into the city was flanked by twin towers. Its massive doors stood open, but the soldiers guarding it destroyed any feeling of welcome. As they approached the gate, Ariana turned her gaze from the soldiers to a large oval building behind the wall to their right.

"What's that?"

Donatus only glanced at it. "The amphitheater."

"What's it for?"

It was made of wood and even taller than the towers built into the walls.

"Mostly to entertain the legion, but other people come to watch as well."

"What do they watch?

"The games." Donatus's eyes remained on her as his mouth curved into a slight smile.

"What kind of games?"

"The usual. Bestiarii fighting wild animals in the morning. Sometimes an execution at lunch time. Gladiators in the afternoon." Donatus waved his bad hand toward Ursus, who rode on her other side. "He's a gladiator."

Ariana shifted to face Ursus. "Did you win the games often?"

A snort was his first answer. "I'm still alive. I fought my last bout there with a retiarius. Right after I killed him, the legate bought me. He took me as his bodyguard when the legion moved into Dacia."

Her hand flew to her mouth as she stared at Ursus. "Men kill men there for entertainment?"

Donatus's voice came from behind her. "I think I saw you fight. You made a quick, clean kill."

Those words triggered a satisfied smile, as if they were great praise.

She forced herself to look at Ursus's proud eyes. "But it's a sin against both God and men to murder someone."

"It's kill or be killed. But if you give the crowd a good enough show, they might want you spared for another fight, even if you lose." Ursus shrugged. "I'll be fighting again in Dacia when the legion builds its permanent camp. There's always an amphitheater."

"Can't you do something else?"

Ursus's head pulled back. His lips twitched as his eyes laughed at her question. "The legate owns me. If he says fight, I fight. If I want to live, I kill."

"Just like a soldier." Donatus's voice was too matter-of-fact.

Ariana twisted in the saddle to face Donatus. He glanced at her, and his calm eyes betrayed his comfort with all Ursus had said.

How many had these two men killed?

"I'm sorry." She slowed her horse a little until they moved half a horse ahead of her. It was better if these battle-hardened men didn't see how truly sorry for them she was.

◆

Donatus turned in his saddle to look back at her. "Marcia Philippa's family has land near here. This is where Gracchus met and married her during Emperor Trajan's first war with Decebalus. She came to join him as soon as she thought it was safe." One corner of his mouth lifted. "The day she showed up at the camp...I've never seen him more shocked and angry and pleased at the same time."

"He loves her dearly. But you know him well, so I don't need to tell you that."

"Know him well?" His first laugh since the knife ruined his arm was more of a snort. "I knew my centurion well. Tribunes are Roman noblemen. I knew him only as my commander. I'm not a friend who knows his private thoughts."

"But the moment Marcia told him we wanted to rescue my brother and sister, he said he knew the perfect man to help. He knows you well enough to pick you without even thinking about anyone else."

He glanced at his bad hand. "Gracchus gave me a chance to recover enough to stay in the legion by working for him for a while. Otherwise I would have been given a medical discharge three months ago. The first time he spoke to me was the first day I worked as his orderly."

"That was kind of him."

Donatus snorted another laugh. "Don't call him kind to his face. Kindness isn't valued in the legions. Fairness is."

"And yet he's still a kind man. You should have seen him with Marcia when she was crippled. I'm glad he hired you to do what only a Roman can."

Donatus turned to face forward without responding. Was it kindness or pity that made Gracchus hire him to help her? But the commander didn't look at him with pity in his eyes, so maybe it was respect from them working together. And even if it wasn't, he would choose to believe it was. No man wanted the pity of another, even if they deserved it

They reached the main gate of the fortress. Directly across the street stood a gate into the city and beyond it the government buildings. Several major roads met in Viminacium, and the Via Militaris continued west to Singidunum, home of the IV Flavia Felix. The Via

Bassiana went on to Sirmium, where even more roads came up from the coast. Which would the caravan have followed? Where was the best place to ask?

Slavers handled the captives after the army rounded them up, and they didn't get their orders from legion officers. But his letter from Gracchus would command help at the fortress that he might not get in the city.

He felt her gaze upon him, and he glanced her way. Trust shone in her eyes. Trust that he knew exactly what to do while he knew there were too many choices to be certain he picked the right one.

But it did no good to think too long when he had nothing to guide him. He slipped from his horse, handed the reins to her, and withdrew the letter from its case.

"Stay here with Ursus. I'll be back as soon as I can."

Then he strode toward the fortress gate. The centurion in charge of the guard today would know where he should go for the information he needed, and a tribune's letter should ensure his willingness to help.

He stepped into the cool shadow of the stone arches, and his jaw clenched. Before his century moved downriver to work on the Dobreta bridge, this fortress had been home. He'd started his twenty-year enlistment within its walls. He'd honed his skills with gladius and shield. He'd learned to move as one with the eight men of his *contubernium*.

He'd planned his future with the retirement grant he'd earn with twenty years of service. He glanced at his hand. One dagger thrust, and all that was history and crushed hope.

The centurion in charge of the gate glanced at him, then switched to a startled stare.

"Donatus? I heard your century was part of the occupation of Sarmizegetusa."

"It is. I'm glad you're on duty, Cordus. I'm on an assignment for Tribune Gracchus, and I need some information."

Cordus's brow furrowed. "Why aren't you in uniform?

"A Dacian dagger." He held out his hand. There was no point in trying to hide it. "I'm out of the legion. I'm only an agent for Gracchus now."

"I'm sorry. Sometimes Fortuna frowns too soon." Cordus crossed his arms. "What did you need to know?"

"There were two slaves in the pens that Gracchus wants to buy, but the caravan left before he got the chance. I'm trying to catch up and buy them before they reach the slave ships. I need to know which road they took."

Cordus blew out a long breath. "That depends. Some go west to Narona. Others go south to Lissus or Dyrrhachium. When would they have come through here?"

"Maybe seven days ago."

"There were two caravans through about that time. One crossed the Danuvius at Lederata. The other came up river from Dierna."

"I'm tracking the one from Lederata."

Cordus curled his fingers for Donatus to follow him into the gate house. The centurion pulled a wax tablet from a stack on a shelf and scanned it.

"Sometimes the caravans sort their slaves and trade between each other here. About half went west to Narona. They'll go straight to Italia, maybe on to Rome. The rest headed south for Lissus. Many go to Delos from there, but some go to southern Italia."

Donatus rubbed his lip. "I'm after an eleven-year-old boy and a six-year-old girl from Sarmizegetusa. Any way to know which group they were with?"

"The boy, he's old enough he might get traded, so he could have gone either way. The girl...your guess is as good as mine, but the ones that young don't always survive the longer trip. Narona's closer, but I've seen young ones go south as well."

"Is there anyone in the city who might know more? I have their names."

"No one keeps track by name. They get changed by their first owner anyway."

"Thank you, Cordus."

Cordus slapped his good arm. "Good luck on the hunt." The centurion turned to the soldier waiting to speak with him, and Donatus left the gate house.

Two caravans, two directions, no way to know which to follow. Not what he'd hoped to tell Ariana. But bad news never got better by waiting. He squared his shoulders and headed back to the horses.

◆

Time dragged as Ariana and Ursus waited for Donatus to reappear. The silence between them was too deep to be comfortable.

Ariana fingered her mare's mane. "I'm glad Donatus is leading us. He always knows what to do next."

"It's good you aren't with him alone. There's too much he can't do with that hand." Disdain dripped from his words.

"Everyone has things that are hard for them. We all need help sometimes."

"He needs more than most."

Her back straightened. "Well, I think it was good of him to give up what he usually does to help me."

Ursus snorted. "What he usually does? He was put out of the legion because his hand doesn't work. With only one hand, who's going to hire him? Fortuna smiled on him when Gracchus took pity on him and gave him this job. The tribune knew he needed it to keep eating."

"No. That's not the reason he hired him. He trusts Donatus to take good care of me and to get my brother and sister freed."

"Then why did he ask the legate for me to go with you?"

"That wasn't the tribune's idea. His wife wanted two men with me for times like this when Donatus would have to leave me to do something. But I'm glad she did. With the two of you, I do feel safer, and there are often times when three are much better than two." She smiled at him. "And it isn't just because you're a gladiator who wins."

Ursus's mouth twisted into a wry smile. "This is better than staying with the legate wherever he goes. No one's going to attack him. His men seem loyal, and his enemies never get close. I'd rather be here or training for the games than doing nothing."

"But you have to kill in the games."

His shrug cut off the question she wanted to ask most, so she picked another. "Did you do something before the games?" She stroked Zapada's neck. "Before the Romans came, my family raised horses." She didn't try to stop the sigh. "But they killed my parents, and that's over now."

He stared at her; then his eyes focused on something she couldn't see. "I helped my father. We had a boat, and we fished. But the boat sank, and Father drowned. I was ten. The man who owned the boat took me and my sisters and sold us to get some of his money back. The lanista bought me to work in the kitchen until I got big enough to train."

Her breath caught. "That's terrible."

"There are worse things than being a gladiator." He shrugged again, but for a moment, his eyes betrayed the truth. Then the proud mask slipped back in place. "When you're good, the Romans can't get enough of you." He grinned. "And I'm good."

He turned his gaze from her to the fortress gate. "He's taking a long time. Maybe his tribune's letter isn't as powerful for getting help as he thinks."

"Perhaps, but I'm sure he'll figure out what to do, even if it isn't."

His 'hmph' and sneer signaled the closing of the tiny window into his soul. He crossed his arms and watched the activity around them, his gaze settling on everything but her.

She leaned over and stroked her mare's neck again. Donatus had a crippled hand and bitterness in his heart, but Ursus's scars ran just as deep. Only God could heal them both.

◆

The moment Donatus stepped clear of the gate, he felt her eyes on him. Ariana straightened in the saddle, anticipation brightening her usual smile.

When he reached her, he rested his good hand on her horse's neck. "We have a problem. Two caravans merged here. Some slaves went south to Lissus. The rest went west to Narona."

Ariana's hands flew up to cover her nose and mouth. Panic danced in her eyes. Then she took a deep breath, and her eyelids closed. She hung her head and froze.

He was about to ask if she was all right when she dropped her hands and straightened.

"We'll go to Narona."

She said it with such certainty, and he had no reason to suggest they choose one port over the other. Now if they went to the wrong one, at least it was her choice, not his, that was to blame.

Her brother and sister were only two Dacians among thousands destined to serve Roman masters until they died. But even though he hadn't cared when they left Gracchus's house, he didn't want her hopes crushed as his had been.

"Are you certain?"

"Yes." Her smile returned as she nodded. "We should go to Narona."

"Then west it is."

Chapter 21

Donatus took his reins from Ariana and jumped to swing his leg across his horse's rump. "I know this road. There's an inn with a stable near the edge of town."

"Can we go farther today? I want to catch up as quickly as possible."

"No. I've marched this road with my legion. There aren't many decent inns other than in the legion towns, and it's more than a day's ride to the next."

"If we can't find any inns, we can just camp, like we have been."

"Troops patrol the road, but robbers can be a problem. And with a pretty Dacian like you..."

Her eyes widened, which only made her prettier. Dressing like a Sarmatian warrior did nothing to diminish that. But he'd been hired to guide and protect her, and that didn't include admiring her as a woman.

"What I mean is any Dacian woman would be a temptation to soldiers who are off duty, especially if they're drunk. It might not be safe for you."

"I'd only tempt drunken soldiers?" Ariana tightened her lips, but that didn't hide her laughing at him turning his unintended compliment into an insult.

His ears warmed. "Drunk, sober...your red hair could invite trouble."

"With you and Ursus here, I'm not worried. Besides, I'll pick a place where it will be safe."

One corner of his mouth lifted. "Just how will you do that?"

Any soldier knew safety and danger could look the same until the trap was sprung.

"I'll pray."

He rolled his eyes. "Gods don't tell people like us things like that."

She arched her eyebrows. "Mine does."

His snort was all the answer her foolishness deserved.

◆

Ariana swung her horse to follow Donatus as he started back the way they'd come.

"I know a good inn the other side of Viminacium, just across the Mlava bridge."

"We're not going through the city?" She twisted in her saddle for a better view through the city gate. "Such beautiful buildings. I've never seen anything like them."

"We'll follow the wall. I'm not taking you in there. The guards on the gate might want to disarm you, and I don't want you to lose your mother's bow if I can't convince them you're harmless. Even if they let you in, a patrol might take it before we got out."

Ursus moved up beside her. "I don't want that either, I'm counting on you to get more rabbits for our dinners."

His cocky grin pulled an eye roll from Donatus.

A stone-arch bridge took them across the river to the inn just beyond. As Donatus reined toward its stableyard, Ariana stopped. "There are still a couple of hours of sunlight. We could go farther today. I want to catch up as soon as we can."

His mouth twitched, and irritation flared in his eyes. "We're traveling twice as fast as slaves can walk. We'll catch up well before they reach the coast. We're going to stay here tonight where none of us have to miss sleep to stand guard and the horses can rest without hobbles."

Her sigh was deep, but he was probably right. It would be nice for the horses to have a night with their legs free.

"I don't mind missing sleep for my watch, but for the horses...I guess we can stop early today."

◆

After Donatus spoke to the stable man, he left Ursus to take care of the horses. He led Ariana into the inn and over to the man who was obviously in charge.

"I'd like two rooms next to each other for the night."

The landlord appraised Ariana, and he obviously liked what he saw. "I only have one empty, but you'll probably enjoy that more"

Ariana moved a step closer to him and looked away from the man. "I'd like to see it."

The landlord led them to a set of stairs on one wall of the dining area. They creaked as if ready to break as the heavy man put his weight on each as they climbed.

He pushed a door open. "Here it is. Best view in the house."

Donatus crossed his arms. "And no way to lock the door." Someone had kicked the door in, and the doorjamb had been torn away where the bolt should catch.

"Take it or not. It's up to you." His smile was too smug. "I always rent it before nightfall."

The room had a single bed with plenty of space in one corner for their saddles and the rest of their gear. The floor was clean and big enough for him and Ursus to stretch out. He went to the bed and flipped the covers back. The lock was broken, but the sheets looked fresh enough.

Ariana leaned close and whispered. "We can still camp."

"In a way, we will be, but you'll be on the bed, and we'll be on the floor." He turned to the landlord. "I'll take it."

They followed him downstairs to pay and returned to the stable to gather their belongings. After taking everything up to the room, Donatus placed his sword on the bed and turned to Ursus.

"You can watch over everything while I take Ariana to eat. When we return, you can go down."

A single nod was Ursus's reply.

In the dining room, Donatus picked a table in the far back corner, but too many men still looked at her too long. It was good she had dressed as a warrior. She'd left the bow and sword in the room, but she still wore the dagger. The ferocity of Sarmatian women was legendary, and in a legion town, many would think her too dangerous to try anything.

She tore apart the loaf of bread, giving each of them chunks that were the right size for eating. He's seen enough of her to know it wasn't because she thought he needed the help. She was only a kind person who tried to take care of everyone when she could.

That triggered a smile. The gentle woman beside him was deadly for rabbits, but whether she'd kill to defend herself... He wasn't sure, but it was his job to make certain she was never in a place where she'd have to find out.

They ate in companionable silence.

He brought the wine cup to his lips and tipped his head back to drain it. "It's time to let Ursus eat."

He signaled the girl cleaning the tables and paid her for their meal. On the way to the stairs, they would have to pass a table of men who'd already drunk too much and looked at her too often. He placed his bad hand against her back. Her head snapped sideways, her eyes questioning, but she didn't move away.

He leaned close to her ear. "To make them think you're mine so no one will try anything."

And to hide his crippled hand, which might make some think he couldn't protect her.

The unease in her eyes shifted to gratitude. She stood on tiptoes, and her lips brushed his ear as she whispered. "Good thinking."

◆

When Ariana entered the room, Ursus was staring out the window. Donatus pulled a couple of coins from the purse hanging from his belt. "This should cover a bowl of stew and a drink." Ursus's hand closed around the coins as Donatus dropped them. Without a word, he headed out the door.

Donatus took the gladiator's post by the window and cradled his arm against his chest. He leaned against the window frame. His mouth was tight, and his eyes closed much longer than a blink would need.

It had been a long day, and he hadn't asked her for a massage since their first break that morning. When he lowered his arm to his waist, his thumb started the slow circles she'd shown him. But his lips stayed tight, and tiny wrinkles at the corner of his eye announced his failure to relieve the pain.

She walked toward him, left hand out. "Before Ursus returns and we all go to bed, let me do that."

His mouth relaxed into its normal frown, but he offered his arm. "What do you do different from what I'm doing? It looks the same to me, but it only helps a little when I do it."

Ariana knew why only her fingers worked, but how should she answer? The tribune hadn't actually ordered her not to talk about Jesus on this trip, but he also hadn't said she could. It was one thing for the house slaves to know (although most didn't), but quite another for a former soldier to find out she followed Jesus.

"Let me watch you. I might be able to tell you then."

She would watch, but she already knew what made the difference. Each time, she asked God to take away his pain and heal the wound that caused it.

Her gaze settled on his face. It looked weary beyond his twenty years. It wasn't only the pain in his arm that she prayed for. He needed God to heal his wounded heart as well.

He made several thumb circles, then offered his arm. She began the massage, then shifted her gaze to his eyes while her thumb kept moving.

His lips relaxed as the pain dulled, then retightened. "It looks exactly like what I do."

It would because it was what he did.

"If I tell you, you mustn't repeat it." That should satisfy Gracchus.

"I won't."

"I pray."

His head pulled back. "To whom? The god you said will tell you where it's safe to camp?"

"Yes."

He rolled his eyes. "Gods don't talk to people, and they don't answer prayers. It's something else."

She offered him a smile as she shrugged. He didn't want the truth now, but they would be traveling many days before they returned to Marcia. Maybe one day he would.

He moved his arm away. "That's enough for now. When you're ready to tell me what you really do, you won't have to do this anymore."

"I did, but I don't mind doing it until you're ready to listen to what I say."

A small shake of his head, and he turned back to the window to watch the sunset.

Until the door creaked, announcing Ursus's return, she sat on the bed and prayed for Donatus to see God's sunrise as well.

Something rustled, and Ariana's eyes popped open. Silence, then something moved in the darkness. "Donatus?" Her whisper felt like a shout.

"What?" His whispered reply came from near the window, not where she'd seen him lie down by Ursus.

"Did your arm get you up? I can massage it."

"It's fine. Go back to sleep."

"Are you sure?"

"Yes. Go to sleep."

She lay down and wriggled a little to find the least lumpy place on the mattress. His arm did get him up, and it wasn't fine at all. But if he didn't want her to help him, there was nothing she could do. Nothing except pray, and there was nothing he could do to stop that.

Chapter 22

THE WOMAN HE NEEDS

Sarmizegetusa, Day 15

Marcia entered the triclinium to find Quintus at the table, dipping his final hard-boiled egg into his favorite sauce. She placed her hands on his shoulders and gave a gentle squeeze.

He tipped his head back to smile at her. "I tried not to wake you, but I'm glad I failed."

"Morning is always better when we eat together." Her fingers kneaded his shoulders, and he relaxed against the back of the chair.

"It was too quiet yesterday." She kissed his temple and resumed the massage. "I miss Ariana. How do you think they're doing?"

"They would have reached Viminacium yesterday. They should be starting toward one of the ports today."

"That's only part of what I'm asking. I wonder how she and Donatus are getting along."

"He'll do all he can to take care of her. You don't have to worry about her."

"It's not Ariana I'm worrying about."

"Donatus? I'm sure he's fine."

"But he wasn't fine when he came here. He's lost everything that was important to him. He's trying to find his way, but with his hand, what's he going to do?"

"If it were my choice, he'd still work for me. He's the best I've ever had as my orderly. His replacement is...less than adequate. I'll be selecting another tomorrow."

"I've been praying for them. You said Ariana would be good for him, and I'm sure you're right. But I don't know what God's going to do."

"Nothing. That's what your god will do. But she is a cheerful presence, and that's good medicine for anyone."

He stood. "I'll be late tonight."

She stroked his jaw. "Be sure to wake me, no matter how late."

The corner of his mouth turned up. "Donatus needs a woman like you. If she weren't a Christian, your Ariana could have been be the woman he needs."

"She still might be. The very best wives are Christian."

His lips brushed her forehead. "One of them is, but she's the exception. And the fact that she is will remain our secret."

She slipped her arms around him for a quick hug. "Of course, dear."

As he left the room, her smile saddened. *Whatever it takes, claim his heart, Lord. Please make him Yours, as I am, and please do it soon.*

Via Militaris, west of Viminacium, Day 15

Ariana awoke to find Ursus still under his blankets and curled into a ball in the corner. But Donatus's blankets were rolled and by his saddle, and he was gone.

Footsteps approached in the hallway, and she drew the blanket up to her nose as the door swung into the room. Her breath released when Donatus stepped in carrying a basket.

She swung her feet out of the bed and took the basket from him. The aroma of rosemary-laced bread wafted toward her, and she lifted the basket to her nose and inhaled.

"This smells wonderful, but there's so much." She moved two loaves to the side and discovered cheese and raisins hiding beneath them.

With expenses paid by Gracchus, he wasn't going to short-ration Ursus or himself. "Food for two men...is there ever too much? Besides, it's for breakfast and lunch. Tonight we should be at Tricornium, and there's a taberna there with a good stew for dinner."

"How far will we go today?" She picked up a raisin and popped it between her teeth.

"Far enough that we'll reach Singidunum early tomorrow. There's an auxiliary fort at Tricornium, so it should be safe in the campground there."

Ursus stirred, then flipped off the covers as he stood. "Ground makes a better mattress than these floorboards."

Donatus took the basket back. "Let's eat and get going."

Ariana rose and smoothed the sheets. "I'll be back in a moment." She hadn't reached the door when Donatus fell in beside her. "The drunks from last night, not all have left. I'll escort you."

"If you think you must, but I don't think it's needed."

The tip of his head toward the door was his only answer.

She really didn't need an escort, but his insistence was a sign that he cared what happened to her. That warmed the place in her heart that this Roman filled more each day.

Ten miles along the Danuvius took Ariana and her escorts across a plain and brought them to Margum, with its earth-and-timber legionary fort just across the Margus river from the town. Five more miles and the plain turned into low hills. They continued to follow the military road along the river, and another five miles brought them to an auxiliary fort at Aureus Mons. At every fort, Donatus described which legion or auxiliary unit was stationed there.

She wouldn't have cared, except he looked at his hand each time and turned silent. He tried to keep the emotion from his face, but a wistful look escaped as they rode by each. Then the frown he'd worn when she first saw him returned for a while.

But at least the frown was no longer aimed at her, and when he caught her watching him, it softened into a sad smile.

It was early evening when they rode up to the earth-and-timber fort at Tricornium.

"You'll see Germans here and maybe some fine horses. The I Flavia Bessorum equitata is mixed infantry and cavalry."

"What I most want to see is some of that delicious stew you described."

"We'll eat fast while Ursus watches everything."

Ursus slipped from his horse and took their reins when they dismounted. "I'll pick a campsite."

"Good." Donatus waved his hand toward the taberna. "The sooner we eat, the sooner Ursus can."

She moved to his right side to distract curious eyes from his hand, and they headed toward the delicious smells wafting through the taberna door. Good food in the company of a good man—that thought made her smile. But his heart was so far from God, and that put a barrier between them she could never cross, no matter how good he might be.

Ariana watched Donatus roll out his bedroll by the pit where Ursus had arranged the wood before going to eat.

"You'll sleep here between Ursus and me."

"If you think that's best." She spread her own bed where he pointed.

Someone in the camp began plucking a lyre and singing in a language Ariana didn't know, but the music was lilting and lovely. "Do you know what he's singing?"

Donatus listened a moment. "No, but it sounds sad."

The only sadness was in his voice, and that plucked at her heartstrings. "Before we sleep, would you like a massage?"

"It's not bad tonight."

His mouth said no, but his eyes spoke the truth. She held out her hand, and he gave her his arm.

As she massaged away the pain, she glanced at his eyes. He used to watch her fingers, but now he watched her face. Each time she looked up, his lips curved with a trace of a smile. When they left Sarmizegetusa, his eyes had been those of an enemy, but they had become the eyes of a friend. And with each circle of her thumb, she prayed God would touch his arm and his heart and heal both.

That night, Donatus took second watch. He sat by the fire, trying to hear any suspicious sounds, but that was almost impossible. Ursus had finished first watch, and now he sprawled on his back, mouth open. His snores rumbled like not-so-distant thunder, and Donatus strolled over to nudge the big man with his foot. The Syrian rolled on his side, and his breathing quieted.

The fire crackled behind him. Hand on his sword, he spun to find Ariana sitting on the log, poking at the coals with a stick.

He stared at her across the fire, arms crossed. "It's not your watch yet."

She raised her eyes from the flames to fix them on his. "I know." Her gaze settled on Ursus. "But the bear was growling loud enough to wake me. I've slept enough already."

The corner of his mouth lifted. "I'm not sure if it's the fire or his snores that keep the wolves away."

"Could be either." She patted the log beside her. "If you're not ready to sleep yet, maybe we can talk a while."

"About what?" He rested his arm against his stomach while his thumb made slow circles around the scar.

"Where we're going. What we can expect." A large branch shifted, sending sparks upward, and her stick repositioned it. "I've never been more than ten miles from home."

He settled on the log next to her, but not too close. "We'll stay on the Via Militaris to its end in Singidunum, then follow the road along the Danuvius until the Via Bassiana branches off toward Sirmium. From there, we head southwest to Narona on the coast."

"Have you been on that road?"

"No, but Gracchus sent letters there. It's the capital of Pannonia Inferior, and the garrison was manned by a detachment from our legion.

"How long to get there?" The fire popped, and she flipped the escaping ember back among the coals.

"Another day and a half to Sirmium. From Sirmium, six, maybe seven days. We're traveling almost twice as fast as the caravan, so we should catch up two or three days before they reach the coast, even if they left the same day Gracchus got you."

A shiver ran through her, so he went to her bedroll and returned with the top blanket. He would have wrapped it around her shoulders if his fingers could grip it, but he had to settle for holding it out to her.

She stood and flipped it around her shoulders. As she drew it close, her smile warmed him better than a cloak in winter. "Thank you...for everything."

"It's only a blanket."

"Thank you for being willing to help me. The tribune was right that I could never have done it alone."

"Whatever he asks, he's a man it's hard to say no to." One corner of his mouth turned up. "He was my commander for two years." He struck his chest with his right arm; crippled fingers didn't prevent that. "'Yes, tribune' is the only correct response to his orders...or requests."

Her gaze lifted from the changing patterns of yellow and orange shimmering on the coals and rested on him. "I know you said kindness isn't valued in the legion, but I think you're both kind men. At least to me."

Any man would want to be kind to her, but he would never tell her that.

"No. If I were kind, I wouldn't be letting you stand watch." He stood and arched his back. "And I'm certainly not kind enough to forego sleep to keep you company." He lowered himself to his bedroll and pulled the covers over him. "Wake me if there's a problem."

He kept his eyes closed long enough that she shouldn't be looking at him. But when he opened them for one last view of her before sleeping, he was greeted by a gentle smile and warmth in her calm gray eyes.

Chapter 23

Day 16

Donatus had started them down the road early. By midmorning, they were approaching Singidunum, and the first view of the castrum made Ariana's breath catch.

Perched atop a distant hill overlooking the Danuvius, the walls of white limestone caught the sun's rays as if lit from within. It was a fitting monument to Roman power. From a distance, it looked deceptively small, but she'd seen legion castra up close, and this home to six thousand legionaries was bigger than anything she'd seen in Dacia.

As the horses walked the dirt track beside the road that brought a legion to conquer her homeland, her gaze followed its straight-line path toward the city.

Head to toe, it would take four of her to span the road that was topped with white limestone pavers. Small stone buildings with closed doors and no windows lined the way. Many were decorated with life-like carvings of people and animals, some doing things that made her blush.

"What are those?"

"The Romans honor their dead with them. They're filled with the burned bones of their ancestors. They carve their images and hope people remember them." Ursus's voice dripped disdain. "Not that it matters what happens to a corpse. Burned or rotted or fed to lions...you're still dead and gone."

Ursus looked away, and she longed to tell him what life could be and that death didn't mean you were gone. Hers would only open a new and glorious life with Jesus and reunion with her parents. But God would tell her when it was time to speak, and that time hadn't come.

A string of stone arches came from the distant hills, passed the castrum, and descended into the city below.

Ariana raised her eyebrows. "Why such a long bridge where there's no river?"

Why had her question made Donatus's mouth twitch to stop a smile?

"It's an aqueduct. It carries water to the camp and the city. There are hot springs nearby as well." He released the smile, but it was no longer one that laughed at her. "When we come back through with your brother and sister, we can stop and enjoy soaking in the hot water at the baths."

The warmth in his eyes cooled. "I'd hoped to get my retirement land here, to grow grapes and sheep and raise a family on the farm I'd earned by my service to Rome." His eyes dropped from the lush hillside to his ruined hand, and he turned his face away.

"Do you have family that you'll be joining after you finish helping me?"

He turned back to her. "The only family still alive is my uncle in Germania. It would take two months to walk there and money for the trip I don't have. I'm not even sure exactly where he lives." His eyes shifted away from her, then returned. "No one cares where I am anymore."

"I care. I'm glad you won't be going to Germania. That's so far away. Perhaps Tribune Gracchus can help you find something to do near us. Marcia says he can solve almost any problem."

He turned both hands palm up and flexed his fingers. His left hand curled into a fist, but not the right. Its little finger curled and the fourth finger bent a little, but the rest of his hand did nothing. "Not even Gracchus can solve this."

He put on a smile. "We're about to cross the Savus. It's named for a river god who pours nectar and feeds Zeus with ambrosia, thus making him immortal. But the gods are just stories people tell. Gracchus is right that the immortals live only in men's minds."

"He thinks that, but it's only because he hasn't met the god who is real."

"No god is real, but even if one was, I don't expect he would change what is already ruined. As I was saying, we're going to cross the Savus." He turned in the saddle to face Ursus. "The legion built a pontoon bridge over it. Ready for another one?"

Ursus tipped his head to look down his nose, but his lips curved into a smile, not a sneer. "I trust Roman bridges now as long as you weren't one of the builders."

Donatus's smile slipped toward a grin. "You trusted my work at Dobreta."

"Before I knew you helped build it." Ursus's grin mirrored Donatus's.

Three abreast, they rode onto the bridge, and the thuds of their hooves over the water's murmurs were melody and harmony that made Ariana smile.

A few miles past the bridge, Ariana's gasped. Her hand shot out to point at a huge boat moving upriver, two rows of oars dipping into the flow. They left a trail of sparking droplets as they lifted from the water, moved forward, and dropped again, like dancers with perfect timing.

Donatus hauled back on his reins. "What?"

"That! What is it?"

Her amazement brought a smile to his eyes. "A bireme of the Pannonian fleet. It's based here in Taurunum. They usually patrol the river, but they helped bring the IV Flavia down to join the VII Claudia for the campaign." He glanced at his hand, and his proud-Roman smile faded. "I had a chance to crew a *liburna* stationed here, but I wanted to become a centurion, like my uncle. I'd still have a future if I'd made a different choice."

He squared his shoulders. "We leave the river in a mile or so. That road goes to Bassiana, and we'll spend the night there."

One kick, and his horse resumed its trot.

She dropped back a little so she could watch him without him seeing. All he'd hoped for had ended with that knife in his arm. But even if he'd stayed a warrior, he might have died in battle before he retired.

He didn't need that legion retirement money to have a future. She had a farm and sheep. They could plant grapevines. They could find someone to help with the things that need two hands. But first he needed to see that one God was real and that God loved him more than he could even imagine. Only then could she ask him to share the future with her.

Chapter 24

To Kill a Man

Bassiana, Evening of Day 16

Ariana sat on the edge of the fountain and dragged her fingers through the water. Donatus had asked at the garrison for a good inn, and good didn't come close to describing it. Red flowers she'd never seen before filled the courtyard with a lovely scent. Wooden benches were shaded by grapevines. Water spouted from a marble sculpture of a strange fish-looking animal Ursus had called a dolphin. He'd seen them in the sea as a boy.

Donatus and Ursus had gone to the public baths, where afternoons were for men only. But the inn had a small private bath for the women staying there, and Donatus had arranged for her to use it. The two Roman matrons who were undressing when she entered had eyed her Sarmatian clothes, but a friendly greeting in Greek had erased the worry from their faces. She'd watched them use the scrapers and oils to remove dirt before entering the hot water and copied everything they did. They all relaxed in the same small pool of steaming water, but their Latin conversation left her to enjoy warm solitude as she prayed. Prayers for Diegis and Roanna but especially for the two men who'd never met the one god worth believing in.

After dinner, Donatus had gone for a walk, leaving Ursus to watch over her. She'd checked on Zapada and the other horses before returning to this garden to enjoy a few moments by the splashing water.

The only thing that would make the evening better would be Donatus's smile. She scooped a handful of water from the fountain's pool and let it run through her fingers. He'd been too quiet after they left the river. Too often he glanced at his hand where it rested on his thigh as they rode. Too often his usually straight mouth drooped into a frown, not of anger but of sadness.

And her heart ached for him. *God, how can he bear such loss when he doesn't have You? I thought I'd lost everyone, but I still had the hope You give me. He has nothing and no one but himself.*

If only he'd let her tell him the wonders of God that she knew, she could fix that. Or rather God could fix that...for both of them.

Sirmium, Day 17

As Ariana and the men rode into Sirmium, her Roman escort was failing in his role as teacher and guide. Instead of his confident voice that had explained everything worth knowing and even more about Singidunum, silence hung over their party.

She'd seen enough to recognize many things: the hippodrome where the chariots raced, the large stone buildings that housed the men who ran the city, the temple to some Roman god, a public bath house, and a theater where performers acted out plays, recited poetry, played instruments, and sang.

But the one thing it lacked brought a smile to her face.

She turned to Ursus, riding beside her. "It's nice to see a Roman city where there isn't an amphitheater."

He glanced at her. "We just fight in the regular theaters where there isn't one."

Why did his words feel like a punch to her stomach?

"What is wrong with you Romans?" She slumped in her saddle. "Is there no place in your Empire to get away from men being kept as slaves just to kill each other?"

The glances exchanged by Ursus and Donatus said it all, even before they shrugged.

Ursus's indulgent smile did nothing to soothe her distress. "We don't just fight in the arenas. I spend more time as a bodyguard."

As if that made it any better that his owner made him kill or die.

"That's good. I like having both of you with me." Her words flipped Ursus's smile from patronizing to pleased. "I'm glad Marcia thought Gracchus should borrow you, but why would the commander of a legion ever need a bodyguard? He's surrounded by soldiers."

Ursus's chuckle raised her eyebrows. "A soldier's loyalty isn't always to his general. No legate can fully trust the men of his legion, even his officers, and even less the auxiliaries. They aren't Romans. Your king was a treacherous snake. He held Longinus prisoner after he tricked Trajan into sending his friend to discuss peace terms. He sent a deserter back to assassinate your emperor. The legate doesn't trust anyone...except maybe your tribune."

"But he must have trusted you."

"He trusts me well enough. I have no ties within his legion, no loyalty to anyone who might help an assassin. When he talks with someone who might betray him, he has me watch that man's friends. You learn to read a man without hearing words when you're on the sand."

"Well, I'm glad he sent you with us. When Donatus leaves me, you make me feel safe."

Ursus's smile broadened. "You should. You're like my little sister."

"But now the war is over, what's next for you?"

"He'll keep or sell me. Either way, I'll fight until the crowd demands that the sponsor of the games sets me free...or I die."

"I would rather die than kill another person."

"Dressed like that, you look like you could kill." One corner of Ursus's mouth lifted. "But it's a good thing you'll never stand on the sand."

He turned his eyes away from her, declaring their conversation over.

Donatus's nod caught her eye and triggered her sigh. These men she'd grown to care about were killers at heart and comfortable with that.

God, no one is too lost for You to reach them. Please let our time together start them both on their way home to You.

Her gaze turned on Donatus, but she looked away before he knew. *Please, Lord, make Donatus Yours, and then make him mine.*

Between Sirmium and Gensis

Ariana leaned back to watch the dancing patterns of light in the leaves overhead. They were passing through thick woods, and these reminded her of home. They would be spending the night north of the *mansio* at Gensis, and they had traveled almost half the distance from Sirmium.

"Tree on the road. I'll get it." Ursus nudged his horse and rode ahead. He'd barely dismounted when his horse snorted, jumped, and cantered back up the track toward Ariana.

She reached for its reins as the mare galloped past. She missed, so she turned Zapada and cantered after it.

When she caught the mare and turned, her breath caught. Donatus was off his horse, standing back to back with Ursus, swords ready for battle. Surrounding her friends were five men with swords drawn.

One stepped in front of a tall beech beside the road. "Drop them. If you don't fight, we'll just take your money and horses. You fight, and we'll take your lives."

She freed the quiver from her scabbard and draped its strap across her chest. With bow in hand and arrow nocked, her legs commanded Zapada to advance, and the little mare cantered forward.

She released the arrow, and it passed through the narrow space between their leader's arm and his ribs, pinning his cloak to the tree behind him.

Almost before that arrow struck, she had another ready to fly. Zapada froze in response to the two-tone whistle they'd practiced in games with Diegis.

"Stop." The quaver made her voice sound too frightened to her own ears. *God, protect us!*

Her voice steadied. "You and your men will leave now and not bother us again, or the next one is in your throat or heart."

He laughed at her and shed his cloak.

"Stop now."

He signaled his men and started toward her friends.

The arrow flew, and his howl of pain rent the forest silence. His sword dropped to the ground as her arrow quivered in his arm exactly where Donatus had been stabbed.

His cry was followed by a string of curses. But he froze mid-curse when he saw her third arrow nocked and pointed straight at him.

"Throat or heart?" Her eyes never left him. "And I have plenty of arrows for your men, too."

He pulled the arrow out and clamped his hand on the bleeding wound. He tipped his head toward the hill behind him. "Go."

With each one glancing over his shoulder at her, his robber band scrambled up the slope.

The robber bent to pick up his sword.

"Leave it." Donatus's icy voice drew the robber's stare. "Where she shot you, you won't be needing it again."

"Go now, and don't even think about coming back." She tried to match his icy tone.

Still clutching his arm, the robber climbed the slope and disappeared over the hill.

Her friends sheathed their swords. While Ursus dragged the tree off the road, Donatus gathered the robber's sword and cloak. He wrapped the sharp blade in the thick cloth and handed it to Ursus, who tied it at the back of his saddle.

Then Donatus crossed his arms and stared at her.

She raised her eyebrows. "What?"

"You said you weren't a warrior."

Her mouth relaxed into a smile. "I'm not, but Mother was before she married Father. She taught me to use her bow."

"Why didn't she marry a Sarmatian warrior? What made her leave her tribe for a Dacian horse trader?"

The still, small voice she knew better than to ignore whispered within her: 'Tell him.'

"She didn't leave them for Father. She left them for Jesus."

His eyes veiled, and the corners of his mouth plunged. "You're a Christian?"

"Yes." Had she made a mistake telling him?

"Does Gracchus know?"

"Yes."

"Marcia Philippa?"

Ariana didn't answer. Was he asking whether Marcia knew or whether she was a Christian, too?

His face relaxed. "If it doesn't bother Gracchus, it doesn't matter to me."

He mounted and moved his horse beside her. "That shot in his arm scared them off, but would you have shot for his throat or his heart?"

Her smile vanished. "I hope I never have to shoot to kill anyone."

He shrugged. "It's only hard the first few times." One kick, and he started them trotting down the road once more.

Ariana lagged behind so he wouldn't see her shaking as she fought tears.

Only hard the first few times? The Roman sword piercing her father. The Roman dagger slitting her mother's throat. The soldiers had killed as if their deaths meant no more than shooting a rabbit or crushing a bug. Had Donatus been so cold-hearted when his hand still worked? Had he only killed other soldiers in the heat of battle? Or had he murdered innocents who had no part in the war, who'd only been in the path of armies clashing because a king and an emperor both wanted to control the land?

At first, she wiped each new tear away before it could run down her cheek. But they became too many, and some trickled down her cheeks before she could catch them.

Ursus turned in his saddle to look back at her. The face of the gladiator softened before he faced forward again.

Donatus started to turn as well, and she braced for the questions she didn't want to answer.

"Donatus." Ursus's voice caught the Roman's attention, and he turned back before he saw her tears. As the gladiator drew Donatus into conversation about what lay ahead before they stopped for the night, she could have hugged him.

Both men lived to fight and kill, but maybe one already suspected that wasn't the way God meant it to be.

Chapter 25

Gensis

Donatus had planned to camp in the forest, but the possibility of the robbers trailing them for a night ambush kept him riding toward the way station of Gensis. It was almost dark when he led their party past the *mansio* and found himself wishing the tribune was with them. Gracchus could have stayed in the government villa that welcomed officials of the Empire and those on official business. Donatus was neither.

A hot meal, the mansio's private bath, clean sheets in a room where he wouldn't have to worry about Ariana's safety—Gracchus could have provided them all.

Drunken guffaws assaulted his ears when a man staggered out the door of the *caupona* just ahead. After leaving his drinks behind at the base of the outer wall, he wobbled back inside.

Donatus covered his mouth as he rubbed his jaw. The door opened again, and a good-natured shriek escaped the building.

Ariana reined in beside him. "Will they have rooms for us this late?"

Ursus's tightened lips and quick shake of his head were in one accord with Donatus's thoughts.

"Even if they do, we don't want them."

"Why not?"

"The women there are…for rent."

Her eyes widened. "Oh."

Another drunk emerged and wove his way down the road. His mouth opened into a sappy grin when he spotted Ariana. He redirected himself straight toward them, and Ursus moved his horse into his path.

"Not for sale. Get out of here."

The man's eyes bounced between Ursus and Ariana before he shrugged and wandered off.

Ursus's mouth tightened. "The mansio, maybe? You have Gracchus's letter."

"Nothing lost in asking."

By the arch into the mansio's stableyard, Donatus slipped from his horse and handed Ariana his reins. If they couldn't stay there, they'd have to ride farther and find a campsite far enough off the road to remain out of sight.

The smile he offered Ariana was a crooked one. "Maybe your god can make them let us stay here. You say he answers your prayers."

She raised her eyebrows. "He's not a servant who does my bidding." Then her eyes warmed. "But I can ask, and we will see."

As he walked through the archway, he glanced over his shoulder. Her eyes were closed, and her mouth curved into that sweet smile she always had when massaging his arm.

If her god was real, he'd sleep well tonight. If not, he still might sleep well. He had more faith in the letter of a tribune than in any god.

Ariana patted Zapada's neck before turning to Ursus. "I hope we can stay here."

Ursus shook his head. "A legate stays in a mansio. An ex-legionary does not." He tipped his head toward Donatus as he returned. "That frown says we'll be camping down the road tonight."

Donatus took his horse's reins from her, but he didn't mount. "There's only one room empty, and we can share it like we did in Viminacium." His lips twitched as he looked up at her. "And getting the last room here doesn't mean your god did anything. Gracchus's letter was enough."

She tried to keep her smile from turning into an I-told-you-so grin. "You can believe that if you want to, but I know the truth."

His eyes rolled, but he said no more before leading his horse toward the stable.

Donatus didn't believe her, but Ursus looked at her with a question in his eyes before a slow nod.

As she rode under the arch, she thanked God for His answer to her prayer. Belief in a little thing was the first step toward faith in the greatest thing of all.

Day 18

Ariana stood by Zapada's stall, stroking the mare's nose. Because of the robbers, they had ridden twenty miles farther than Donatus intended, and she could see why he wanted to give the horses a half-day rest that morning. But somewhere ahead of them, Roanna and Diegis were getting closer each day to the auction and the slave ships that could take them from her forever. He'd insisted there was half a day to spare, but still…

Donatus came to stand beside her. Like so many other times, he remained silent.

Zapada reached over the gate and bumped his chest with her nose. She got a scratch of her forehead and some fingers drawn through her forelock for her trouble.

"She's a good horse. Someone trained her well. From canter to full stop with a whistle—are all Sarmatian horses trained to do that?"

"Maybe. I trained her, and she is a wonderful horse."

Zapada turned back to Ariana. When she nuzzled Ariana's shoulder, she got her cheek stroked in exchange.

"I'm glad the tribune bought her. I'd hate to see her with a mean owner." A sigh welled up. "All our horses were lovely animals. I hope they ended up with people who treat them well."

The corner of his mouth lifted. "For all our faults, we Romans know how to value a good horse."

"Who taught you to ride?"

"My uncle. He was a centurion with Gracchus on his first tribune posting." He stroked Zapada's neck. "Good thing for me. It's why Gracchus was willing to try a one-handed orderly while I waited to heal."

"Good thing for me, too. He had to know you to choose you to help me, and he couldn't have chosen better."

He said nothing, but his slight smile spoke louder than any words could.

She stepped back from the stall. "It's a while until they serve lunch and we can leave. Join me for a walk?"

A nod signaled his willingness. As she headed for the archway that led to the road, he walked beside her, slowing his stride to match hers.

She glanced at him several times as they strolled, keeping each glance too quick for him to return it. He was a good man. A better man than he thought, and a woman would be lucky to have him as her husband, injured hand and all.

Help him see he needs you, Lord. Then help him see he wants me.

North of Ad Drinum, Evening of Day 18

The road had climbed off the river plain and was once more crossing tree-covered hills that reminded Ariana of home. She liked sleeping under a clear night sky, and who wouldn't feel safe when protected by men like Donatus and Ursus?

Ursus had first watch. She should be sleeping, but she wanted to watch the stars a while. She and Diegis had often lain on the grassy knoll just past the corrals and watched them appear, one by one, as the sky darkened after sunset. Soon they would do that again, and that thought drew a contented sigh.

Her gaze settled on Donatus, asleep across the fire from the fallen tree she shared with Ursus. He'd let her massage his arm until the pain had almost disappeared, and he'd gone to sleep almost as soon as he stretched out under his blanket. Now he lay on his side, head on his arm, his useless fingers lying along the back of his head.

She'd offered so many prayers for his healing, and still there was no sign of it. But God always moved at the right time in the right way. Perhaps Donatus wasn't yet ready to be healed.

Ursus cleared his throat, and she turned her eyes on him.

"I've been wondering." He poked at the fire, and sparks flew upward. "Why were you crying yesterday? That robber probably murdered other travelers. He deserved to die, and all you did was hurt him some."

It was hard, but she kept her smile from turning into a grin. The opening she'd been praying for had come.

"God says we're to love each other, like He loves us. I hate hurting anyone for any reason. I only did it because they planned to kill you and Donatus. At the very least, they wanted to take our horses so we couldn't have reached the coast in time to rescue Roanna and Diegis. For the sake of others, I shed blood."

The fire snapped, and Ursus flicked the ember that had escaped the pit back into the coals. "Your brother and sister are lucky to have someone who loves them like you do. It makes no difference to anyone whether I live or die." His mouth twisted into a wry smile. "Crowds chant my name. Noble Romans want to eat with me before the games, but that doesn't mean they won't demand I die if I ever lose a bout. I've been in the arena twelve years. I've seen it a hundred times."

"I care."

He stared at her eyes. Then his focus returned to the fire. "You're the only one. Even my father's family didn't care. My uncle had more than enough money to buy me and my sisters at the auction. He didn't even bid."

"I'm sorry." Her heart ached for the boy condemned to a life of killing by an uncle who didn't want him.

"No one has ever cared for me like you do for your brother and sister, like the tribune's wife must care for you. Gracchus is spending a lot of money with no guarantee you can reach them in time to pay the redemption price to free them. No one would ever want to pay it for me."

Her breath caught. *God, give me the words he needs to hear.*

"But someone already paid that price, if you want to accept it. He paid it for me, too."

His head cocked as his eyes probed her face. "The tribune? He only borrowed me. He wanted you for his wife, but after we return, he has no reason to want me."

"That's not what I mean. God brought the tribune to the slave cages to save me from a life of bondage, but it's Jesus, the Son of God, who freed me. With His own life, Jesus paid the price that set me free from death because of my sin. He made me a child of God. God wants you to become His child, too."

His head pulled back. "Paid for you with his life?" His mouth curved into the cynical frown he wore when their journey began. "Even if the gods were real, one would never die for one of us. But Donatus is right. They aren't real, and they have no children. And even if they did, they wouldn't want me."

He stood. "Time for Donatus to wake up and for me to sleep. You, too. Your watch will come sooner than you realize."

"Goodnight, Ursus."

She slipped into her own blankets and pulled the cover up to hide her mouth. She didn't want Ursus to ask why the big smile. A man who'd been betrayed found it hard to trust, and he'd built a shell around his heart. But tonight, she'd seen the first crack in the shell. God was patient when someone resisted at first, and so was she.

In the flickering light of the fire, her gaze settled on Donatus's face, and her smile faded. It was only when he slept that she couldn't see the pain so close to the surface. If he caught her watching him, he'd demand to know why she wasn't sleeping. But his eyes would soften the harshness of his words.

She willed her body to relax. She'd be no good for her watch if she was too tired. Until sleep overtook her, she asked God to open the hearts of these precious friends and give them His peace.

◆

Donatus had lain as still as a man waiting for an enemy patrol to pass, but his mind had been racing. He wasn't that different from the gladiator now. With his useless hand, he was a man no one wanted. Like Ursus, he had no close family left. Would it make any difference to anyone if he lived or died? He'd asked that question too many times in the last four months, and he never liked the answer.

Until now. A small voice deep inside his head had started telling him yes. It would matter to Ariana. It might matter a great deal.

"Donatus." A big foot nudged his back. "Your watch."

He stretched, stood, and stretched some more. "Anything I should know before you sleep?"

Ursus tightened his lips and shook his head. "Should be a peaceful night." The big man knelt, flopped onto his back, pulled up the covers, and began to snore.

Donatus rubbed his forehead. He used to go to sleep like that, like he hadn't a care in the world. But a peaceful night and Ursus on his back would never happen together. His foot pushed on Ursus's shoulder until he rolled on his side. His breathing remained deep and slow, but now it was silent.

And in the silence of the night, Donatus's eyes drifted between the stars and the woman who was capturing his heart. Both beautiful, both peaceful, and both beyond the reach of a one-handed man.

Chapter 26

THE ONLY ONE WHO'S REAL

South of Ad Drinum, Evening of Day 19

In Ad Drinum, the mansio had been full, and Donatus had pronounced the caupona too rowdy for her safety. But Ariana didn't mind. They had ridden another ten miles before stopping for the evening. That was ten miles closer to her reunion with Roanna and Diegis, and every mile made her heart lighter.

After spit-roasted rabbit and some fresh bread from the taberna in Ad Drinum, Donatus had pronounced it a good dinner and gone to bed.

Ariana had no intention of sleeping yet. Ursus only talked in the flickering light of an open fire, and eternity might hang on their next conversation. At least that had been her prayer all day.

Ursus dumped an armful of small logs that would keep the fire going for her and Donatus's watches. She moved over to make room for him on the fallen log. He chose instead to sit on the rock across from her.

The silence stretched out between them as she prayed.

"About what you said last night..." Ursus stared at the fire, only glancing at her before returning his gaze to the flames. "About your god loving you. About him wanting us to love other people because he does."

He whacked the biggest log with his stick, and sparks spiraled upward. "About him wanting to love a man like me."

His gaze locked on her. "You have no idea the things I've done."

"No, but I saw what soldiers do when they killed Mother and Father. Is it that different?"

"Not much. That's why Donatus and I understand each other. He killed for Rome, but it's still killing. And there's nothing personal about it." A quick glance at her, and he stared into the fire again. "I've killed men who were my friends."

Her hand shot to her mouth before she thought to stop it.

He raised open palms toward her. "That was only in the arena. I'd never hurt you or Donatus."

"I know." She moved a loose strand of hair behind her ear and lowered her hand.

Another whack sent more sparks skyward. "It bothered me a lot when I started"—he shrugged—"but after a while, it doesn't feel any worse than when I worked in the kitchen and slaughtered a pig I'd raised for the men to eat."

But his eyes told her otherwise. "I know you had to do it to stay alive. But people are made in the image of God, and He told us not to murder. Jesus even said if we were so angry we wanted to murder someone, even if we didn't, that disobeyed God's command, too. We're supposed to love other people as much as we love ourselves. Not just our friends, but our enemies as well."

"I watched how Donatus looked at you when we started. He saw an enemy, but you treated him like a friend. How could you do that after what the Romans did to you and your family?"

"Jesus told us we have to forgive if we want to be forgiven. It doesn't start out easy, but the more I try, the easier it gets."

"This god of yours, tell me about him."

It was all she could do to keep her smile from turning into a grin. As Ursus's shell shattered, praise and thanksgiving surged through Ariana. *Give me the right words, Lord.*

"He's the one who created everything. He's the only God who's real. He made Himself known first to the Jews, but He's the God of everyone."

"I've heard of the Jewish god. Some Jews lived near us when I was a boy. They never fished on Saturday, but they still caught more than we did."

"God used the Jewish prophets to tell people about Himself, but He made us all so we could know Him and love Him. And He wants us to love each other like He loves us."

"Loves us? Like the gods of Rome who come to make love to women?"

"No. Those are just stories, and that's not love. This is real. It's love where He wants the very best for us, even though we keep pushing Him away and doing things that He commanded us not to, things that hurt other people and even ourselves. Doing things that put a barrier between Him and us...that's called sin. There's a penalty to pay to take that sin away so it doesn't keep us from Him."

She scooped up a handful of twigs and tossed one at the fire. She missed.

"Penalty? Like giving the gods your money or sacrificing an animal?"

"Money can't pay for sin. God gave some of His commands to Moses hundreds of years ago, and He said only blood sacrifice could cover up sin so we could be in His presence."

"So killing an animal fixes the problem."

"No, it only covers it. The sacrifice has to be absolutely perfect to erase sin."

The next twig fell closer to the coals and began to smolder.

"What your god commands is impossible. No animal is perfect."

"But even if it was, it wouldn't be enough. The sin is mine, not the animal's. It's only a substitute for me. All the animals sacrificed for hundreds of years only covered sin for a while. It was still there...until Jesus of Nazareth made Himself the perfect sacrifice when Pontius Pilatus crucified Him. Jesus told His followers that He came as the sacrifice to pay for everyone's sin before it happened, and when He rose from the dead, He proved everything He said was true."

A tiny flame appeared on the end of the twig closest to the fire.

"But no person is perfect, either, so how could one man dying do anything?"

"You're right. We never can be perfect on our own, and God knew that. So He came as Jesus, became a man, lived a life without sin, and gave Himself as the perfect sacrifice to erase my sin. All I have to do is believe He did that for me, and my sins are paid for as if they never happened."

Ursus eyes narrowed. "What could you ever have done that needed something like that to pay for it? You're the kindest person I've ever known." He stirred the coals before looking at her again. "You're nothing like me. I've killed twenty-two men in the arena, and I've even enjoyed doing it. How could any sacrifice, animal or man, erase that?"

Deep within his eyes, hopelessness battled longing.

"I don't know how it works. I only know what God promised, and He never breaks His word. I know I feel Him with me every day. I trust Jesus's word when He says God loved the world so much that He gave Jesus, His only son, so anyone who believed in Him would have eternal life with God. All I have to do is confess my sins, ask God to forgive me, and believe Jesus died to pay for my sins so I could be forgiven."

The final twig hit the white-hot coals and burst into flame.

"And I know it's all true because He's here with me right now. His Spirit is in me, and I feel His love around me. He made me His child." She leaned forward. "And He wants you as His child, too."

Ursus snorted. "No god would want me. Just ask Donatus. A gladiator is an *infamis*, scum at the bottom of the Roman classes. Even if the legate frees me, I can never be a citizen. I'll never be higher than a slave. The noble Romans seek out my company when I'm winning, but I'm less than a man to them."

She straightened "But God doesn't see you that way. He sees you as a man worth dying for. When Jesus was dying on the cross, a robber who'd murdered people hung beside Him. When he asked Jesus to remember him when He came into His kingdom, Jesus told him he'd be with Him in Paradise that day. That murderer believed in Jesus, and that was all it took for God to see him without all his sins."

Ursus tightened his lips. "It sounds too easy." He shook his head.

"It is simple, but if we really believe, then we want to live like God tells us. That can be hard. That means we don't keep doing the things we know God says are wrong."

"Like killing in the arena just to entertain."

"Yes."

He ran his fingers through his hair. "But I don't put myself in the games. My owner does. And if I enter the arena, I have to kill for him."

"The greater sin is his for ordering you to kill."

His mouth set to a grim line. "But the only way not to kill is to choose to die instead."

What could she say? He was right, and she fought tears over the choice he faced.

Ursus drew a deep breath and blew it out. "That's seems too high a price to pay."

"Following Jesus…that's never a safe choice. When Gracchus came to the slave pens, he asked if any were Christians. When I stepped forward, I expected him to have me killed. But God had other plans." Their gazes locked, and he leaned toward her. "And telling you about Him is part of those plans. The joy I know now and eternity with Him—that's worth losing my life for, if I have to."

"I'm not afraid to die."

She believed him.

"But what comes after, that I fear. If the Romans are right, I'll be tortured in Tartarus forever." His smile was sad. "Gladiators don't go to the Plains of Asphodel with the good and pious. No Elysian fields like a soldier killed in battle."

"But like the robber who died beside Jesus, you could be with Him in heaven forever. With me and my family and everyone who has ever followed Him."

He rubbed his mouth with the back of his hand. "If what you say is true, I could. And if Jesus truly is God and he did sacrifice himself to free me, I can't ignore his commands. But making that choice…that would cost everything."

One more whack on the biggest log and he tipped his head to watch the rising sparks until their glow faded. "I need to think about this before I decide anything."

"When you're ready, He's waiting for you."

Ursus rose. "Time for you to sleep." He tipped his head toward Donatus. "He'll scold you for not resting for your watch."

She lay down and pulled the blankets over her. "Goodnight, Ursus. I'll be praying for you. I always do."

The smile that lit his eyes made her heart sing. He hadn't yet spoken his decision to believe, but that was so close that the angels in heaven must already be singing.

◆

Donatus's thoughts churned as silence descended around him. Ursus was right. There wasn't that much difference between them. How many had he killed for Rome? More than Ursus's twenty-two. He'd been a soldier fighting warriors, and each knew only one would walk away. Before the heat of battle, it helped to work up some hatred for the enemy.

Just being Dacian had fueled his anger toward Ariana before that first time she massaged his arm. She'd insisted on helping even when he tried to drive her away. Despite what his fellow soldiers had done to her family, she treated him like a man she cared about. Like she felt how much he hurt.

Forgive your enemies? He would never forgive the Dacian who ruined his hand. Could she really forgive like she said?

It was no wonder Gracchus's wife seemed to love her. Who wouldn't care about this woman who'd do anything to help you? Even Gracchus was fond of her.

Donatus didn't know a single man more loyal to Rome than Gracchus, and Donatus knew Christians were considered enemies of Rome. But his commander had deliberately brought one into his house. He'd even given her to his helpless wife. He teased Marcia Philippa about praying with Ariana, and he must know which god they prayed to.

Gracchus's wife was a Christian now. That thought slammed into Donatus and left him stunned. She'd become a Christian, and the woman who was supposedly crippled for life had walked out to greet them in the stableyard.

Had the physician been wrong? Had that healing been natural... or not?

He felt the scar on his arm. No matter what he did, he never got it to hurt as little as it did when Ariana massaged it. His lips tightened. Massaged it and prayed. She told him more than once that was the difference.

Gracchus was right that the Roman gods weren't real. But only a real god could heal a crippled woman.

Could that real god heal him, too? And what would it take to get him to do it?

Chapter 27

The Gracchus house, Day 20

The bread was still warm from the oven when Quintus tore off this first piece. The scent of something other than rosemary teased his nostrils as he took the first bite.

He glanced over his shoulder when Marcia's favorite perfume replaced the hot herbal scent.

She kissed his temple and leaned over him to take a grape from the silver bowl. "I wonder what Ariana and Donatus are eating this morning."

"Bread and cheese. It's the easiest when you ride far and fast."

She slipped into the chair beside him. "When do you think they'll get back? I want to have a special celebration as soon as they return."

"Depends on which port they followed the caravan to. You'd better wait until they actually return to plan it."

"The date, maybe, but not what we'll do." She chose another grape and popped it into her mouth. "I've been praying for them, and I expect they'll have something delightful to tell us when they get back."

"They'll tell us about the trip, I suppose."

She tore off some bread and nibbled it. "I asked the cook to try tarragon, and I do believe I like it a little better than the rosemary. Perhaps I'll have her alternate."

"They're both fine. Do whatever you like."

"Both fine. Yes, I expect both Ariana and Donatus to be fine when they come home."

His brow furrowed. Why a woman bounced from one topic to another had always been a mystery. One thing that had attracted him to Marcia was how seldom it happened.

He rose. "The legate is having the officers to dinner tonight. I'll be home late."

She stood and tucked her arm in his. "It's such a blessing to have a fine husband." A playful smile curved her mouth. "Ariana's going to agree with me."

As she walked him to the stableyard, Quintus tried not to roll his eyes. Even the best of women were too much like...women sometimes.

Between Ad Drinum and Aquae, Day 20

The afternoon sun warmed Ariana's shoulders as they rode across a clearing in the woods lining the road. They'd made good time with Donatus alternating periods of walking and trotting.

But he'd been silent most of the day, so she dropped back to ride beside Ursus as they slowed to a walk. He wasn't a talkative man, either, but at least his silence was friendly instead of brooding.

"This is such beautiful country. It reminds me of home. I can't wait to get back there."

Ursus scanned the woods and nearby hills as if he hadn't seen them before she spoke. "It's nice, but I've always liked the sea." His gaze settled on her, and he smiled. "What will you do when you return with your brother and sister?"

"If I have a choice, I'd like to return to our home when Gracchus thinks it's safe for a Dacian woman to be outside his house. He and Marcia didn't want me there while I might be taken as a slave again. But as soon as he says it's safe, I want to go back."

"Didn't the Romans take everything?"

"Only the horses. I still have sheep in the mountains. Diegis is eleven and big for his age. The two of us will be able to raise enough food for our family. There are plenty of rabbits as well."

"I'd like to eat your rabbit stew sometime." He grinned as he rubbed his seat. "Sometime when we haven't spent all day in these saddles and you have time to make it."

His grin broadened her own smile. "I'd like that, too. I should have let you ride one of my saddles. They're much better than these Roman ones."

She leaned forward to pat Zapada's neck. "I have good corrals. Maybe Marcia can get the tribune to let me breed Zapada and the other two mares with his stallion to start a herd again. He'll own the horses, but maybe he'll share the profits with me. But even if he doesn't, nothing satisfies like working with horses, and I want Roanna to learn how. Diegis can train even the wildest ones. He's already more expert than anyone I know."

"I'd like to go out on the sea and be a fisherman again. Maybe raise a family. But that will never be." His smile faded. "I don't want to kill anymore. Being admired by men who revel in blood and death is worth nothing. I want to be with people like you. Are all Jesus's followers like you?"

"Many are better."

"How would I find them? The legate doesn't keep me locked up. I go to the baths and the races, and he trusts me to return."

"I don't know, but there are a few of us everywhere. The man who helped Diegis and me memorize the writings by Jesus's closest follower, Apostle John, and by Paul, the man Jesus called to tell the whole world about Him—he came from Thessalonica."

"I've been there. Where did they meet?"

"He worshiped at the home of Aristarchus, who had a merchant fleet and several estates. His house was big enough for many to gather. But even worshiping God with one other person is glorious. Once we follow Jesus, we're all brothers and sisters."

"Brothers and sisters." The corner of his mouth rose, but it was a sad half-smile. "I've spent most of my life in a *familia gladiatoria*, but it's no family. The men are not my brothers, and I lost my sisters when they were sold. But every man needs some place to belong. As long as I fight, it will have to do."

◆

Silence settled on the group, and Donatus was not sorry. Talk of family and homes and futures...he had no part in that and no hope he ever would.

"Donatus."

Donatus looked across his shoulder at the gladiator behind him. "What?"

"What will you do when we return?"

"I don't know." Donatus kicked his horse into a trot, ending the conversation.

Shoulders squared and chin high, he fought the dark uncertainty over what waited for him in Sarmizegetusa. He didn't know what to do before this expedition. Nothing would have changed when he returned.

An owl hooted in the darkness beyond the circle of firelight. Ariana sat on a rock and stared at the dancing pattern of orange, yellow, and white in the hottest part of the coals. Except for the owl, she might as well have been the only living creature there.

Donatus had barely spoken since Ursus asked his future plans. Ursus had gone silent, too, and now he stood with his back toward her, scanning the woods around them. Not because there was anything out there. It was only to keep counsel with his own thoughts rather than share them with her.

It was not going to be a night for conversation like the two before had been. She didn't need to miss sleep only to keep herself company.

She sighed before rising. "Goodnight, Ursus."

His quiet 'goodnight' drifted over his shoulder without him facing her.

She flipped back her top blanket, smoothed the bottom one, and slipped between them. The ground beneath her was rocky, and she shifted to find a place where nothing jammed into her side.

Before closing her eyes to begin her prayers, she watched Donatus's chest slowly rise and fall. What did the future hold for him? Loneliness and loss had echoed in his 'I don't know' that afternoon. If he'd only let her tell him about Jesus, she could show him the path away from both. A path they could share.

Mentally she shook herself. He'd never said anything that showed he cared for her as more than a friend. But sometimes his eyes would rest on her, and she'd almost swear they warmed like Father's had when he looked at Mother. Then the warmth would fade, replaced by a cold sadness before he turned away.

She closed her eyes. *God, please reach him. Give him Your hope. Give him a future, and let it include me.*

Chapter 28

Catching Up

Northeast of Aquae, Day 21

That evening, Donatus planned on a hot bath and a good night's sleep in Aquae. It was only a two-day ride from there to Narona, so they could catch up with the caravan at any time.

The slaves had been walking for three weeks now. As a legionary, he'd done that more than once, but the ones they followed weren't soldiers trained for the hardship of a long march. He scanned the brush under the trees to the side of the road. So far, he hadn't seen what he expected.

And when he did, it was sure to upset Ariana.

She was riding beside him, and he jumped when she grabbed his arm. Then she pointed.

Tossed to the side like garbage, a dead child lay face-down at the edge of the bushes.

"Her shirt and blouse. They look like Roanna's."

Ariana slipped from her horse and approached the corpse, tears washing her face. She bent at the waist and reached toward the crumpled form, then pulled her trembling hand back. She crouched and was stretching her hand toward the girl once more when Donatus reached her. He drew her to her feet and wrapped his arms around her.

"You shouldn't touch her." The smell of death—he knew it too well, and it would cling to her hand and haunt her.

Tears turned into sobs, and she slipped her arms around his chest. She whispered into his shoulder. "I need to see if it's Roanna."

"But you don't need to touch her. I will." Ursus crouched by the dead girl and turned her over. "Did your sister have an old scar on her left cheek?"

"No."

"Then this isn't her." Ursus turned the dead child face-down again.

Donatus expected Ariana to release him then, but she didn't. The torrent of tears continued, soaking his tunic where her cheek pressed against his chest. And even though he hated to see her suffering, some part of him was glad she still clung to him for comfort.

When the torrent turned to a rivulet and finally stopped, she still made no move to leave his encircling arms. He shifted his good hand so he could slowly rub her back. He rested his cheek on the top of her head, and she seemed to welcome it with the deepest sigh.

As Donatus continued rubbing her back, Ursus crossed his arms and frowned like a protective father. Donatus returned the frown and shook his head. The gladiator should know by now that he'd never choose to hurt her.

Too soon, she sniffed and tipped her head back, turning red-rimmed eyes upon him. "Can we bury her?"

"We have nothing to dig with." Ursus shrugged, but his eyes spoke his regret.

Another shuddering sigh made letting her go out of the question for Donatus. There would be more who died as they approached the end of the journey. They couldn't bury them all, but this one…

He scanned the area and spotted a fallen tree. As its roots had pulled free from the earth, they left behind a hole much larger than the child.

He tipped his head toward the pit. "But we can put her there and cave the walls in. Then we can cover the grave with some of those rocks."

She relaxed against him, and her whispered 'thank you' held a warmth far beyond what he deserved. With his good hand resting on the back of her head to keep her from watching, he held her tight while Ursus dragged the child to the hole and rolled her in.

With a large branch, Ursus loosened the sidewalls, and the dirt showered down on her. He worked his way around the hole until the body was well covered. "It's ready for the rocks."

Ariana stepped back, freeing herself from Donatus's embrace, and turned toward the rock pile. As she picked one up, Donatus's useless hand rested against the spot on his chest where her tears had soaked into his tunic.

This child was a total stranger. What would it do to Ariana if they caught up with the caravan, only to find they'd trailed the wrong group or her sister or brother had died on the way?

Aquae, Night of Day 21

The faint smell of sulfur drifted through the streets of Aquae as Donatus walked back to the horses, but he didn't care. It would feel good to soak in the hot waters of the public bath, and he'd just rented two rooms at a decent inn with a private bath for Ariana.

But best of all, the innkeeper had told him the caravan of slaves had passed through only one day ahead of them. Tomorrow they would catch up.

"Good news." He mounted and started toward the stableyard.

"What?" He'd barely settled into his saddle before the word burst from her smiling lips.

"The caravan spent the night here yesterday. We'll catch up tomorrow."

Her mare fidgeted beneath her, sensing the excitement he could see in her glowing eyes and beaming smile. "If we don't stop here, can we catch up tonight?"

"If they traveled at their usual pace, no. It will be late tomorrow."

Too many times he'd seen success snatched away by cruel fate. Just as rejoicing began, catastrophe snuffed it out. If he could shield her from life's crushing blows, he would.

"We'll catch a caravan, but don't forget there were two that left Viminacium. It is possible we followed the wrong one."

"I'm sure we followed the right one. God told me to go to Narona."

A single nod declared Ursus's agreement, but for Donatus, that remained to be seen. It was hard enough to believe any god was real. Had hers actually spoken to her? Or had she only imagined someone told her which way to go?

Ursus had been so eager to believe what she was saying about her god by the campfires. A gladiator might be easy to fool, but a Roman tribune was another matter. Even with Marcia Philippa suddenly walking again, Gracchus didn't believe in the Christian god. Without undeniable proof to the contrary, he would side with the commander he respected on the existence of any god.

For Donatus, a hot bath and a good dinner in the company of friends was a satisfying ending for a long day in the saddle. Except for the dead child, it had been a good day.

Two adjacent rooms at an inn with solid locks meant a night off guard duty. Not that he would get more sleep. Ursus standing first watch let him sleep some before the bear's snores made that impossible. And he liked watching Ariana sleep while he stood guard. Even in repose, a slight smile curved her lips. The man who married her someday would find so many pleasures in her company.

But that wouldn't be him. He suppressed a sigh.

As Ariana walked at his side, she smelled faintly of roses from the bathing oils. She stopped by the fountain along the path to their rooms.

"Your arm is hurting."

"Not much."

"Any is too much. I haven't massaged it today."

She held out her hand, and he gave her his arm, as he'd done so many times.

"You promised you'd teach me how to do that right. When are you going to tell me what you do differently that makes it work?"

"If I tell you, will you still let me do it sometimes?" Her eyes danced with a tease.

He couldn't stop his own smile. "Whenever you want to."

"All right. I'll tell you." She signaled for him to move closer, then stood on tiptoes. He tensed as her breath warmed his ear.

"I pray."

She dropped back on her heels. Her laugh was like fingers stroking his hand so lightly they tickled, and he didn't mind at all that it was directed at his skepticism.

Whatever she did differently, it worked. He still needed to learn the real secret before he returned her to the tribune's house, and sometime she'd probably tell him.

But what would he do when her fingers no longer stopped the ache in his arm and her laughter never again dulled the pain in his heart?

Halfway between Aquae and Narona, Evening of Day 22

Donatus would have stopped an hour ago, but Ariana couldn't wait to catch up. When Ursus sided with her, he'd agreed to keep riding. If her sister and brother were alive and with the caravan, she'd be ecstatic. But if they weren't, he'd rather she have one more night of happiness before her hopes were crushed. He was an expert on crushed hopes, and the last thing he ever wanted to see was the hollow emptiness in her eyes that he'd seen in his own.

When they caught up with the caravan just before nightfall, the slaves were already bedding down for the night. Donatus led them toward the clusters of exhausted men, women, and children.

"Diegis!" Ariana's voice rang out beside him.

"Don't do that."

Brow furrowed, she stared at him. "Why not?"

"If your brother or sister hears and tries to get to you, the slaver in charge of that group might think they were trying to escape and do something to stop them. They could get hurt."

"You're right, but it's so hard to wait."

"We'll watch for them as we pass. You'll probably have to spot them. We can look for a girl dressed like the one we buried, but we don't know what your brother looks like."

"He has red hair that's a little darker than mine, and he always has a slight smile."

He stared at her. From what he'd seen, almost every Dacian boy of eleven had red hair, and no one in his right mind would be smiling while he marched to a slave ship.

They had passed two thirds of the way along the caravan when Ariana gasped and pointed. "That's her!"

She slipped from her horse and darted into the group of small girls. Donatus dismounted and handed his reins to Ursus.

He followed her into the group in time to intercept one of the guards who was hurrying toward the pair, shaking out his whip as he strode toward them.

Donatus blocked his path. "We've been looking for that particular girl, and we only want to speak to her for a few moments. Then we'll be leaving to set up our own camp."

The slaver looked down his nose as he fingered the whip. "No one is allowed to do that."

"Do you mean no one is allowed without paying?"

A twisted grin showed two missing teeth. "Yes. That's exactly what I mean. For a...sestertius, you could talk, but not for long."

Donatus withdrew that amount from his purse. He dropped it into the outstretched hand, and the slaver sauntered back to his companions by their fire.

When Donatus reached Ariana, she was hugging and rocking her sister. Her eyes glistened, but those must be tears of joy.

Roanna recoiled when she saw him, pressing herself tightly against

Ariana. With his straight, dark hair in its military haircut, his gladius hanging from the strap across his chest, and the military dagger on his belt, he looked too much the Roman soldier towering over her. He dropped to one knee, hoping it would make him less frightening.

Ariana stroked her hair. "This is Donatus. He helped me find you. He's my friend, and he won't hurt you."

The small girl still cast furtive glances his way as she relaxed in Ariana's arms.

"We're going to buy you and Diegis, and then we'll go home." Joy echoed in each of Ariana's words.

Sudden tears filled Roanna's eyes. "But I saw him walking away with the other caravan in that big stone town by the river." Her lip quivered. "He's gone."

Ariana's beaming smile froze, then crumbled. She drew Roanna against her so the girl couldn't see as agony twisted her features and tore Donatus's heart.

She closed her eyes, and he would have bet anything she was praying. Tears flooded her face as she silently rocked her sister, who was sobbing. Ariana's scrunched face finally relaxed, and only when it looked calm did she move back and cradle Roanna's face between her palms.

"As God has protected you, I'm sure He's protecting Diegis. He can work all things for good for those of us who love Him."

She swept the tears from her own cheeks, then from Roanna's "We must always remember that."

Roanna nodded as she tried to smile.

"Can we take her tonight?" Ariana's red-rimmed eyes filled with hope as she directed a trembling smile at him.

"No. I have to arrange to buy her tomorrow." He pointed to the trees just past the huddled slaves. "We're going to pitch our camp right over there where you can see us, Roanna."

His eye caught movement, and he turned. The slaver was coming to end their conversation. It was time to leave before he got angry.

"While you say goodnight, I'll take care of him. Meet me back with Ursus."

As the sisters exchanged final hugs, he intercepted the slaver.

The man fingered the whip hanging from his belt. "If you want to talk tomorrow, it will be another sestertius."

"Of course." Donatus kept himself between the man and a clear view of Ariana. It was best if he didn't think too much about the pretty free sister of one of his slaves. When the slaver turned back toward his fire, Donatus followed her to the horses.

She stood by Zapada, her forehead resting against the mare's cheek.

"I'm sorry we couldn't rescue both." It wasn't enough, but he didn't know what else to say.

She drew a deep breath and released a shuddering sigh. "It's good we came for Roanna. Diegis's faith is strong. Whatever comes, he'll always know God is with him. He was always telling me God will work all things together for good for those who love Him, even when we can't see how." Another deep breath, another shuddering sigh. "Somehow, Diegis will find the good."

Then the dam burst, and tears poured down her cheeks like they had in the forest where they buried the girl.

He drew her into his arms and held her tight as her chest heaved with the sobs shaking her body. She clung to him as her warm tears soaked into his tunic. It was too long until her sobs faded to tears and the tears finally stopped. And still he held her as her breathing steadied and slowed. Soundlessly, her lips began to move, and her face relaxed.

Praying to a god would change nothing, but whether anyone listened or not, it gave her peace.

If only he could shelter her from everything bad in life. Taking care of her—he could imagine nothing better, but he didn't even know how he would take care of himself when they returned.

When her eyes opened, the gentle smile he'd grown to love appeared. "Thank you."

For what? He'd done nothing special to deserve her thanks.

"Let's go set up camp. Tomorrow will come sooner if we do." With his good hand, he reached to move a loose strand of hair behind her ear but stopped himself. "I can take your watch tonight."

"No. I'm not going to sleep well until Roanna is by my side." Her smile slipped toward teasing. "Maybe I should take yours."

Ursus started toward the trees. "We'd better get camp set up if I'm going to take mine."

She stepped away from Donatus, scooped up her horse's reins, and followed Ursus.

Donatus's gaze shifted to the slaver's fire. They'd found Roanna, but they didn't own her yet. The slaver had been too quick to reach for that whip, too willing to use it on Ariana. Until Donatus had the bill of sale proving Roanna was his, something could still go wrong. It was too soon to declare victory and lower his guard.

Chapter 29

So Close But Not Yet

Northeast of Narona, Day 23

The early-morning clouds were still awash with pink when Donatus tossed the saddle blanket on his mare. After straightening it, he lifted the saddle into place. Ariana appeared beside him to tighten the straps.

"Where are you going?"

"To see if I can buy Roanna before we reach Narona. I need to talk with their leader, and my guess is he'll still be where we saw their fire last night."

He mounted and reined away from her.

She called after him. "We'll have everything ready before you return."

Three men still sat by the slaver's fire when he reached them. The man from Roanna's cluster of slaves was nowhere to be seen.

He dismounted. "Who is in charge?"

A short man with a scar stretching from ear to chin rose to face him. "I am. What do you want?"

"You have a girl who was supposed to stay in Sarmizegetusa. I've come to find her and take her back."

The short one's mouth pulled sideways into a leering smile. "That must be some girl to ride this far. Nikonos here is in charge of the young women."

"She's only six."

His head pulled back. "Six? Demetrius has charge of those." His eyes narrowed. "You came this far for a child?"

Donatus shrugged. "Woman, girl, boy. What the man who pays me wants, that's what I'll deliver. We found her last night. I'd like to buy her and start back."

"You'll have to go on to Narona. The owner usually doesn't sell any before they go up for auction. He gets a better price that way. But you can try to convince him to make a special sale."

"I will. We'll travel along with your caravan. We brought her sister to identify her. She will probably want to walk with the girl some."

"That's fine as long as she doesn't do anything to slow us down."

"I'll make sure she doesn't." He mounted. "Thank you."

The scarred man raised his hand, then sat by the fire again.

Donatus nudged the mare into a trot. Going to Narona for the auction was not his first choice, but he had plenty of money for one small girl. There should be no problem outbidding anyone else who might want her.

Two days traveling at the snail's pace of the caravan—that wouldn't be his first choice, either. They could ride on ahead, but something made the hairs on his neck tingle, like they did when someone watched the marching legion from the trees.

Letting Roanna out of their sight might not be wise. He squeezed his lips to stop the wry smile. Ariana would never let them leave her anyway.

It was only midafternoon, and it already felt like two days beside the caravan. It moved slower than a walking horse, so slow that Donatus and Ursus alternated riding with walking alongside the horses.

But for Donatus, it was worth it for the smiles on Ariana's face. She'd taken some of their food to share with Roanna and some other children at lunchtime. He'd give her his full portion, as had Ursus, and the glow in her eyes as she thanked him quenched any hunger pangs he might have had.

But his gaze kept drifting to Demetrius. The slavers rode mules, and they moved up and down the caravan, urging their captives onward. Most simply yelled, but Demetrius liked to snap his whip. Sometimes he flicked it close to someone and grinned when they cringed. Other times he caught them with the tip. But mostly the children didn't cry out. They knew better.

One did, and Demetrius added an extra strike for good measure.

Donatus ground his teeth. The man needed a good lashing himself.

He mounted, and Ursus did the same. They hadn't ridden a hundred feet when the girl in front of Roanna tripped and fell. She started to cry.

Ariana had just leaned over to help her up when Demetrius trotted over. The first crack of the whip was followed by the girl's scream of pain.

Ariana arched her body over the crying child, and the second strike hit the leather strap that held her scabbard. Ursus kicked his horse and raced toward them. When he drew alongside, he lifted the slaver from his mule and tossed him over its head. Then he dismounted beside Ariana and helped her to her feet.

Demetrius rose, cursing, and gathered his whip. As he drew back to strike, Donatus came from behind and grabbed the whip. He kicked the horse to a trot and dragged Demetrius until he let go of the whip handle.

He returned to Ursus and tossed him the whip. "Cut it up."

With a huge grin, Ursus pulled his dagger and cut the whip into foot-long pieces, tossing each in the air as he cut it.

Demetrius charged over, and Donatus drew his gladius.

"These are children. No grown man needs a whip to control a few children, and you will not whip any of these again."

Niconos had ridden over to watch, and his grin declared his neutrality in the fight.

Demetrius stormed over to him and held out his hand. "Your whip."

Niconos shook his head, still grinning. "They'll just cut mine up, too. He's right. I control grown women without needing to use a whip. You should be able to control children without yours."

With a string of curses that brought color to Ariana's cheeks, Demetrius stomped off to catch his mule.

"You'd better stay by your woman and her sister. He won't forget what you did, but it's not you he'll go after." Niconos turned his mule and trotted back to his own post along the caravan.

Donatus rubbed his lip as he watched the distant Demetrius. "Tonight, Ursus and I will split guard duty here with the children. We'll give him no chance to do anything before the sale."

His gaze returned to Ariana's pale face and worried eyes. "And you'll stay right beside one of us as well. Tell the children they need to start walking. I said we wouldn't slow the caravan down, and the sooner we get to Narona, the safer everyone will be."

Ariana clapped her hands and called out instructions in Dacian, and the children trudged forward once more.

It was a good thing he'd listened to the hairs on his neck and stayed.

Narona, Day 24

The caravan reached Narona in the late afternoon and worked its way past the forum, theater, and temples to the auction yard down near the docks.

Ariana stayed beside Roanna. Less than four weeks ago, she'd been talking with Mother as they prepared dinner together. The laughter of Roanna and Diegis as they played tag in the farmyard had drifted through the window, marking the end of a day's labor and the beginning of an evening enjoying each other.

Now the cold stones of a Roman city pressed in around her. Diegis would soon be auctioned and shipped only God knew where. Tears stung her eyes as her last vision of him being herded into the boys' cage in Sarmizegetusa rose before her. Would he ever be free to laugh like that again?

Ahead lay the slave cages. She knew too well the fear that gnawed at all those who'd made the trek with Roanna. Her sister might have to spend tonight there.

But only tonight. Tomorrow Donatus would buy her and set her free.

Her eyes sought out her Roman protector, riding a little ahead of her while Ursus rode behind her, leading Zapada. Every step of the way, he'd known what to do, just as Gracchus had said.

He dropped back to ride beside her. "The cages are just ahead. Time to step away from the caravan. I don't want you locked up with the rest."

She kissed Roanna's forehead. "We'll get you tomorrow."

Roanna bit her lip, but she kept walking when Ariana stopped.

Donatus slipped from his horse to stand beside her. "It will only be tonight, and maybe not even that. As soon as they get everyone in the cages, I'll go see if I can buy her ahead of the auction."

"Can you do that?"

"I can ask. The head slaver didn't think it likely, but I won't know until I try."

"If anyone can, it's you."

His mouth curved up only at the corners, but even though his smile was small, her praise warmed his eyes.

"Where are the slave ships?" She wanted to see what Diegis would be sailing in, but she also didn't.

"Over there on the river. You can see their masts."

"On the river?"

"Ships often come a few miles up a river to a port town on the main roads, like Narona. Even Rome isn't right on the coast. If you want, before we head back, I'll take you to the shore."

"I'd like that. Roanna should see the sea, too, before we head home to our Dacian mountains."

Ursus had caught up, and he handed her Zapada's reins. "I always liked the sea. Going out in our boat, setting the nets with my father. I wouldn't mind working as a sailor, traveling the Empire and visiting all the main ports."

His eyes turned wistful, and she wished with all her heart he could.

The lead slaver stood by an open cage door as the last of the women walked in.

Donatus dismounted and handed his reins to Ursus. "Time to see if I can buy Roanna today."

"I'll be praying for you."

"You do that. Maybe it will help." His skeptical smile said more than his words.

As he strode toward the slaver, Ariana offered up the prayers she promised. Prayers for Roanna's freedom...and for his.

◆

It was only half a block from the cages to the auction office. The hinges creaked as Donatus opened the door and stepped inside.

"The slaves that just arrived. I'd like to see about buying one of them."

Two Greeks turned to face him, one thin with tired eyes and one plump wearing gold rings the size of Gracchus's signet on three fingers.

"I'm their owner." He tipped his head toward the thin man. "My auctioneer will start the sales tomorrow at three hours after dawn."

"The men who brought them here, do they work for you?"

"They do." The fat Greek deigned to give him a superior smile.

"Perhaps you'd like to know about a problem with one of them."

"A problem?" The Greek's eyebrows lowered.

"We traveled for a day with your caravan. One of your slavers was whipping children who weren't trying to cause trouble. He was damaging your merchandise, and if it were me, I wouldn't employ a man who couldn't care for my property better."

"Do you know his name?"

"Demetrius."

"Hmm." He turned to the thin man. "Have you seen anything?"

The thin Greek cleared his throat. "Well, there have been more children coming in with whip marks than normal. But I thought Dacians were just harder to handle."

The owner scowled. "I should have been told. Make sure that stops immediately."

A hard swallow was followed by two quick nods. "I can look for a replacement."

"Do it now, and don't let him near this crop of slaves again before they're sold."

The fat Greek turned an oily smile on Donatus. "You have my thanks for bringing this to my attention. I won't forget."

"I'm glad I could help. It can be hard to find reliable workers when you can't watch them work yourself." Donatus offered a genuine smile. A favor well done deserved one in response. "I came in to see if I could buy one of the slaves today rather than wait for the auction. I need to start back to Dacia as soon as possible."

The fat Greek smiled as he shook his head. "I never do direct sales. Slaves bring more at auction."

Donatus froze the smile on his face before it flipped into the frown the man deserved. "Then I'll be back tomorrow."

The Greek responded with a tip of his head and a smug smile before turning back to his auctioneer.

Donatus strode from the office. Disgust swirled within him as his jaw clenched. The owner deserved to have Ursus toss him on his head as he had Demetrius.

The ingrate would be making more money with the cruel slaver gone. He should have shown his appreciation by selling Roanna immediately.

He stretched his jaw, and it relaxed. At least the children in the next caravan wouldn't have to suffer as much. That was worth something.

He joined Ursus and Ariana, her eyes eager as if she was certain he'd made the purchase.

"We have to wait for the auction." Her smile faded. "But Roanna and the others won't be harmed tonight. He's dismissed Demetrius and ordered him kept away from the cages."

His nostrils flared. "That worm of an owner wants to maximize his profits, and uninjured slaves bring more than injured ones."

"I asked at the taberna for a decent inn with a stable, and I have directions." Ursus pointed back past the cages. "One block that way and right three blocks."

"Let's go. The auction starts three hours after dawn. We want to be back here two hours early so we don't miss the start."

As they passed by the cage where Roanna was, Ariana started over. An armed guard stepped into her path. "Come in the morning. Inspections start an hour past dawn."

Ariana craned her neck to look past him. "We'll get you tomorrow."

A raised hand and trembling smile were Roanna's response.

Donatus moved beside her. "It's time to go."

As they walked away, she kept looking back over her shoulder. Roanna stood by the cage wall, her hand raised in a motionless wave lest the guard see.

When they turned the corner to go to the inn, the tears Ariana hadn't let her sister see trickled down her cheeks.

And Donatus's anger at the cruelty of it all surged once more.

Chapter 30

The Auction

The slave auction, Day 25

For two hours, Donatus stood with Ariana by the wooden platform where the slaves would be offered for sale. Two turntables, one for men and boys, one for women and girls, stood empty, but not for much longer.

During those two hours, buyers had inspected the Dacians who would be shipped all over the empire, but he kept Ariana by the platform. No need for her to watch people poked and prodded and handled like animals.

When the auctioneer appeared, Ariana smiled up at Donatus. "I hope they bring her out quickly. It's so hard to wait."

The first two slaves climbed the stairs at the back of the platform and stepped up on the turntables: a young man near his own age and a pretty woman near Ariana's. Each wore a wooden plaque around their necks.

"What are those wood things?" Ariana pointed.

221

"They describe the slave: where they came from, good points, weaknesses."

When the handler pulled the tunic over the man's head and dropped it on the floor, Ariana gasped and turned away. "He's wearing nothing!" Her whisper quavered as her face turned red.

"They'll all be naked."

"Women, too?"

"Yes, but you don't need to watch. I'll tell you when Roanna gets here."

"If it weren't for Gracchus, that would have been me."

She moved a little closer to him and stared at his feet.

He'd seen auctions before, and he never thought much about what was done. He always thought a buyer had the right to see what he was buying. He'd never thought about how a woman might feel.

The auctioneer alternated the sales between men and women. After the first batch of adults, he sold a batch of boys and girls. When the next group of men and women came on the platform, Ariana gripped his arm. "Did we miss her somehow?"

"No. She'll probably be in the next batch of children."

His anger with the owner surged again. If he'd shown the gratitude of any decent man, he would have sold Roanna yesterday, and Ariana wouldn't have to endure this.

Finally, the person on the turntable was a pretty girl of ten. Several men bid on her, driving the price up from 150 to 400 denarii before the auctioneer pronounced her sold.

And the next one up was Roanna.

The auctioneer's voice carried over the murmurs of the crowd. "One Dacian, six years of age, sound of limb and mind. Starting bid is one hundred fifty denarii."

Donatus raised his hand "I bid one hundred fifty."

Ariana gripped his tunic, closed her eyes, and was probably praying.

"Do I have a bid for two hundred denarii?"

Silence. "One seventy-five?"

No voice was raised, no hand waved.

"Sold for one hundred fifty denarii. Pay over there and present the bill of sale to claim your purchase."

The handler tossed Roanna her tunic and led her down the stairs.

Ariana touched his arm, and he looked down to find her brightest smile.

"God just gave us a bargain, and now we can go home."

"Whether he did or not, she's yours again."

At the table, he paid and was handed a bill of sale in his name. He would transfer title to Gracchus when they got home.

Bill of sale in hand, he led Ariana to the pen where Roanna was waiting, holding her plaque. The guard opened the gate, and she was released into Ariana's arms.

Donatus picked up the plaque where it had fallen at their feet and tossed it back in the pen. He was a free man, but one glance at his hand declared his own defect to all without any plaque.

They were walking away from the auction when Roanna grabbed Ariana's sleeve and pointed at the boy who had just climbed onto the platform. "There's Bikili! Can we buy him?" Her voice dropped to a whisper. "He's a brother."

"Donatus."

He turned at her voice, eyebrows raised, "What?"

"I want to buy that one, too." She pointed at a red-haired boy with a fresh ragged scar on his cheek and an empty socket where his eye should be. "Gracchus said we could buy two."

The auctioneer's voice rang out. "One Dacian, ten years of age, one eye missing but otherwise sound of limb and mind. Starting bid is one hundred fifty denarii."

Donatus's mouth settled into a frown, and he shook his head. "He gave me money to buy your sister and brother."

She rested her hand on his arm as she stood on tiptoes. Her whisper reached his ear. "But he is my brother in Christ, and if I can't rescue Diegis, I can at least rescue him."

"Do I hear one hundred twenty-five?" The auctioneer's voice boomed behind him.

"Love runs much deeper than blood relationship, and a brother in Christ is closer to my heart than a brother by blood who didn't love Jesus ever could be."

"Do I hear one hundred? A bargain even with one eye." The pitch of the auctioneer's voice had risen.

Her eyes were so eager. It wouldn't cost much to save the boy...and Gracchus had expected to buy her brother. Why should he care which boy she brought home?

"Seventy-five denarii? Only half what he's worth."

Donatus released a sigh. "All right."

"Fifty denarii? He's worth at least fifty if only to use training guard dogs."

He strode to the edge of the platform. "I bid fifty."

"Fifty here." The auctioneer pointed at Donatus. "Do I hear seventy-five?"

Silence and then, "Sold for fifty denarii. Pay over there and present the bill of sale to claim your purchase."

The boy was cheap, but he wasn't what Gracchus had sent him for.

But if Ariana claimed he was her brother, perhaps it wouldn't matter.

She slipped her arms around him, and her hug swept away his concerns.

He paid at the table and got his second bill of sale.

Roanna ran ahead of them to the pen. "Bikili. You're coming home with us."

After inspecting the bill of sale, the guard opened the gate for the boy. He'd no sooner stepped out than Roanna had him in her arms. She'd barely released him when Ariana drew him into an embrace.

His beaming smile faded as he eyed Donatus, who was tucking the bill of sale into the pouch with the one for Roanna.

Donatus slipped the pouch inside his tunic. "Back to the inn. Our business here is complete." The corner of his mouth lifted. "Unless you have some more you want to buy."

Ariana hugged his arm. "I'd buy them all if I could, but Gracchus might only be content with two. Let's go home."

He left the auction yard with Ariana beside him, her arm around Roanna, and Roanna holding Bikili's hand. But Bikili eyed him with suspicion and stayed as far away as Roanna's reach allowed.

As the three chattered happily in Dacian beside him, his jaw clenched.

He had succeeded in the quest to recover her sister, and now it was time to return. But he didn't want this trip to end. Each day worked was two more denarii, and eight more days he'd be able to eat after the job was over. But mostly he didn't want to be separated from Ariana.

He loved her, but he had nothing to offer her. It wouldn't be right to ask her to leave the security of Gracchus's household to be with him.

Another future he longed for had been destroyed by the knife in his arm before it could even begin.

Chapter 31

The three entered the stableyard walking ahead of Donatus. A nicker from his left drew Roanna's gaze, and she scurried over to Zapada's stall.

The white mare lowered her head over the half-door to get a nose rub. Roanna looked over her shoulder. "Did you find any of the others?"

"Tribune Gracchus found Zapada. Maybe the others are where she was." Ariana pointed at the next two stalls. "We brought those two as well."

"Three horses for four people?" Surprise colored the little girl's voice.

Ariana had reached the stall and placed her hands on her sister's shoulders. "Five, actually. You haven't met Ursus yet."

"We'll get more. We'll need two rooms tonight as well." Donatus smiled down at the serious-faced Bikili, who stood back from both him and the horse. "He's not as mean as his name sounds, but he does snore."

"Is he your slave, too?"

"He's a gladiator the legion commander lent us. And you won't be anyone's slave after we get back to Dacia. We bought you to free you."

Bikili's eyes widened, and his straight mouth curved into a smile before spreading into a grin. Then the smile vanished as quickly as it had appeared. "But where will I go? My family is dead. I can't go home."

Ariana wrapped her arms around him from behind and pulled him against her. He turned his single eye on her face.

"You are home. You're going to stay with Roanna and me."

Roanna slipped her hand into his. "You'll be my brother forever."

His shoulders relaxed, and the smile returned to his lips. "God can work anything for good for those of us who love Him."

As the three embraced, Donatus felt the wall between these followers of Jesus and him. A wall that he'd put there, not them. What would it be like to have such hope even when everything had gone wrong? Was it just a trick the mind played on itself? Was their god only a story or was he real?

What would it cost to find out? Was it more than he was willing to pay?

They entered the courtyard.

"Donatus."

He turned to find the innkeeper approaching, holding out a key.

"Your big friend gave me your key to hold in case he didn't get back before you did."

"Thank you." Donatus took the key and herded the children toward the stairs.

The key rattled in the lock, and he pushed the door open.

Ursus's gladius and scabbard lay on the bed. A wax tablet rested against it. Donatus opened it, and as he read, his mouth set to a thin line.

"What does it say?" Unease colored her voice.

He handed it to Ariana, and she handed it back. "I only read Greek."

"I decided to follow Him. I'll look for Aristarchus. Give Donatus my sword. Thank you and goodbye, little sister."

He closed his eyes, and a sigh drained his lungs. "Ursus has run away." He scrunched his eyes as he rubbed his forehead. "I have to report him while there's still time to catch him."

"No! You can let him go. He doesn't want to kill anymore, and he doesn't want to die. This is the only way for him."

She gripped his arm. "Please, Donatus. Have mercy on him. He's done nothing but help us. He could have stolen your money and the horses and left us stranded. He could have killed us so we could never tell. Without him, the robbers might have killed us."

"That was more your arrows than anything he did."

Her hand pushed his words away. "He helped protect Roanna from the slaver. He's our friend, and he's become my brother. Please let him go. Give him a chance at a new life where he doesn't have to choose between killing and dying."

"If he were mine, I'd let him go. I'd even free him legally. But he's not mine. Gracchus borrowed him from his own commander. What will losing the man cost him?"

He shook his right hand at her. "No one would hire me with this. Gracchus took a risk when he gave me this job. He trusted me, and I've failed him."

She took his crippled hand and stroked the back of it. "You didn't fail him. He hired you to help me get my family back, and you have. Roanna is free now, and Bikili."

He pulled it away, and she took it again. "Tribune Gracchus is a fair man. He won't blame you for something you couldn't control. I never suspected Ursus would leave like this. He couldn't have been more reliable all the way from Dacia."

"But I'm still responsible."

"It's not your fault." She took a deep breath. "But it might be mine."

His brow furrowed. "Yours? You weren't even here when he left."

"No, but we talked about what he did as a gladiator, how killing for sport is wrong. I told him what God had said about loving each other like we love ourselves. He told me he didn't want to kill anymore. But he didn't want to die, and that's what he'd have to do to stop."

"Your conversations by the fire...I heard them."

"Then you heard me tell him how much God loves him and how He wants Ursus to love Him back." She wiped the corner of her eye. "No one has cared about him since he was a boy. He didn't think anyone could after all the men he's killed. But he was so wrong. Jesus loves him. He loves us all enough to go to the cross to pay for all our sins so we can know God's love."

She wiped another tear away. "He was hearing God calling him to believe in what Jesus did and become God's child. He wanted to, but he knew what answering yes would cost if he stayed."

Donatus stared at her. He'd never seen tears trickling down a face that shone with joy.

"That's what he means by 'I've decided to follow Him.' He's my brother in Christ now, just like Bikili. And the angels in heaven are singing for joy over that."

She swept the tears from her cheeks and offered a watery smile.

"So you see, it's really my fault, not yours, and Gracchus will blame me, not you, when he knows what happened."

"His wife...she's a Christian now. Is that your fault, too?"

A sheepish smile replaced the watery one. "I didn't tell her about Jesus, but she met the man who did because of me. So indirectly, yes. Gracchus told me he'd crucify me if I told her anything, but God found a way to reach her without me saying a word. So Gracchus has seen how God can claim someone's heart whether he likes it or not. When we tell him Ursus became a Christian, he won't be surprised at him choosing to run instead of kill."

He drew a deep breath and held it. A chance at a new life. Ursus had seen it and grasped it. He looked at his hand. The future he faced would never be what he'd hoped for. But he could give Ursus a chance for the future he wanted.

"I'll let him go."

She slipped her arms around his chest and squeezed. "Thank you."

When she stepped back, her joyful eyes triggered his smile and warmed him inside.

They still had a long ride to get home. His job was only half done, and it would be harder without Ursus to help. But this day had a shine on it he'd never forget. Today he set three people free.

Chapter 32

BRINGING GOOD FROM BAD

Ursus was gone, but they still needed another horse for the ride home. While Roanna and Bikili stayed at the inn, Donatus and Ariana headed for the horse market.

A port town on a major trade road had many people fresh from a ship looking to buy a horse, and there were plenty of dealers and animals to meet the need. Donatus scanned the rows of corrals and blew out a breath.

"I don't want to spend too much of Gracchus's money, so let's find the cheaper ones."

"That's not wise. A cheap horse could break down before we get home. We should buy a better horse that we can sell back in Dacia for more than we pay. We can make enough profit to cover the extra you paid for Bikili."

"You're the horse breeder." His good hand swept the market before them. "I yield to your better judgement."

She strolled among the corrals, watching both horses and people. Finally, she stopped where a chestnut mare paced the sides of the corral. It was taller than most, with a flowing mane and tail that were two shades lighter than its coat."

As she leaned on the rail, the owner strolled over. "I have others over here. That one is broken to saddle, but she's too much horse for a woman or boy. No one but an expert horseman can ride her."

Ariana turned smiling eyes on him. "How much is she?"

"Normally, six hundred denarii. But today, a special sale price of only five hundred."

"But if no one can ride her, no one will pay that. And every day you don't sell her is money out of your pocket because you have to feed and stable her. I might be willing to pay...two hundred, if she'll let me hobble her."

"She's worth three times that."

"Only if you can sell her, and you've already told us almost no one can ride her." She waved her hand at the people looking at other vendors' horses. "I don't see any Sarmatians or Persians or anyone else likely to want a horse too spirited for most to ride."

He frowned as he rubbed his chin. "Two hundred fifty."

She looked at Donatus, and he nodded. "Two hundred twenty-five, but only if she lets me hobble her."

The dealer crossed his arms. "Agreed."

She made a sucking sound. The mare stopped pacing and stood watching her. Ariana held out some hay and repeated the strange sound. After eyeing her curiously, the mare sauntered over. It took a bite, and Ariana's soft Dacian words held its attention as it chewed. After the second bite, Ariana placed her free hand on the horse's cheek.

A silent exchange as they looked into each other's eyes, and the mare walked away.

"What kind of hobbles does she like?"

"I don't know."

"Has she ever been hobbled?"

"Not by me."

She held out her hand to the owner. "Your longest hobbles, please."

He handed her a pair, and she climbed into the corral. The mare let her approach and run her hands along its back, down its neck, across its shoulder, and down each of its legs. It stamped its foreleg once, then stood still.

She draped the hobbles across the mare's withers, then jumped to lay her stomach on the horse's back. As she twisted into riding position, the mare turned its head to watch her. A gentle kick to its sides, and it started walking.

Ariana swung her leg over its neck and slipped off. Cooing softly, she put first one hobble, then the other around its legs. Then she stood and led the hobbled horse over to a trough filled with fresh hay. One soft slap on its shoulder, and Ariana strolled to where the horse dealer and Donatus leaned on the rail.

"We'll take her for two hundred twenty-five, if you throw in those hobbles."

The dealer's mouth pulled into a wry smile. "Sold. If you ever want work taming horses, come see me."

"I'm heading home to Dacia, or I might do that. Now we need to get a saddle."

He pointed across the market square. "Leander will give you an honest price. Tell him I sent you."

Donatus fell in beside her as she wove her way through the shoppers. "Amazing, the way you talked him down. But if only you can handle her like that, will Gracchus get his money back?"

She smiled at him. "Don't worry. Roanna will ride Zapada, and I'll train Pneuma for others as we go." The smile turned into a teasing grin. "A spirited horse deserves a matching name. She's big enough for you to ride, and she'll be gentle enough before we get home. We'll get a Scythian saddle so she'll be comfortable to ride as well."

"Not interested. I'll take Ursus's brute, and Bikili can ride mine. I'll leave the spirited ones to you and Roanna."

She flashed him a smile before starting to deal with Leander for whatever she'd need.

Arms crossed, he watched her. She'd calmed that horse's restless spirit. She had the same effect on him. Two weeks and they'd be back at Gracchus's house, and he'd have to leave her.

How was he going to get through each day when she was gone?

As they lead Pneuma into the stableyard, Roanna skipped over to join them. "She's pretty. What's her name? Do I get to ride her?"

The music of Ariana's laughter washed over Donatus.

"Pneuma and not yet. She needs a little gentling first."

Donatus bent over to get at Roanna's level. "What she means is the trader sold her for a third of what she was worth because no one else can ride her." He straightened. "But now we have four horses, we could ride over to the coast so you can see the sea before we leave."

Roanna's bouncing and Bikili's subdued smile proclaimed their approval of the plan.

Donatus glanced at his hand. "I'll get someone to saddle the other horses."

Ariana rested her hands on the boy's shoulders and squeezed. "Bikili will help you if you just tell him what needs to be done."

Drawing a deep breath, Bikili stepped forward. "I haven't saddled a horse before, but I can try."

Donatus accepted the offer with a quick nod. "I've never taught anyone before, but I can try, too.

He led the boy upstairs to get the Roman saddles. He lifted the one for his horse and handed it to Bikili. The boy wrapped both arms around it, and Donatus stacked the blanket on top. Then he draped Ursus's blanket on his own shoulder before swinging the saddle up to balance on top of it.

With the boy right behind him, he descended to the courtyard and led him to the horses' stalls.

"We'll do yours first."

"Because he's shorter or friendlier?" He eyed the horse where it munched hay in the stall.

"They're both friendly."

Bikili raised his eyebrows as he drew a deep breath. "I'm ready."

Donatus dropped his saddle outside the stall where Ursus's horse stood watching him and opened the stall to his old mount. He was well practiced at getting the blanket in position and lifting the saddle into place with one good hand. "The straps are the part you have to help me with."

Bikili's gaze moved from Donatus's face to his hand and back. "How did that happen?"

"A knife right here." He touched the scar.

"That doesn't look like much to have caused that. Does it hurt?"

Donatus made some circles around the scar with his thumb. "Yes, but Ariana rubs it to make it feel better. Looks like you've been hurt recently as well."

"My eye?" His lips lost their slight smile.

"Yes. How did you lose it?"

"The slaver in charge of us. One of the little girls was too tired to keep walking. Demetrius started whipping her, and I tried to stop him."

He touched the edge of the socket of his missing eye. "I didn't know how well he could aim it. The first lash hit my cheek. The second took my eye. He just laughed and said he'd take the other if I got in his way again." His mouth turned down; then a slight smile returned. "But God can bring good out of bad. When he turned on me, he stopped hurting her. She was all right after a night's sleep."

Donatus stared at him as silence stretched between them.

Bikili reached under the horse's stomach and picked up the hanging belly strap. "What do I do with this big one with the ring on the end?"

"Pull it up here. Slip this strap through the ring, then..."

As Donatus pointed and explained, Bikili followed every direction until the saddle was firmly held in place.

"Did I do it right?" The boy's eye shone with his eagerness to please.

Donatus tousled his red hair. "I couldn't have done it better myself, even with two good hands."

The Mare Nostrum west of Narona

Donatus led them along the river and down to the sea. A ship was entering the river channel as they reach the shore, its sail still filled by the wind as it moved into the fresh water.

The children stopped to watch, and Ariana slipped from her horse. "Let's walk a while."

As they led the horses along the shore, she tipped her head back and breathed in the salt air. "Ursus said he loved the sea. I hope he finds somewhere to live where he can enjoy it again." Her fingers rested on his arm. "Thank you for not reporting him."

"Under Roman law, I should have. But you were right about it being pointless. He was as useless to the legate as if he'd been killed on the sand. We saved Gracchus's commander the embarrassment of having his man stand there like a sheep at a butcher shop."

"There's always some good we can find, even in the bad things that happen."

"Maybe. Even Bikili believes that. 'God can work anything for good for those of us who love Him.' That's what he said about staying with you when he had nowhere else to go."

He'd have to agree with the boy that staying with Ariana would be good. More than good. It was the best thing he could imagine.

"Apostle Paul told us that in one of his letters, and I've found it to be true. Sometimes it takes a while to see the good, but if I wait long enough, I can."

"I don't love your god. I don't even know if he's real, but you have me looking for the good in the bad, too. At least some times, even though I know I'll only be disappointed."

"I know it can be hard, but I try to thank God in all things. He helps me thank Him for what's good while giving me strength to bear the bad. So many times, that season of pain is the seed for joy in the future. Like the ground laying fallow in winter, with seeds planted and waiting to sprout in the spring when conditions for growth are best."

He'd worked on a farm before joining the legion. A man could starve waiting for the next harvest.

Her eyes focused on something distant. "Sometimes what you want most in the word isn't possible, like setting Diegis free, but I trust that somehow God will bring good out of evil. Like me getting to rescue Bikili from the horrible life he'd have as a half-blind slave. If we'd bought Diegis, would you have let me buy Bikili?"

Her gentle gray eyes warmed him as they waited for his answer.

"No. Probably not." But maybe he would have. It was hard to refuse her anything.

"Like me becoming a slave so Marcia would be healed, but even more so she would know the joy of loving and being loved by God."

◆

His arm was resting, palm up, against his stomach, a sure sign it was aching again. Ariana placed her thumb on the scar and made some of the circles that always helped. "Like me knowing how to ease your pain because our neighbor broke her arm." Her thumb stopped moving when she raised her eyes to his. "Like your wound making you leave the legion so you could be the one who helped me get Roanna back. No one could have done better. I trust your judgement, and I feel safe with you."

She felt more than safe. She felt happy even in the midst of all that had gone wrong.

"Gracchus said he knew the perfect man to guide and protect me in the hunt, and he was right."

"Even if you think of me that way, other people don't." He lifted his right hand and shook it at her. "They only see this. They see a cripple, not a man. What didn't look like much of a wound has ruined the rest of my life."

"Maybe it really set you free."

His head snapped back. "What are you talking about?"

"Maybe it freed you from a life spent killing for a life of…only God knows what."

"I certainly don't know what kind of life I can have with this, and if your god does, he isn't telling me."

"He doesn't usually tell us when we demand an answer, but He makes it clear at the right time."

"Hmph." Donatus turned and led his horse away.

His shoulders started square, but they sagged a little after the first few strides. She blinked fast and stopped the tears he must never see. The last thing he needed was to think her tears of longing for a future with him were tears of pity instead.

Chapter 33

Everything She Told Him

Day 26

It was early morning when Donatus led his troop out of Narona. They would ride more than halfway to Aquae and spend the night in the forest. Tomorrow, a leisurely soak at the baths and a hot meal awaited them. The thought of both brought a smile.

As she had with Ursus, Ariana set the pace as she taught Bikili to ride the trot without bouncing and the canter without fear.

The boy wore a giant grin as he trotted back to take his place beside Donatus.

"You really look like one of her family now. I've been wondering if Ariana is part centaur since we started this trip, but maybe she isn't if she can teach you to ride just like her."

Bikili's gaze settled on Ariana, riding ahead of them with Roanna at her side. "I hope I can be the brother she needs."

"Diegis was eleven, so you're almost the same age."

"Is eleven. I'm sure God has him in His care somewhere. I'll always be praying for him, for God to bless him with a family again like I have been."

"You will?" Donatus kept his eyes from rolling…barely. Her brother would be on a slave ship soon, and slaves taken in war seldom saw freedom again.

"Oh, yes." He cocked his head. "And you will be, too."

"I don't pray to your god."

"But you will. God brings good out of bad, and there's nothing better than following Him." A grin split his face. "Roanna thinks you will, too."

Roanna turned in her saddle. "Bikili. Come ride by me."

With a bounce of his eyebrows, he kicked his horse and trotted ahead.

Donatus shifted his gaze from the happy trio ahead of him to the woods that surrounded them. The undergrowth at the edge of the road was thick. A man would get scratched up badly if he tried to push his way through. Behind it rose the trees, a mix of pines and leafy trees of medium height. But one oak overshadowed them all.

He'd loved climbing trees as a boy. One like it towered over the villa next to his grandfather's small farm. It had seemed like he could see forever when he climbed high enough. A tree like that inspired dreams. Sitting in its branches, he'd made his plans to travel the Empire in the legion, then get a farm himself.

But climbing trees took two good hands. He'd be earthbound forever, and reality replaced dreams when you stood on the dirt.

The children's laughter drifted back to him. Only three days ago their future must have seemed hopeless, but they hadn't lost hope.

Were they right that their god could bring good from bad? Was he real, with power to change what seemed inevitable? Donatus gave up believing in any gods when he was only a little older than Bikili. Like Gracchus, he saw the Roman gods as the imaginary characters they were. But what if one god was real? If a man refused to even consider that, could he ever know the truth?

A lunch of bread and cheese had satisfied Donatus's hunger. The children were watching frogs in the small stream while the horses grazed.

His arm was hurting, and Ariana always seemed to know. Without any words, she held out her hand. As soon as he placed his arm on it, she began the slow circles that eased his pain and warmed his heart. Her eyes closed, and that smile he'd come to love appeared.

When the pain was mostly gone, he took her hand. "I know you say you pray, but what exactly do you say to your god that makes this work?"

"I ask God to take away the pain. The pain in your arm..." She touched his chest. "And the pain in your heart."

"The pain does go away for a while, and everything seems less hopeless...until I start thinking again about what I can't do without my right hand."

"One of God's greatest gifts after we become His children is hope."

"Hope." His mouth turned down. "I lost that when I lost the use of my hand."

He stared at his useless fingers. "Those nights you thought I was sleeping...I listened to you and Ursus. I've been thinking about what you said. I'm more like him than you might think. When he said no one cared if he lived or died...I could have said those same words."

She slipped her fingers around his palm and squeezed before releasing it. "But I care, and God cares, too."

If only his fingers could grip, he would have held her hand for as long as she'd let him.

"I know you do. And maybe Gracchus does, at least some, or he wouldn't have hired me. He knew I was in trouble." His mouth pulled into a wry smile. "He even pretended he didn't have time to finish his lunch when I came to his office, but he never ate that much when I was his orderly. He had it all there for me." He rubbed his jaw. "And if your god is real, maybe he cares, too."

"He's real, and He does. He cares even more than I do, and I care so very much what happens to you."

Her eyes spoke the truth of that, and it warmed him more than she could imagine. "Like you cared about Bikili when you'd never even seen him before."

"I couldn't leave him there. I was afraid what they'd do to him with only one eye."

"With good reason. If no one bought him, he would have been dead within the week, maybe even before dinner. His owner wasn't the kind to keep around any mouths to feed that he couldn't make money with."

She shuddered. Then her smile returned. "I think God timed Roanna coming out so we'd still be there when Bikili was sold. Things we never expect, God uses those to help His children. He brought the tribune to the slave cages to save me from a life of bondage, but it's Jesus who freed me with His own death. Not just for me, but so I could tell others."

He offered his arm again. "Like Ursus."

"Yes, and Marcia. God used me to save Marcia from feeling worthless, from wanting to kill herself, from going to hell when she died. She would have been separated from God for all eternity, living in torment. Now she's my sister forever and filled with joy."

She touched his scar and made a few more circles. Then her eyes locked on his. "You could have that, too."

Joy. One corner of his mouth lifted. He wasn't even sure what she meant by that. Happiness—he'd had that as a child, at least some. And pleasure—plenty of opportunities for that. But joy? Maybe you had to experience it to know what it was.

"And hope." Her eyes warmed with that word. "Diegis and I memorized the writings of some of Jesus's apostles. I started writing them down for Marcia before we left. Apostle Paul had so much to say about hope. He was writing to Christians in Rome when he quoted the Jewish prophet Isaiah from hundreds of years before Jesus was born, and then he explained it. 'And again Isaiah says, "The root of Jesse will come, even He who arises to rule the Gentiles; in Him will the Gentiles hope." May the God of hope fill you with all joy and peace in believing, so that by the power of the Holy Spirit you may abound in hope.' Root of Jesse, that's Jesus, and the Holy Spirit...He lives within us after we choose to follow Jesus."

His eyes narrowed. "Your god lives within you? How can that be?"

"I can't explain how, but when He's in you, you'll know. And the peace and joy and hope will fill you."

"You say your god filled Marcia Philippa with joy." He paused, hoping he knew the answer to his next question. "Did he also heal her legs?"

"Yes. My friend Cotiso prayed with her for her legs to be healed and for God to claim her heart."

"You know that powerful a healer? When we get back, could he pray for my hand?"

"Cotiso doesn't have healing powers. He only asks God, and God does the healing. Any Christian can ask God to heal."

His lips tightened. "But you've been asking, and nothing happens."

"I told you at the first mansio that God isn't a puppet. He's in control, and He decides when it's time for healing. Marcia was ready to believe and follow Jesus when she was healed."

Believe. Was he ready to do that? Gracchus said his wife was permanently crippled. Only a real god with real power could have made her walk again. All that Ariana had told Ursus about forgiveness and peace and hope...it sounded so good, and she gave all the credit to her god.

"You told Ursus we were separated from God by the choices we'd made. That Jesus had sacrificed himself to end that separation."

"Yes, and if you believe in Him, you'll have peace and hope and joy now and eternal life with God. All you have to do is confess your sins to Him, ask Him to forgive you because Jesus paid the penalty for you, and then follow Jesus as your Lord."

"How would I do that?"

"Jesus said the greatest commandment is to love God with all your heart and soul and mind and strength and to love others like you love yourself. Tell Him the things you've done that don't live up to that, and ask Him to forgive you for those sins. Thank Jesus for paying the penalty so you can be forgiven. Then thank Him for becoming your Lord."

"Out loud?" There were things he'd done he didn't want her to know.

"God knows your every thought as much as He hears every word. I usually talk with Him inside my head."

"This might take a while."

"God has more patience than you can ever imagine."

He squared his shoulders and blew out a deep breath. Then, as he'd seen her do so many times, he closed his eyes.

They popped open again. "Will you start for me so I'll know God is listening?"

"Yes, and then I'll pray silently until you finish."

She held out both hands, and he placed his in them.

Head bowed, she closed her eyes. "Donatus stands before You, Lord, ready to choose to follow You. Fill him today with Your Holy Spirit. Forgive him and heal him in body, mind, and spirit, and claim him as Your own child forever."

It took a while to name all the things he'd done that God needed to forgive. Finally, he was ready.

God, please forgive me for all these sins and for the many I probably forgot to mention. I thank You, Jesus, for dying to pay for them for me. Thank You for forgiving me. I don't know what it will take, but I'll try to follow You as Lord from this day forward.

Shimmering light surrounded him, and love and peace flowed through him. Words he didn't know bubbled up in his mind as everything dark drained away.

When he opened his eyes. Ariana stood there before him, eyes closed with that slight smile on her lips. And he knew exactly why she smiled.

"Ariana."

Her eyes opened, and the brightest smile he'd ever seen lit her face.

"You met Him, didn't you?"

"Yes." He couldn't stop grinning. "Everything you told me...it's all true."

She slipped her arms around him. "And now you're my brother forever." A quick squeeze, and she stepped back.

He closed his eyes, and stretched his arms heavenward. Despair was gone. Pain was gone.

He lowered his hands and flexed his fingers...and the three that hadn't worked still didn't.

He turned to her, brow furrowed. "I feel great. I feel God right here with me, and the pain is completely gone. But my hand still doesn't work. Did I do something wrong?"

She took his hand and drew it to her chest. "No."

"Then why didn't He heal my hand like He did Marcia's legs?"

"I don't know. God is the great healer, but in His own way and His own time. He is so far above us that we don't always understand why He does something." A shadow of sadness took her smile. "Or why He allows something else. I still can't understand why He let my parents die, or why Diegis had to go the other way so we couldn't free him. But I trust God to someday bring good from bad."

She wiped the corner of her eye. "My heart is still breaking because Diegis is gone. Until the day I die, I'll be lifting my brother up to God, and someday, we'll be together again. God does what's best for us, even when it isn't what I'd choose myself. I have to trust in that."

She rested her hand on his cheek. "Diegis is going to love you when he meets you, like I do."

He gave her the smile she wanted, but he didn't want her love to be like a brother's love. He wanted her to love him like he already loved her, like a man loves the woman he wants for his wife, to spend a lifetime together and beyond.

He rubbed his scar, now pain-free, and the presence of God filled him again with hope and a peace like he'd never known.

But his hand remained crippled. God must have His reason for that, and maybe he'd know why someday. God works all things together for good for those who love Him. Those words kept playing in his mind.

God was trying to tell him something, but what? He'd met God, and he could honestly say he loved Him now.

Still, what he wanted most on earth remained beyond his reach. He could never ask Ariana to tie her life to a man who couldn't take care of her. She said God did what was best, even when she didn't understand why. She must live her life without her beloved brother...and he would live his without her.

Chapter 34

Not Future, but Now

The Gracchus house, Morning of Day 27

Quintus placed a slice of cheese on the tarragon bread and took a bite. "The new orderly is better than the last one, but he's not as good as Donatus."

Marcia took one sip and returned her goblet to the table. "Donatus seems like a nice young man. You might need to figure out something for him to do."

"Why?"

She reached for some of his cheese. Her eyes turned teasing as she nibbled it. "Because he and Ariana are going to marry, and I'd like her to stay nearby so we can visit."

His chuckle echoed in the room. "When they left you were worried because he looked at her like an enemy. Now you think they'll marry? A Dacian ruined his hand. He's not likely to marry one."

"But all Jesus's followers are brothers and sisters. We don't let hatreds born of old loyalties ruin that. Jesus forgave us, and He tells us we have to forgive, too."

"Some things can never be forgiven, and some people don't deserve forgiveness. Justice matters."

"It does, but mercy is more important. And mercy and forgiveness walk hand in hand."

Her fingers touched the back of his hand and drew his smile.

"When I was bringing your Ariana home, I told her I was not a forgiving man. It's not the Roman way."

"And I'm sure she believed you." She leaned over and kissed his cheek. "But you always forgive me."

"That's different. You're my wife." He pushed some hair behind her ear. "And you've probably forgiven me a few times as well."

Her grin broadened his own smile.

"It's harder to hate when you're trying to forgive. Ariana didn't hate us when you brought her here. Donatus won't hate her by the time they return. He'll be a follower of Jesus, too. Just wait, and you'll see."

She pushed back her chair and stood. "I need to talk with the cook about something for dinner. I'll be right back."

He watched her until she disappeared into the storeroom connecting the triclinium and kitchen. Conversations with Marcia were sometimes surprising since she turned into a Christian, but no man ever had a better wife.

Aquae, Evening of Day 27

In Aquae, Donatus lead his party to the same inn. A night on a bed instead of the ground would be most welcome, and the aroma of roasting pork that wafted from the kitchen promised a meal far better than bread and cheese.

He left Ariana and the children in the stableyard and returned with a single key.

Ariana raised her eyebrows when he waved it at her.

"There's some festival at the local temple, and the whole town is full. I got the last room."

"But at least the baths should be lovely. Roanna will love the rose-scented oils."

He reclaimed his horse's reins from Bikili. "As soon as we unload the horses, we should bathe. It might get crowded later."

Bikili stayed with the horses while they ferried their bundles up to the room. With too many people in town, the horses would have to double up in the stalls. Ariana paired Pneuma with Bikili's horse and Zapada with Donatus's. There was barely room for two to turn, but with plenty of hay and water, it would still be a good night for them.

But not so good for him. Their room was up under the eaves with a low ceiling and not much floor space, even with the narrow bed.

As Ariana stacked the saddles four deep and balanced bundles and bags around them, Donatus tousled Bikili's red hair. "Good thing you aren't as big as Ursus yet. One of us would be sleeping outside alone. As it is, we'll have to be careful not to make that stack avalanche on us."

Ariana slipped past him to stand outside the open door. "I pray all is well for him. I miss our bear."

"I do, too, except for the snoring. He was a good friend, but I'm glad he's gone."

Bikili's head tipped, and his brow furrowed. "How can you be glad a good friend is gone?"

"Sometimes it's better for someone to go away. But we'll always pray for him. He's a brother now."

Ursus wasn't all Donatus missed from their first time in Aquae. The splashing of the fountain below their balcony had accompanied her caring for his arm. He didn't miss the pain, but he missed the closeness he'd shared with her each time she made it stop.

It wouldn't be long before he'd have to leave, as Ursus had, and it wasn't only Ariana he'd be missing. Bikili followed him like a puppy, and Roanna gave good hugs. But they didn't need to know yet. There was no reason to spoil the time they had left with him. They would have good memories, and they'd still have Ariana. He'd be left with only memories.

Dinner had been as delicious as it smelled. He'd checked on the horses, and it was time for bed. Ariana already had the children bedded down, Roanna in the bed she would share with her sister, Bikili in Ursus's blankets on the floor. Ariana kissed Roanna's forehead. "Slide over against the wall. I'll be back in a moment."

Donatus was about to bolt the door when Ariana's whisper warmed his ear.

"I have something to tell you." She slipped her hand into his and led him onto the balcony.

At the railing, she turned. "I have a confession."

His brow furrowed. "What?"

"I started praying for you the first time I massaged your arm. But I was only praying for the pain to go away. Then I started asking God to heal your fingers."

"He took most of the pain every time." The corner of his mouth turned up. "You said it was prayer that made it work, but I didn't believe you. I was so sure you were doing something secret with your fingers that you wouldn't tell me."

Her mouth curved to match his own. "It wasn't long until I started asking God for something else."

"Did He give it to you?"

"Not yet, but I have every hope He will. He's done the first part, but you have to do the second."

"If I can. What did you ask for?"

"A future...with you. I asked Him to claim your heart, and He has. I asked Him to make you His...and then to make you mine."

His head pulled back; then he raised his useless hand. "You don't want this. I can't give you the future you deserve. I couldn't find work before this trip. I don't know if I can after I take you home to Gracchus. How can I take care of you? Of the three of you?"

"You don't have to take care of me. We'll take care of each other. You said twenty years in the legion would get you a farm, some sheep, some grapevines, and a family. Well, I should still have a farm, and I have sheep. We can plant grapevines. Bikili, Roanna, and us...there couldn't be a better family, and who knows how many children God will give us?"

She took his bad hand and pressed it to her cheek. "Everything you ever dreamed of you can have with me. Not in the future, but right now." She lifted his hand from her cheek and kissed his palm. "And nothing would give me greater joy than being your wife."

She placed his hand on her cheek once more and leaned into it. "I pray every day that you'll want me as much as I want you."

"Are you sure?"

"Does God make the sun rise every morning?"

"He does, and my love for you is as certain as that sunrise." With his good hand, he tucked a strand of red hair behind her ear. "I want nothing more on earth than to be your husband."

"Then I consider myself betrothed." She stood on tiptoes, and her lips brushed his cheek. "We'll tell the children tomorrow."

He pulled her against him and lowered his lips to hers. Her breath caught, then she relaxed in his arms.

When he released her, her shining eyes triggered his grin. "A promise of things to come. But before we do all I want and more than we should, it's time to get some sleep."

He opened the door, and she crept past the sleeping Bikili to slip into bed with Roanna.

After rolling one blanket into a pillow, he pulled the second over him. As he shifted to get comfortable on the wooden floor, his thanks flew heavenward, and God's peace descended.

God had truly worked all things for good.

Chapter 35

A Blessed Man

The Gracchus house, Day 38

Marcia sat under the canopy in the courtyard, trying to read some Tacitus. But it was hard to stay focused on the history of Rome when it was almost time for Ariana to return. Quintus said it took almost two weeks to reach the coast by horse, and two weeks back. It was almost four weeks since Ariana rode out with her two escorts. She must be almost home.

One of the housemaids stuck her head through the archway. "She's back, mistress."

She set the scroll aside and hurried to greet her sister and best friend.

Arms spread, she walked toward the four horses and their riders. "Welcome home."

Four, not five. She scanned the faces. Ariana was beaming, and Donatus looked pleased. A boy and girl sat the other two horses as if they were part of them, so they must be Roanna and Diegis. But where was the gladiator?

Ariana slipped from her white horse and rushed into Marcia's arms.

"It's so good to be back." She turned and signaled the others to join her.

Roanna came first, but she wrapped her arms around Ariana and hid her face. Slowly, she turned it just enough to peek at Marcia.

Marcia crouched and held out a hand. "You don't have to be afraid, Roanna. Ariana is my sister in Christ, just like you are. This is your home now, and you can stay as long as you want."

The little girl placed her fingertips on Marcia's, then snatched her hand back, but her eyes held no more fear.

Hand on the boy's shoulder, Donatus stood a few feet away, a friendly smile curving his lips.

"Welcome home, Donatus." Marcia rose. "And this must be Diegis."

"No. Bikili." The boy's words were confident, his voice strong, even though his single eye looked uneasy.

"We went to Narona, and they took Diegis to Lissus." The catch in Ariana's voice and Roanna's sniff brought Marcia's hands to her mouth.

"I am so sorry!" She bit her lip as her eyes grew too moist. "If only we'd known that might happen, maybe Quintus could have sent someone with you to follow the second caravan."

Ariana's lips trembled, then steadied "That probably wouldn't have helped. There were so many boys his age. I don't know how a stranger could have found him."

She turned a warm smile on the solemn boy at Donatus's side. "But Bikili is our brother in Christ, so we brought him home instead. And somehow, somewhere, even if I never know it, God can work all things for Diegis's good."

It was time to shift the conversation before the tears stinging Marcia's eyes escaped and got them all crying.

"Well, are you two hungry?" Bikili's nod and Roanna's shy smile said all Marcia needed to hear.

"The kitchen's right there. Dinner is almost ready, but you can tell them I said you needed a little something to tide you over until then."

"They can wait." Ariana's raised eyebrows sent a mother command they instantly read and obeyed. "But I can't. I have a question I've been eager to ask you for too long."

"What is it?"

"Under Roman law, since I was never officially a slave, will Rome recognize me as owner of my family farm?"

"I don't know, but Quintus would. He'll be home soon."

Ariana reached out to Donatus, and he moved up beside her. She interlaced her fingers with his. "If Rome won't recognize it as mine because I'm Dacian, would it recognize it as Donatus's if he's my husband?"

Marcia's smile grew into the broadest grin. "I told Quintus this would happen. I'm not an expert on Roman law, but I believe it would. If need be, Quintus can almost certainly arrange that."

She held out her hand to Ariana. "Come inside. We'll sit and chat until dinner. You must be tired after such a long journey, and I can't wait to hear about your adventures."

"Did you want to chat?" Donatus fought the grin as he looked at Bikili.

A single eye roll said it all before the boy shook his head.

Marcia couldn't help but laugh. "You two are just like Quintus." She wrapped her arm around Ariana's waist and led her and Roanna into the courtyard. "But now you can tell me everything it would embarrass your future husband to hear."

◆

Quintus rode through the gate to find Donatus with a one-eyed, red-haired boy beside him. The boy's smile vanished the moment he turned and saw a Roman officer. It was the response Quintus expected from any Dacian. The boy took Donatus's limp hand, but he stood with chin raised as he met Quintus's gaze.

Donatus met him with a broad smile, which triggered one of Quintus's own.

Reaching across his chest, Donatus tousled the boy's red hair. "That's Quintus Fulvius Gracchus, the man who freed you. He's not your enemy anymore."

A tentative smile, then "Thank you, Quintus Fulvius Gracchus."

Gracchus swung his leg over his stallion's neck and slid off. "So this is Ariana's brother."

Donatus rested his bad hand on the boy's shoulder. "He is now."

"Now?"

"The slave caravan split at Viminacium. Diegis went south to Lissus. God told Ariana to go to Narona. We rescued Roanna and Bikili there."

Quintus's mouth turned down. "Her god told her which port?"

"Yes. We caught up two days before the auction. One small girl and a one-eyed boy didn't cost much, so I can return most of your money. I had to buy another horse. It was on the wild side, but Ariana gentled it so you can sell it for at least twice what I paid." He drew a deep breath. "But I must report that Ursus didn't return with us, so you will need the rest and maybe more to buy him from the legate."

His thumb massaged the scar by his elbow. "It may take a long time, but I'll pay you back."

"Why would you do that? You didn't kill him, did you?"

"No. He ran when we were at the auction, and I didn't report it."

Quintus's frown deepened. "Why not?"

"He decided he'd killed too many already, but that was over. Next time, he'd choose to die. The legate had already lost his gladiator. Nothing would be gained by dragging him back, so I let him go."

Gracchus rolled his eyes. A Roman was required to help capture any runaway. "That sounds like something Marcia would do."

Donatus's smile broadened. "It would. We follow the same God now." He offered his right hand, palm up. "Ariana told me what happened to Marcia. Like with her, He healed me and set me free."

Quintus rubbed his mouth. Marcia had said this would happen, but how did she know?

"Make a fist."

"I can't."

Gracchus didn't even try to stop the snort. "Then how can you say that her god healed you?"

"The pain is gone, here..." He touched his forearm. "And here." He tapped his chest. "I'm still learning, but if you want to know—"

"Not now. If your god ever makes your fingers work again, then we can talk."

Marcia burst through the courtyard door and came to wrap her arm around Quintus's waist. "I've ordered a special dinner to celebrate their return, but first I need you to answer a question for me."

"What?"

"We're not sure whether a free Dacian still owns her family land, but if she doesn't, would her Roman husband own it? If not, could we buy it and give it to them as a wedding present?"

Quintus's gaze bounced between beaming Marcia and smiling Donatus.

She slipped her fingers around his hand and raised it to her cheek. "That and a few horses to start their herd again. Maybe her other mares are still where you got Zapada. We could partner and share the profits."

"Hmph." He opened his mouth, but his objections couldn't stand against the glow in her eyes. "I expect I can work something out."

She slipped her arms around him and squeezed. "I knew you'd know how to solve their problem. You always do."

"Not always, but I do this time." He rested his finger on her lips. "I seem destined to be surrounded by Christians, but I still don't want anyone else learning you worship that god."

"I know. We'll all be careful."

"You'd better be."

Why did he doubt they'd be able to keep that promise, even if they meant to?

Day 39

Donatus stood at the window, watching the clouds flame and then fade as the sun, already hidden by the mountains, finally set.

He and Ariana had declared themselves husband and wife in the presence of Gracchus and Marcia Philippa. That was all it took under Roman law, but the love in her eyes as she declared her desire to be his forever was all he needed.

Marcia had insisted they spend their wedding night in her best guest chamber before moving to the cottage that had been Ariana's home. But for him, a palace, a barn, or a bedroll beside a warm fire...it was all the same. All he would notice that night was the warmth of her lying beside him, cradled in his arms.

Ariana had worn the embroidered tunic her mother had worn for her own wedding, and not even the finest silk with threads of spun gold could have made her more beautiful. The women had set up a screen in the corner of the room, and Marcia had given Ariana something to wear that she said was one of Gracchus's favorites. Ariana's soft humming reached his ears as she prepared for their first night as husband and wife.

When she finally slipped from behind the screen, he knew why the tribune liked it so much. Her thick red hair, freed from the single braid she always wore, cascaded over her shoulders and down her back. She took a step toward him, then hesitated.

He closed the space between them in three strides. It was time for the surprise he'd been saving since his morning prayers. A gift for them both, straight from God. He hadn't expected it, but God had a way of giving a man exactly what he needed, whether he expected it or not.

"I have a surprise for you. Are you ready?"

Her gray eyes shone with more love than he could ever deserve. "I'm ready for a lifetime with you, whatever may come."

With the back of his right fingers, he stroked her cheek. "Whatever comes, God will be with us. Close your eyes."

He focused on a strand of her hair as he brought his right thumb and forefinger together. Savoring the silky softness, he rolled the hair between them. Then he slipped it behind her ear.

Her eyes popped open as her eyebrows shot up. "Your hand! It's working. When—"

His finger on her lips silenced her. "A wedding gift from our God this morning." He traced her lower lip. "I can't do much with it yet, but you told me God is the great healer in His own way and His own time. Who knows what He still plans to do?"

She buried her face in his chest and snuggled in. "He works all things together for good for those of us who love Him, even when we can't see it at the time." She tipped her head until she could look into his eyes. "And whatever He gives us, we'll rejoice in that."

He kissed her forehead, then lowered his lips to hers.

As she melted against him, he gave thanks...for the knife in his arm, for Gracchus hiring him, for the trip that had rescued him more than anyone, for the future with Ariana he'd never dreamed possible.

His hand might never heal completely. Only God knew if that was best. But even if it never did more than it could at that moment, he was still a blessed man.

Finis

I'd Love to Hear from You!

If you enjoyed this book, it would be a real gift to me if you would post a review at the retailer you purchased it from. A good review is like a jewel set in gold for an author. Other great places to share reviews are Goodreads and BookBub. If you've read others in the series, it would be great if you post a review of those, too.

I'd also love to hear from you at carol-ashby.com or directly at carolashbyauthor@gmail.com.

Want to hear about upcoming releases in the Light in the Empire series and free gifts only for newsletter subscribers?

For free gifts and other special offers, advance notices of upcoming releases, and info about my latest writing adventures, I hope you'll sign up for my newsletter at carol-ashby.com.

Dangerous times, difficult friendships, lives transformed by forgiveness and love

Honor Bound is the eighth volume in the Light in the Empire series, which follows the interconnected lives of four Roman families during the reigns of Trajan and Hadrian. Each can be read stand-alone. The nine novels of the series will take you around the Empire, from Germania and Britannia to Thracia, Dacia, and Judaea and, of course, to Rome itself.

Brutus and Africanus will return in *Honor Bound* in AD 122,
four years after *True Freedom*

For a preview of the opening chapter
of the seventh volume in the series,
coming in November 2019, read on!

Honor Bound

When the honorable path isn't clear, how do you find your way?

Marcus Brutus owns estates, ships, and gladiator schools that increase his fortune daily, but his greatest treasures are his honor and his wife. When she reveals her faith in Jesus before dying after the birth of their son, he's consumed by hatred for the unnamed Christian woman who led his beloved to abandon the Roman gods, making him lose her in this life and the next.

For fifteen years, Licinia's father hid her Christian faith. But now her father is dead, and a ruthless political enemy is hunting for anything to destroy her brother's career. When she becomes the target, her brother sends her to their estate in Germania. But is that far enough to protect her from an evil man who will stop at nothing?

When a carriage accident leaves Brutus injured and his best friend near death after rescuing Brutus's son, Licinia welcomes and cares for them. But her strange habits and his friend's unexpected recovery make Brutus suspect she's the Christian who corrupted his wife. When her brother's enemies come for her, does honor require him to protect her or turn her over as an enemy of Rome? And when Licinia's heart is drawn toward the pagan man who makes money off death, can she reconcile her growing affection with her love for Christ?

Chapter 1

GOODBYES

Rome, Fall of AD 122

The ring of steel on steel echoed across the practice arena of the *Ludus Bruti,* Marcus Brutus's gladiator school in central Roma.

When Brutus lowered his *gladius* and backed away from his favorite sparring partner, he wiped some sweat from his forehead with his forearm. "A good match, Africanus, but were you holding back today?"

The muscled, curly haired Nubian who was four inches taller than Brutus raised his eyebrows. "Holding back, Master Brutus?" He pressed his lips together to stop a guilty smile. "Don't you always want our best efforts, practice or combat?"

"So, the answer is yes."

Africanus shrugged. "You seemed tired today."

"I couldn't get to sleep, so I read most of the night. Camilla's time draws near."

"I found waiting for my first hard. By the third, it becomes easier."

"Your wife is strong and healthy. Camilla…" He chewed his lip. "The third try almost killed her."

"But all has gone well this time. Not like the others."

Brutus pulled a deep breath and blew it out through pursed lips. "True, but I'll have no peace until she hands me the baby and calls me 'Father.' I'll relax then, not before."

The rapid slaps of sandals drew Brutus's eyes to the hallway beside the armor room. His jaw clenched when one of the slaves from his villa trotted onto the arena sand.

"Stabularius. Why are you here?" His whole body tensed, fearing the answer.

"The mistress's labor started a few hours ago, master."

"A few hours? Why didn't someone come for me immediately?"

"Mistress Camilla said you'd be home soon enough anyway, but then the physician decided you should come as soon as possible…because of the mistress's problems in the past."

Brutus handed his gladius to Africanus. "Bring my stallion back to the villa."

He trotted down the hall to his office to snatch his tunic and belt. He pulled the tunic over his head as he strode toward the stable yard. He was still fastening his belt when he entered it.

The horse Stabularius had ridden from the villa lifted its head from the trough, water dripping from its muzzle. Brutus scooped up the reins, grabbed a handful of mane, and hurled himself onto its back.

"Open the gate."

The stable slave scurried to obey and held it open as Brutus trotted through.

Labor took many hours, and the first baby was the slowest to come. But the physician had said as soon as possible, and fear gnawed at him. What if as soon as possible wasn't soon enough?

◆

Africanus sucked air between his teeth as Brutus trotted down the hallway. Then his gaze shifted to Stabularius.

"Is the physician overcautious, or is something wrong?"

The villa stable slave shrugged. "I don't know. They only told me to get here quickly."

"Go saddle Master Brutus's stallion and my horse as well. I'll ride back with you."

Stabularius nodded and disappeared into the hallway.

Africanus turned toward the red-haired gladiator who'd been wielding a wooden practice sword against one of the heavy wooden stakes around the edge of the arena.

"Rufus."

Rufus turned, eyebrows raised.

"Go tell my wife I'm going out to the villa. I doubt I'll be home for dinner."

Rufus nodded. "Fortuna smiled on you, giving you such a good cook for a wife."

Any other time, Rufus's comment would have drawn a smile. "Tell her I want you to eat what she's prepared for me."

Africanus carried the steel *gladii* into the armor room and placed them in the rack. Then he selected two wooden ones that were used for practice by the gladiator slaves. Brutus would want to spar to relieve the tension as he waited.

They usually sparred with metal swords, but he'd rather not fight the master, even with dull-edged steel, when Brutus was distracted. He ran his hand down the weighted wooden blade. Wooden swords should be safe enough.

If the mistress did not survive the delivery and the master needed to fight in anger and grief, he'd rather not die as well.

It had been several hours. Brutus paced in the peristyle, staring often at her closed door on the balcony above. Africanus sat on a chair, tipped on its back legs, with the wooden swords across his lap.

Her every cry cut like a sharpened sword nicking him when his timing was off while sparring.

Then her scream blended with another sound, higher pitched and angry. A piercing, lusty wail.

Their child.

He slapped Africanus's shoulder as a grin split his face. Two steps at a time, he bounded up the stairs and trotted down the balcony to her door.

His palm pushed against it...and it didn't budge.

Why latched?

He knocked softly, but it didn't open. Several harder raps with his knuckles, but still it remained closed.

His fist pounded on the carved door panel. "Open this door. Now!"

A slow, scratching sound as the bolt was drawn back, then Camilla's maid, Capria, opened the door and stepped behind it.

Brutus stood in the doorway, taking in the vision of Camilla cuddling a tiny bundle at her breast. Her hair was soaked with sweat, and she seemed pale, but he'd never seen her more beautiful.

She tipped the baby to turn its face toward him. "See your father, Marcus?" Her lips brushed the baby's cheek.

Brutus strode across the room and sat on the bed beside her, grinning like a fool.

"Reach out your arms. Hold our son."

He took the tiny bundle and gazed into their baby's eyes.

Camilla lifted her hand to stroke his tiny cheek. "He has your eyes. Raise him to have your honor and courage, and he'll be the finest man."

He grinned at her. "We'll raise him to have your wisdom and humor, too."

Her eyes locked on his, and something changed. Their expression shifted from joyful to...wistful?

She shifted in the bed. "Capria, take our son. Everyone, leave us."

Her maid stood before him, arms outstretched, and he transferred the precious bundle to her.

Physician, maid, and two other slaves filed out of the room and closed the door.

Brutus's gut twisted. "Why did you do that?"

"I have some things to tell you that only you should hear."

He shifted on the bed to face her, resting his knee against her side and taking her hand in his. "What?"

"The bleeding isn't going to stop."

"You don't know that. It stopped last time. Why not—"

Her fingers rested on his lips, silencing him.

"I just know. I want you to promise to bury me by the olive grove where we watch the sunset. Don't cremate me, and don't have the usual Roman funeral rites." She drew a deep breath. "I'm a Christian, and I want to be buried like one."

He stared at her as his whole world crumbled. A Christian? It couldn't be. That would bar her forever from the Plain of Asphodel, the place of reunion in the afterlife, reserved for the good and pious. To lose her now would rip his heart out, but to never see her again?

Her fingers shifted from his lips to his cheek. "You haven't promised."

He forced his voice to sound calm, pushing down the surging anger. "I promise. But who convinced you to become one?"

"I won't tell you her name. You'll try to find her, and I don't want her hurt."

"But what could she have said to turn you from the gods? I was the one who questioned whether they were real, not you."

"It didn't start with what she said. It's what she did. I told her I wanted to give you a son more than anything, but after losing three babies, I knew the gods were against me. Just before you went to the Lousonna estate, she prayed to her god for me to conceive. Before the last words of that prayer, I knew something was different inside me. When I begged you to lay with me the night before you left and you gave in, I knew we would have a son."

"But that doesn't mean her prayer did anything. You conceived three times before."

"That was only the start. I wanted to know the God who has real power. She told me how much God loves me, that he came as Jesus to let me become His child if I just believed, that I would feel that love when I did. And she was right. God gave me love and peace and joy. I used to fear death, but not now. I'll be with Jesus when I die."

Her thumb stroked his cheekbone. "God truly blessed me because He gave me the son I always wanted for you. My only regret is I won't be with you to raise him."

Married for fifteen years, and he'd thought they kept no secrets from each other. How could she hide this?

"Why didn't you tell me before?"

"I wanted to. I almost did, several times. But then you'd mock the Christians who died for their faith in the arena, and I knew it wasn't the right time. But time has run out."

Her fingers stroked his hair. "I wish I'd told you. Then you'd know how wonderful it is, and we'd be together for eternity. I'll keep praying for you to come to Jesus, too."

He tried to hide the emotions from her as he oscillated between pain and anger. Come to Jesus? He would never want to worship the god who took her from him.

Again and again he'd told her he didn't need her to give him a son. He could adopt one, and he knew several men willing to give him one of theirs. Nothing was worth losing her in childbirth. Why had some Christian convinced her it would be safe to try again?

Her fingertips drifted down his cheek to his lips. "I don't want you to grieve too deeply or too long. Promise me."

His jaw clenched. His nod drew her smile. "I'll try." *But the best part of me dies with you. How can I not grieve until death swallows the rest?*

A wave of shivers swept over Camilla. "I feel so cold."

Brutus lay down beside her and drew her trembling body against his own. "Better?"

"Much." She turned her head enough for their eyes to meet. "God has truly blessed me with you."

He kissed her forehead and wrapped her tighter in his arms. As he willed the warmth of life to flow from him to her, her contented sigh was a dagger slicing into his heart.

Her breaths grew shallower...and stopped.

He held her for several minutes before he rose and strode from her chamber.

Africanus stood, grim-faced, in the peristyle below, his arms hanging, each hand holding a wooden gladius. Brutus charged down the stairs. His slave yet closest friend held one out as he neared.

Brutus's knuckles whitened as his grip tightened on the hilt.

The clack of wooden sword on sword echoed through the house until sweat soaked Brutus's hair and his arm was too leaden to raise the sword one more time.

And with every strike, he cursed the Christian woman who'd taken his beloved from him…in this life and the next.

Portus, seaport of Rome, that evening

Licinia's fingers gripped the ship's rail. The sun had vanished below the edge of the sea an hour earlier, but the wharves of Portus still swarmed with slaves unloading and loading cargo by torchlight. None of them wanted to be there, and neither did she.

A deep sigh drained her lungs. "I know you only want to protect me, Sextus, but to leave with only one day's warning? To be parted from everyone I care about like this?" She bit her lip. "I didn't even get to tell Camilla goodbye."

Her brother's brow furrowed. "It's too dangerous to delay."

She blinked hard to force back the tears she was determined not to shed where her brother could see. "You and Father have kept my secret for fifteen years. I still don't think his death has to change everything."

Sextus rested his hand on hers and squeezed. "I wish it didn't, but it does. Father let everyone think he couldn't bear to give you in marriage because you were so much like Mother. Some thought that foolish, but no one questioned his right to do it. But I've been *paterfamilias* for two months now, and I can't use that excuse. Eyebrows are already raised because I haven't arranged a marriage for you yet."

He withdrew his hand. "You're twenty-seven, and most women have half-grown children by your age. Many think marriage to a Licinius Crassus has great political value...and they're right. I've already had several inquiries about you."

"I could keep my faith secret from a husband. Camilla has."

Sextus's head drew back. "No, you couldn't. What would you do the first time he asked you to offer a libation to his household gods? Or go with him to one of the temple ceremonies? Or host a dinner with male and female slaves to entertain his guests?" A frown accompanied the shake of his head. "You'd never go against what your god commands just to make a husband happy."

He rubbed the back of his neck. "Gnaeus overheard one of Manius Sabinus's allies asking a few of my clients why I didn't want you to marry...what was wrong with you. One of those clients was fishing for information about you when he came to the salutation yesterday." His mouth turned down. "For enough money, Fidelis will betray us.

"No one important is asking me dangerous questions...yet, but what can I say when they do? I'm not a good liar. Sabinus is looking for any way to undermine me. Even if that means getting you killed."

His eyes turned away from her. "As *praetor*, it's my job to judge and condemn the Christians brought before me. Imagine the scandal if it comes out that my own sister has been one for years." His jaw clenched. "Nothing would give that reptile greater pleasure than exposing you to hurt me. Emperor Hadrian wouldn't care about your religion if you were a slave or some shopkeeper's wife, but a daughter of one of the noblest families, the sister of one of his magistrates…he'll demand action against you."

Licinia's lips tightened. "And that would keep you from ever becoming a provincial governor."

The pain in his eyes at her words made her wish she'd never uttered them. She reached for his hand and squeezed. "I'm sorry I said that. I know that's not why you're sending me to the Octodurus estate."

His eyes clouded, but the pain was gone. "Uncle Gaius barely escaped his estate with Priscilla and his children before the soldiers came to arrest him. He was no more threat to Rome than you are, but that doesn't seem to matter to the ones who want you Christians converted back to worshiping the Roman gods…or dead." His eyes closed as his lips tightened. Sadness darkened them when he fixed them on her again. "I hate condemning them just because some Christians won't make a meaningless sacrifice to the genius of the emperor and the Roman gods, but I have no choice when that's the law."

She drew a deep breath, then let it out slowly. No more sighs…she didn't want to make sending her away harder for her brother than it already was.

"I only wish I could stay in Rome until Camilla's son is born. For years, it's been her deepest desire to give Brutus an heir."

A skeptical smile accompanied the shake of Sextus's head. "What if she has a girl?"

"She won't. When I prayed for her to conceive, God told me it would be a son."

His laughing snort was exactly what she expected.

"Laugh if you want, Sextus, but I know I'm right. You'll hear when the newest Marcus Antonius Brutus is born. When he is, I want you to deliver the special blanket I wove for him to Camilla. I promised her I'd

be there for the delivery. I was going to give it to her then, but now..."
A tear tried to escape again.

"I will, but it will have to be an anonymous gift. I don't want to draw Brutus's anger if he discovers you've corrupted his wife by getting her to become a Christian, too."

"It's not corruption. It's liberation from silly superstitions to freedom and joy in the presence of the only true God."

Sextus rolled his eyes. "So you've told me for years, but that's not how Brutus will see it. He's an honorable man, so I don't expect him to openly support Sabinus. But if he suspects you, he might refuse to support me. Brutus is only an equestrian, but his wealth and network of connections make him a political force. I don't want him as an enemy."

He rested his hand on her cheek. "Time to bid you farewell, little sister. I don't want anyone to know which ship you're on, so I'd better leave before someone recognizes us. Stay in the cabin out of sight until you're out to sea." His thumb caressed her cheekbone. "I'll miss you. Don't forget to write to me as freedman Sextus Licinius Gratus. I can't be certain your letters won't be intercepted by one of Sabinus's agents, and he must not discover where I've sent you."

She shook the sleeve of the plain white tunic he'd borrowed from their steward. "You may thing the famous Senator Crassus is recognized everywhere, but I think you can pass incognito without your purple stripes."

Her teasing relaxed the grim lines around his mouth, just as it always had.

"I'll write as soon as we reach the estate." She took his other hand between both of hers. "And I'll pray for you every day."

The corner of his mouth pulled up. "You can pray for my health and success, but I want you to promise you will not be praying for my conversion."

She stood on tiptoes to kiss him on the cheek. "That's one promise I will never make."

Their hands slipped apart as Sextus stepped back. Then he strode down the gangplank and wove his way through the cargo on the wharf. His pace quickened as he climbed the ramp to the road. He paused in a circle of light beneath one of the torches and raised his hand. Then his figure was swallowed by darkness.

Licinia clenched her teeth, but some tears escaped anyway. Would she ever see the brother who'd teased and taught and defended her again? *Please, God, protect him until you claim him as your own.*

She swept the teardrops from her cheeks and squared her shoulders. Father was dead, and life in Rome was over.

She glanced at the cabin door. Primula, her maid and sister in Christ, awaited her in the cabin, and the four male slaves traveling with them were brothers as well. The life she'd known was gone, but she wasn't completely alone.

She belonged to Jesus, and even though she couldn't see it now, maybe this was God's plan after all.

THE ROLE OF WAR IN THE SLAVE ECONOMY
OF THE ROMAN EMPIRE

There were three basic types of people in the Roman Empire: Roman citizens, free noncitizens, and slaves. The first had many special rights, and the last had no rights at all. Under Roman law, slaves were simply property that could be treated like other animals.

There were several ways a person might become a slave: born to a slave mother, abandoned as a baby because the head of the family didn't want the child, sold into slavery by a poor parent, captured outside the Empire by slave traders, kidnapped within the empire and sold, and captured in war.

From the time of the Roman Republic through the expansion period of the Roman Empire, war was a major source of slave labor. After a battle or the sacking of a city, the defeated were collected and guarded by soldiers. The commanding general then decided their fate. Although some were released to become subjects of Rome, death or enslavement was more likely. When Corinth was conquered in 146 BC, all adult males were killed, and the women and children were made slaves.

Slaves were just one more kind of plunder to be used for the profit or glory of Rome and its military leaders. Right after a battle, the defeated warriors and often civilians were collected and guarded by Roman soldiers. By the middle of the first century AD, manacles with chains had become a standard part of a legionary's equipment. Soldiers often received a personal share of the plunder, which might include people. In 52 BC, Julius Caesar gave each of his legionaries one slave to be kept for personal use or sold to the traders who followed the army.

Romans regarded anything taken from an enemy as their rightful property, including people. Usually, the questor, who was responsible for the financial affairs of a legion, took charge of the captives and sold them to slave traders who followed the legions as they advanced against Rome's enemies. Sales of captives were called sales under the spear (*sub hasta*) or under the garland (*sub corona*) because war slaves in the second century AD wore a garland on their heads while being auctioned.

Slave traders transported the captives from the conquered territory to many parts of the empire. That often started with a long walk to a coast where the slaves could be loaded onto ships for transport around the Empire. It was common for men to have metal shackles clamped around their necks. Chaining slaves together made it harder to escape on the long treks. Women and children were considered less likely to try to escape and weren't always chained.

From the Republic through the Empire, military success was measured in part by the number of slaves taken and sold. The money from such sales paid the expenses of the Roman state, including paying her armies, building public facilities, and funding future wars.

The numbers of people enslaved following a successful Roman campaign were staggering. In 167 BC, over 150,000 slaves were taken from Epirus, a relatively small area spanning parts of present-day Albania and the western coast of Greece. In 57 BC, Julius Caesar took 53,000 from a single tribe in Gaul (present-day France). During his Gallic wars between 58 and 51 BC, he might have taken as many as one million Gauls as slaves.

In the First Jewish Revolt of AD 66 to 70, 97,000 slaves were taken from Judaea. Emperor Vespasian used the wealth plundered from the Jews to replenish a Roman treasury depleted by the civil wars of AD 69 and for public building projects. Many Jewish slaves were used to build the Flavian Amphitheater (Colosseum), started by Vespasian and finished by his son Titus, only to be killed in the games in the amphitheater they helped build.

After Trajan's Second Dacian War (AD 105-106), between 400,000 and 500,000 Dacians were enslaved, allowing the new Roman province of Dacia to be largely repopulated by Romans and their allies. Combined with the wealth from Dacia's rich gold and silver mines, slave sales helped fund Trajan's many public building projects, from the massive public Baths of Trajan (larger than eighteen American football fields) to a huge forum (1000 x 600 feet). A hill was flattened to make room for the forum's construction.

Trajan's Forum included a huge basilica along one side for government activities and public gatherings. Along the adjoining side was a six-story building (large parts still standing) of shops and offices that served as an ancient shopping mall. Two libraries (one Greek, one Latin) stood behind the basilica with a courtyard between them. In that courtyard was Trajan's column. The column (still standing) is ninety-eight feet tall and has carved scenes of the First and Second Dacian Wars spiraling up it. In vivid detail, the scenes tell the story of those conflicts from the preparations for the first war through the Roman triumph in the second. Since no account written at the time of Trajan's Dacian wars still survives, the column is a vital source of information about those conflicts in particular and Roman military practice in general.

One can only imagine the cost of such magnificent building projects, and slaves were one important source of the wealth that funded them.

Slave prices in the early second century AD varied considerably, depending on the age, fitness, and skills of an individual. A denarius was a silver coin worth about one days living wage. The very young were cheap (75 denarii for a 3-year-old boy) because mortality for children under five was high. Young slaves ranged from 175 to 600 denarii. One seven-year old boy cost 200 denarii, and a girl sold for 210. A young woman might sell for 250 to 675 denarii and a male slave for 350 to 700 denarii, depending on age and skill set.

Once the captives were sold to a trader at the questor's first auction, they entered the slave trade as a commodity for resale. At the next auction, they would wear wooden plaques around their necks that described where they came from, what skills they possessed, and what defects they had, both physical and mental. They would be displayed naked so the bidders could see what they would be buying. It was common for a new owner to rename a newly purchased slave to emphasize the break between a former life as a free person and a new life as property.

Hope Unchained begins with Ariana, her younger brother Diegis, and her little sister Roanna held in separate cages sorted by age and gender, awaiting the questor's auction. Although she is taken from her cage before that first sale and soon freed, her brother and sister start the march to the sea for a second sale that could take them anywhere in the Empire. *Hope Unchained* follows her attempt to find and buy her loved ones out of slavery before it's too late to save them.

For more about life in the Roman Empire at its peak, please go to carolashby.com.

The Daily Life of Gladiators:
Celebrities Yet Social Outcasts in the Roman World

Perhaps the most widely recognized symbol of ancient Rome is the Colosseum, started by the first Flavian emperor, Vespasian, in AD 72 and finished by his son and successor, Titus, in AD 80. During the Imperial era, Romans called it the Flavian Amphitheater after the dynasty that build it. Nothing epitomizes the Roman attitude toward the value of human life better than this marvel of Roman architecture that let more than 50,000 people watch as men fought and died, urged on by the roar of the blood-thirsty crowd. Perhaps as many as four hundred amphitheaters were spread across the Empire, ranging from wooden structures, which might seat one to ten thousand, to stone or concrete marvels that are still in use today for bull fights, concerts, and film festivals in Arles and Nimes in France and Pula in Croatia.

The typical schedule for the Roman games involved more than gladiatorial contests. The morning was filled with animal events, ranging from hunts to *damnatio ad bestias*, the feeding of condemned criminals to beasts. Irenaeus (AD 130-202, Bishop of Lugdunum in Gaul) reported that Ignatius of Antioch was fed to the lions in Rome in AD 107 for the crime of refusing to worship the Roman gods. Condemned criminals or prisoners of war might be forced to fight each other until only one remained to be killed by a gladiator. But the real excitement came in the afternoon, when professional gladiators met in one-on-one combat, fighting until one was dead or so badly injured he was forced to admit defeat.

A loser who fought well enough was often spared to fight again, so the odds of surviving a single fight were about five to one. The typical gladiator fought only two or three times a year. Half died during their first year in the arena, but for those who survived their "rookie year," life after the arena was a real possibility. That life might even be long; a memorial stone in a gladiator cemetery in Ephesus was erected by the family of a retired gladiator who died at age 99.

But how did someone become a gladiator, and what was life like during the 360-plus days of the year when a gladiator wasn't entertaining the masses in mortal combat?

While gladiators were admired for their courage and fighting skills, they were social outcasts. Like a prostitute, a gladiator was an *infamis*, a person of low repute. He couldn't vote or hold public office, and many burial grounds refused to accept a gladiator's remains.

Many became gladiators through no choice of their own. Over half of the fighters in a gladiatorial school (*ludus*) were slaves. Many were taken as prisoners of war and sold into the arena with some fighting skills. Some were slaves who had proven too hard to handle. Some were condemned criminals. These came in two categories: condemned to the sword (*damnatio ad gladium*) and condemned to the games (*damnatio ad ludos*). While those condemned to the sword would be killed during their first appearance in the arena, men condemned to the games could survive as long as they fought well enough and might even hope to be freed someday. If the sponsor hosting the games decided to free a gladiator, he could pay the purchase price to the owner and award a wooden sword to the fighter as the symbol of his freedom.

Some gladiators were free men who were paid a sizable sum of money to sign a contract with a ludus for a fixed period of time, typically four or five years. During the term of the contract, they belonged to the ludus as if they were slaves, swearing the gladiator oath to submit to anything the ludus owner wanted, including having them killed. These voluntary gladiators were called *auctoratii.*

Some auctoratii needed the money to pay debts before they were sold into permanent slavery to pay them. Sometimes former soldiers, especially those who had been dishonorably discharged and were already *infames,* chose to become gladiators if they had no other job prospects. Some were gladiator slaves who had been freed and chose to continue in their profession after receiving their freedom.

While the vast majority of gladiators were men, women gladiators have been pictured in mosaics and listed as special attractions. Whether these were slaves or auctoratii isn't known.

The head trainer of a ludus was the *lanista,* a man who had been a successful gladiator himself. While the lanista was an infamis at the bottom of society, the wealthy Roman who owned the ludus was usually a well-respected member of Roman society. A large ludus might have several hundred fighters, and the money to be made feeding the Roman lust for bloodshed was attractive to many businessmen in the equestrian order. A sponsor of the games hired the gladiators through the schools. For every fighter who died, the sponsor paid a fixed fee based on the ranking of the gladiator, so win or lose, the owner of a ludus made money on every match.

The training regimen for a gladiator was vigorous. Many hours were spent daily practicing with wooden swords weighted to be twice as heavy as real metal ones and shields heavier than those used in combat. Muscles were built up to a level that bones were deformed. Attack and counter-attack were practiced until responses were reflexive and instantaneous. Stamina, strength, and intimate knowledge of how an opponent would fight could make the difference between life and death. Bouts seldom lasted 30 minutes and might be over in a minute, but a longer, fiercer fight might impress the crowd enough that the loser might be spared to fight again. A new gladiator usually trained for a year or more before his first appearance in a professional bout.

The intense training burned many calories, so gladiators were fed large quantities of a mostly vegetarian diet. The gladiator diet differed from the civilian diet in several ways. While wheat bread was a staple for most Romans, gladiators ate mostly barley. Some fruit and vegetables were combined with ample servings of barley porridge (polenta). The goal was to have a layer of fat overlying vulnerable blood vessels and nerves so a shallow cut wouldn't prove disastrous. Fat tissue can bleed impressively, making spectators marvel at the fighter's ability to continue the battle, while not being a crippling injury. To build strong bones, a drink made from the ashes of bones and charred wood was served.

Gladiators and former gladiators worked outside the arena as bodyguards, debt collectors, and enforcers to settle disputes. They also served as sparring partners and personal trainers for men and for women who wanted to fight privately.

Memorial stones in gladiator cemeteries provide ample evidence that many gladiators married and raised families. The stones usually list the names of the relatives erecting the stones and the number of fights, the number of wins, and the age at death. Many died in battle in their twenties or early thirties, but others lived to die a natural death.

The popularity of the games didn't wane until Christianity became the dominant religion. Emperor Constantine replaced sentences that condemned a criminal to die as a gladiator with condemnation to work in the mines, and Emperor Valentinian III banned gladiatorial contests in AD 438.

In *Hope Unchained*, Ursus was sold to a ludus as a child to pay his dead father's debt. In young manhood, he was trained to fight. After more than a decade "on the sand," he was bought by a legion commander to serve as his bodyguard. But with the war over, he expects to be fighting again. When he becomes a Christian during the trip to recover Ariana's sister, he can no long kill other men for the entertainment of the crowds. But that leaves him with a hard choice: return to his owner and choose to die in his next bout, or run away and suffer the consequences, which could be returning to the arena, if he is ever caught.

For more about life in the Roman Empire at its peak, please go to carolashby.com.

1) The story begins with Ariana in the slave cage, facing a life of bondage. Her parents have been murdered, her brother and sister taken as slaves, but she was still praying and expecting God to respond. Have you ever been in a situation where your life felt like it was crumbling? What did that do to your faith?

2) Even though the Roman army had destroyed Ariana's family and future, she saw the tribune as more than a cruel soldier in his love for his crippled wife. She quickly began to care about the wife of the commander of those who destroyed her family. When you look at someone who has hurt you deeply, do you try to see the good as well as the bad in them? How does that affect the way you approach them? The way you respond to those they care about?

3) Ariana was determined to keep her word to the tribune, even when she could set herself free by breaking it. Have you ever been in a situation where keeping your word meant losing something you truly wanted? How did you decide what to do?

4) Marcia was ready to give up on life. Then she heard that a god she didn't believe in might have healed someone, and she was willing to see if he would heal her, too. Have you ever known someone who was desperate enough to seek help from anywhere? How could you respond to that?

5) Tribune Quintus Gracchus welcomed the healing of his wife, but he didn't want to consider the possibility that God had any part in it. Have you had friends like this? Have you found ways to share with them what God does that makes them more open to God?

6) His crippled hand destroyed the future Donatus had planned. When Gracchus hired him, it solved his short-term problem, but he still faced the future without hope. Why did that change? What can we do to bring hope to someone who has none?

7) When Donatus first met Ariana, he saw her as a Dacian enemy, but as she showed him kindness, that changed. Have you ever had the chance to show kindness to someone who dislikes you? How did they respond?

8) Betrayed by an uncle who refused to save him and hardened by years as a gladiator, Ursus thought he was a man no one could care about. What changed his mind? If you know someone who feels no one cares, what might you do to help them?

9) When Ariana learned her beloved brother was gone forever, how did she respond? Why was she able to do that? How do you think you would respond?

10) *Hope Unchained* is a story of hope when the future might seem hopeless-and how sharing God's love with others can open hearts to follow Him. What touched you most? What made you think about what your own choices would be?

Who would you like to see in a future story?

I grew to love several of the characters in *Hope Unchained* while I was writing. That usually happens, and often the next story for a character takes shape in my head even before I finish. I knew Ariana would need her own story after introducing her as Leander's beloved but long-lost sister in *True Freedom*. But there are many people in *Hope Unchained* that I would like to spend more time with, and I hope there are some for you, too. Who would you most like to see in a future story? What was it about them that made you want more of them? I'd love to hear what you think.

I'm going to write the story of what happens next to either Ursus or Gracchus to give to newsletter subscribers. Which would you rather have?

Please go to my website, carol-ashby.com, and share your thoughts in the comment box. Sign up for the newsletter, and you'll get the story when I finish it. Looking forward to hearing from you!

Glossary

Aureus: gold coin worth 25 *denarii*

Auxilia: auxiliaries, large military units of soldiers who were not Roman citizens

Ballista: a machine, often shaped like a crossbow, for hurling stones and firing arrow-like bolts

Bestiarius: a man who fought wild animals in the arena

Caliga: Roman military sandal with hobnailed sole and laces to tie it on

Castrum: a fortified military camp ranging from legionary fortress to marching military camp

Caupona: inn, canteen, tavern; sometimes a place to find prostitutes

Centurion: 1st level officer over a century, a unit of 80 men (10 *contubernia*)

Cisium: two-wheeled cart with forward-facing seat located above the axle

Contubernium: military unit of 8 men, 1 mule, and equipment

Denarius: (plural *denarii*) silver coin worth about one day's living wage

Gladius: short Roman military sword

Familia gladiatoria: members of a gladiator school (*ludus*)

Infamis: Lowest class of free people; barred from legal protections of Roman citizenship, punished like slaves; includes gladiators, prostitutes, pimps, and actors

Lanista: the head trainer of a gladiatorial school

Legate: commander of a legion

Liburna: a warship with two rows of oars (bireme) used on rivers

Ludus: (pural *ludi*) training school for gladiators

Mango: slave dealer

Mansio: roadside guest quarters for traveling Roman officials

Paterfamilias: oldest living male of an extended Roman family; the patriarch who owns everything

Pneuma: spirit

Retiarius: a gladiator who fought with a weighted net, trident, and dagger

Taberna: tavern or shop selling prepared food

Triclinium: dining room of Roman house with three couches arranged in a U shape

Scripture References

What Ariana, Roanna, and Bikili always remembered:

Rom 8:28 (ESV) and paraphrased: "And we know that for those who love God all things work together for good, for those who are called according to his purpose."

Chapter 11: 1 Peter 3:1-2 paraphrased

Chapter 25: Matthew 5:22, 6:14-15; John 3:16; Romans 10:9; and Luke 23:43 paraphrased.

Chapter 32: Romans 15:12-13 (ESV): "And again Isaiah says, 'The root of Jesse will come, even he who arises to rule the Gentiles; in him will the Gentiles hope.' May the God of hope fill you with all joy and peace in believing, so that by the power of the Holy Spirit you may abound in hope."

ESV = English Standard Version

Acknowledgements

First, I thank God for this opportunity to tell a story of how He can use someone who loves Him to help lost souls hope again when the only future they see seems hopeless. I loved writing how God brought good from the bad for Ariana and Donatus, giving them both a future they never expected, and how Marcia and Ursus came to faith. Nothing gives me more pleasure than writing about lives being transformed by forgiveness and love.

No one can write the best book possible without the help of many others. I want to thank Andrew Budek-Schmeisser for being my critique partner and good friend. Despite serious health problems, he's given unstintingly of his knowledge of good writing, his spiritual insight, and his expertise with horses, combat, and low-tech field medicine. When I so often wanted to bounce something I'd just written off someone at 1:00 or 2:00 in the morning, he was usually online and willing to help. He's helped me with *The Legacy, Faithful, Second Chances, True Freedom, Hope Unchained, Honor Bound* (the next in the series), and many brainstorming sessions about characters in future volumes. This book wouldn't have been the same without him.

I'm especially thankful for my alpha beta and treasured friend, Lisa

Garcia, who's a true kindred spirit and wise woman of God. She's also so good at spotting typos that I'll never need a copy editor.

My critique partner, Katie Powner, who's an award-winning author herself, helped me spot and fix things only an author would see. Terry Shoebotham, my local writing buddy and prayer partner, also beta-read the manuscript. Thanks also to Mesu Andrews for being my prayer partner for inspiration and meeting deadlines.

My line editor, Wendy Chorot, has once more blessed me with her skill as an editor and her insights for making the deep spiritual scenes reflect real life. She's a joy to work with as well.

Each time I think Roseanna White couldn't possibly design a better cover than the last one, and each time she proves me wrong. It takes amazing talent to start with a collection of separate images and meld them together to get something that looks like the Romans had color photography. When she couldn't find the right hairstyle, she braided her daughter Xoë's hair and digitally dyed it to get the perfect Ariana. Once more, she came up with a design that both men and women can love. I can't wait to see what she does with the next one in the series.

I especially want to thank my wonderful son, Paul, and my beautiful daughter, Lydia, for their love and patience with my obsession with writing.

But my special thanks go to my amazing husband, Jim. Too often, I'd keep writing and skip dinner if he didn't bring me a bowl of his delicious green chile stew. It takes a special man to listen to the latest twist in a plot for the umpteenth time with only a slight eyeroll, always accompanied by a smile. He makes it so easy to write about men who are smart, funny, kind, patient...men who are just like him.

About the Author

Carol Ashby has been a professional writer for most of her life, but her articles and books were about lasers and compound semiconductors (the electronics that make cell phones, laser pointers, and LED displays work). She still writes about light, but her Light in the Empire series tells stories of difficult friendships and life-changing decisions in dangerous times, where forgiveness and love open hearts to discover their own faith in Christ. Her fascination with the Roman Empire was born during her first middle-school Latin class. A research career in New Mexico inspires her to get every historical detail right so she can spin stories that make her readers feel like they're living under the Caesars themselves.

Read her articles about many facets of life in the Roman Empire at carolashby.com, or join her at her blog, The Beauty of Truth, at carol-ashby.com.

Light *in the* Empire Series

*Dangerous times, difficult friendships,
lives transformed by forgiveness and love.*

The Light in the Empire Series follows the interconnected lives of four Roman families during the reigns of Trajan and Hadrian. Join them as they travel the Empire, from Germania and Britannia to Thracia, Dacia, and Judaea and, of course, to Rome itself.

Forgiven

Are some wounds too deep to forgive?

With a ruthless father who murdered for the family inheritance, Marcus Drusus plans to do the same. In AD 122, Marcus follows his brother Lucius to Judaea and plots to frame a zealot for his older brother's death. But the plan goes awry, and Lucius is rescued by a Messianic Jewish woman. Her oldest brother is a zealot and a Roman soldier killed her twin, but Rachel still persuades her father Joseph to put his love for Jesus above his anger with Rome and hide Lucius until he heals.

Rachel cares for the enemy, and more than broken bones heal as duty turns to love. Lucius embraces Joseph's faith in Jesus, but sharing a faith doesn't heal all wounds. Even before revealed secrets slice open old scars, Joseph wants no Roman son-in-law. With Rachel's zealot brother suspecting he's a Roman officer and his own brother planning to kill him when he returns, can Lucius survive long enough to change Joseph's mind?

Blind Ambition

Sometimes you have to almost die to discover how you want to live.

It's AD 114 in the Roman province of Germania Superior, and being a Christian carries a death sentence. Tribune Decimus Lentulus is on the fast track for a stellar political career back in Rome. When he's robbed, blinded, and left for dead, a young German woman who follows the Way finds him. Valeria knows it's his duty to have her and her family killed, but she chooses to obey Jesus's command to love her enemy and takes him home to care for him.

It's not his miraculous recovery that shakes Decimus to his core. It's the way they love him like family and their unconcealed love for Jesus. In spite of himself, he falls in love with the Christian woman Rome wants him to kill. Can Valeria hide her faith to follow him into the circles of Roman power? Or should he abandon his ambition to help rule the Empire and choose to follow a different way?

The Legacy

When Rome has taken everything, what's left for a man to give?

Betrayed by a ruthless son who'll do anything for power and wealth, Publius Drusus faces death with an unanswered prayer—that his treasured daughter, Claudia, and honorable son, Titus, will someday share his faith. But who will lead them to the truth once he's gone?

Claudia's oldest brother Lucius arranged their father's execution to inherit everything, and now he's forcing her to marry a cruel Roman power broker. If only she could get to Titus—a thousand miles away in Thracia. Then the man who secretly told her father about Jesus arranges for his son Philip to sneak her out of Rome and take her to the brother she can trust.

A childhood accident scarred Philip's face. A woman's rejection scarred his heart. Claudia's gratitude grows into love, but what can

Philip do when the first woman who returns his love hates the God he loves even more?

Titus and Claudia hunger for revenge on their brother and the Christians they blame for their father's deadly conversion. When Titus buys Miriam, a secret Christian, to serve his sister, he starts them all down a path of conflicting loyalties and dangerous decisions. His father's final letter commands the forgiveness Titus refuses to give. What will it take to free him from the hatred poisoning his own heart?

Join the people you met in *Second Chances* eight years earlier in this tale of betrayal, hatred, love, and forgiveness, where even bad things can work together for good.

Faithful

Is the price of true friendship ever too high?

In AD 122, Adela, the fiery daughter of a Germanic chieftain, is kidnapped and taken across the Roman frontier to be sold as a slave. When horse-trader Otto wins her while gambling with her kidnappers, he entrusts her to his friend and trading partner, Galen. Then Otto is kidnapped by the same men, and Galen must track them half way across the Empire before his best friend loses a fight to the death in a Roman arena.

Adela joins Galen in the chase, hungry for vengeance. As the perilous journey deepens their friendship, will the kind, faithful man open her eyes to a life she never dreamed she'd want?

A trip to the heart of the Empire poses mortal danger to a man who follows Jesus, especially when he must seek the help of an enemy of the faith for Otto to survive. Tiberius hunted Christians when he governed Germania Superior and banished his own son when he became one.

When Tiberius learns sparing Galen offers a chance at reconciliation, he joins the trio on their journey home. Can his animosity toward the followers of Jesus survive a trip with the Christian man whose courage and faithfulness demand his respect?

Follow the continuing saga of the people you met in Blind Ambition from the frontier of Germany to the heart of the Empire.

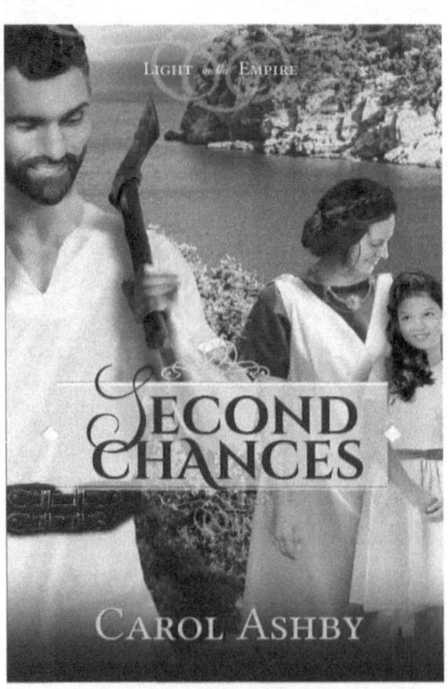

Second Chances

Must the shadows of the past destroy the hope of the future?

In AD 122, Cornelia Scipia, proud daughter of one of Rome's noblest families, learns her adulterous husband plans to betroth their daughter to the vicious son of his best friend. Over her dead body! Cornelia divorces him, reclaims her enormous dowry, and kidnaps her own daughter. She plans to start over with Drusilla a thousand miles away. No more husbands for her. But she didn't count on meeting Hector, the widowed Greek captain of the ship carrying her to her new life.

Devastated by the loss of his wife and daughter, Hector's heart begins to heal as he befriends Drusilla. Cornelia's sacrificial love for Drusilla and her courage and humor in the face of the unknown earn his admiration...as a friend. Is he ready for more?

Marriage to the kind, honest sea captain would give Drusilla the father she deserves...and Cornelia the faithful husband she's always longed for. But while her ex-husband hunts them to drag Drusilla back to Rome, secrets in Hector's past and the chasm between their social classes and different faiths erect complicated barriers to any future together. Will God give two lonely hearts a second chance at happiness?

Join the people you met in *The Legacy* eight years later in this tale of hope and a future never imagined until God opens the door.

True Freedom

The chains we cannot see can be the hardest ones to break.

When Aulus runs up a gambling debt to his father's political enemy, he's desperate to pay it off before his father returns to Rome. His best friend Marcus suggests they fake the kidnapping of Aulus's sister Julia and use the ransom money. But when the man they hired kidnaps her for real, Aulus is catapulted into a desperate search to find her.

Torn from his childhood home by Rome's conquering armies and sold as a farm slave to labor until he dies, Dacius's faith gives him strength to bear what he must and serve without complaining. After a deadly accident makes him one of Julia's litter bearers, he overhears Marcus advising her brother to kidnap her. When Dacius almost dies thwarting the kidnapping, a Christian couple pretend Julia and Dacius are their children to keep her brother from finding them before her father returns.

But pretending to be free again makes returning to slavery more than Dacius can bear, while acting like a common woman opens Julia's eyes to dreams and destinies she never knew existed. With her brother closing in and her father almost home, can she find a way around Roman law and custom to free them both for the future they long for?

Find out what happens to Ariana's brother Diegis twelve years later in this tale of hope and a future never imagined until God opens the door.

Coming in May 2020

Honor Bound

When the honorable path isn't clear, how do you find your way?

Marcus Brutus owns estates, ships, and gladiator schools that increase his fortune daily, but his greatest treasures are his honor and his wife. When she reveals her faith in Jesus before dying after the birth of their son, he's consumed by hatred for the unnamed Christian woman who led his beloved to abandon the Roman gods, making him lose her in this life and the next.

For fifteen years, Licinia's father hid her Christian faith. But now her father is dead, and a ruthless political enemy is hunting for anything to destroy her brother's career. When she becomes the target, her brother sends her to their estate in Germania. But is that far enough to protect her from an evil man who will stop at nothing?

When a carriage accident leaves Brutus injured and his best friend near death after rescuing Brutus's son, Licinia welcomes and cares for them. But her strange habits and his friend's unexpected recovery make Brutus suspect she's the Christian who corrupted his wife. When her brother's enemies come for her, does honor require him to protect her or turn her over as an enemy of Rome? And when Licinia's heart is drawn toward the pagan man who makes money off death, can she reconcile her growing affection with her love for Christ?

Join some of the people you met in *True Freedom* four years later in this tale of loss and discovery, anger and forgiveness, and the truth that sets people free.

I'd Love to Hear from You!

If you enjoyed this book, it would be a real gift to me if you would post a review at the retailer you purchased it from. A good review is like a jewel set in gold for an author. Other great places to share reviews are Goodreads and BookBub. If you've read others in the series, it would be great if you post a review of those, too.

I'd also love to hear from you at carol-ashby.com or directly at carolashbyauthor@gmail.com.

Want to hear about upcoming releases in the Light in the Empire series and free gifts only for newsletter subscribers?

For free gifts and other special offers, advance notices of upcoming releases, and info about my latest writing adventures, I hope you'll sign up for my newsletter at carol-ashby.com.

Who would you like to see in a future story?

I grew to love several of the characters in *Hope Unchained* while I was writing. That usually happens, and often the next story for a character takes shape in my head even before I finish. I knew Ariana would need her own story after introducing her as Leander's beloved but long-lost sister in *True Freedom*. But there are many people in *Hope Unchained* that I would like to spend more time with, and I hope there are some for you, too. Who would you most like to see in a future story? What was it about them that made you want more of them? I'd love to hear what you think.

I'm going to write the story of what happens next to either Ursus or Gracchus to give to newsletter subscribers. Which would you rather have?

Please go to my website, carol-ashby.com, and share your thoughts in the comment box. Sign up for the newsletter, and you'll get the story when I finish it. Looking forward to hearing from you!

Carol Ashby